Henry VIII and Katherine of Aragon:

The Cannon Conspiracy

Fourth Book in the
Nicola Machiavelli Series
by
Maryann Philip

RealHistoryMysteryPress.com

On the Cover:

Front top left: *Portrait of young Katherine of Aragon* by Michael Sittow, year uncertain. This portrait has also been described as being of Henry VIII's sister Mary.

Front top right: Illustration based on the painting *La donna velata* ("The veiled woman") by Raffaello Sanzio (Raphael) of his mistress Margherita Luti, c. 1514–1515.

Front bottom left: *Portrait of Henry VIII* by Joos van Cleve, c.1530-35.

Front bottom right: Illustration based on a photo by the author, of the cannon designed by Leonardo da Vinci displayed at the da Vinci Museum at the Château du Clos Lucé, Leonardo da Vinci's home in France.

Back, left: Illustration of a Tudor cannon salvaged in 1836 from the wreck of the *Mary Rose*, Henry's warship that infamously sank in 1545.

First edition, Sacramento, California: ©Real History Mystery Press, 2020

TABLE OF CONTENTS

THE HISTORY BEHIND THE MYSTERY

The Renaissance ignited in England with the crowning of Henry VIII and his beautiful and brilliant first queen, Katherine of Aragon. The English loved them and Europe admired them, for good reasons: young Henry was nothing like the mistrustful tyrant he later became, nor was Katherine the harridan he portrayed during their rancorous divorce. The backdrop to this mystery is a portrait of the glamorous and devoted couple they were, at the beginning of a promising reign. Historical events occur around a Tudor Christmas celebration, when they did in real life.

The history is accurate, except as noted in the Afterword, which also reveals when the story takes sides on historical controversies, and tells a few stories of its own.

Though the mysteries solved by Nicola and Queen Katherine are fictional, the background murders and executions actually happened.

Cast of Characters (in order of appearance)
Italics denote a *historical person*

Nicola Machiavelli, illegitimate daughter of the infamous ***Niccolò Machiavelli*** (as in "Machiavellian"). In previous Nicola mysteries, she learned the secrets of gun manufacture with help from ***Leonardo da Vinci,*** while working for her "Aunt" Caterina's armory.

Sir Charles Brandon, close friend of ***Henry VIII***, later ***Duke of Suffolk*** and second husband **to *Henry's sister Mary.***

Sir William Burgoyne, a British knight.

Henry VIII, 19 year old king of England, crowned the year before this narrative begins.

Queen Katherine, formerly Katherine of Aragon, 24 year old queen of England and ***King Henry VIII's*** first wife. Daughter of ***King Ferdinand and Queen Isabella*** of Spain.

Margaret Pole, also known as Margaret de la Pole, and later, Duchess of Salisbury. Presently, a lady in waiting to ***Queen Katherine***. Niece of both ***King Edward IV*** and ***King Richard III***. Cousin to ***John, Edmund, Richard and William de la Pole,*** Yorkist claimants to ***King Henry VIII's*** throne. Sister to a previous Yorkist claimant who was executed by ***Henry VII***. Much later, beheaded herself on order of ***Henry VIII***.

Edward Stafford, Third Duke of Buckingham, direct descendant of the youngest son of *King Edward III,* and therefore a possible claimant to the throne of *Henry VIII.* Later beheaded on his order.

Father Thomas Wolsey, presently a priest and almoner (distributor of alms) to **Henry VIII.** In the future, he becomes *Cardinal Wolsey*: Papal Legate, Lord Chancellor, and the second most powerful man in England. He had two acknowledged sons, one of whom was born the year this story occurs. Much later, died on the way to his trial for treason, ordered by *Henry VIII.*

Lena, dark-skinned body servant to *Queen Katherine.* Likely a Moor, a slave, or both.

Maud Parr, Lady in waiting to *Queen Katherine.*

Elizabeth Boleyn, lady in waiting to *Queen Katherine* and mother of *Mary Boleyn*, one of the many mistresses of *Henry VIII,* and of *Ann Boleyn*, his second wife.

King Henry's Spymaster. Surely a real person, but the author of this tale has been unable to find the name of the individual who served in this post so early in *Henry VIII's* reign.

Vice Chamberlain Sir Henry Marney, Captain of the Yeomen Guard. The nobleman charged, among other things, with the security of *King Henry VIII.*

Lambert Simnel, a young commoner who physically resembled one of the sons of **Edward IV,** the princes locked in the Tower of London by *Richard III.* Promoted by unscrupulous nobles as a "pretender" to the throne of *Henry VII,* father of *Henry VIII.* Realizing his innocence, *Henry VII* put him to work in the palace kitchens. He later became one of *Henry VIII's* falconers.

Maria de Salinas, Spanish lady in waiting to *Queen Katherine*, and one of her closest companions.

Reginald and Geoffrey Pole, youngest of *Lady Margaret Pole's* five children. Both beheaded by order of *Henry VIII* in adulthood.

Lady Cathryn (Katherine) Stourton de la Pole, Wife of **William de la Pole,** who married her for her considerable fortune. (Please pardon the misspelling of her name, done to avoid confusion. There are too many Katherines in this book.)

Peter Fitzpole, bastard son of **William de la Pole. Alice Fitzpole** is Peter's wife. **Michael Fitzpole** is their son.

Sir Thomas Wheeler and Sir Edward Beacham, knights and friends of Henry VIII.

William de la Pole, third of the four **de la Pole brothers**, and the only one likely not involved in a series of Yorkist attempts to dethrone **Henry VII and Henry VIII**, over several decades. He spent 37 years in the Tower of London, the longest of any prisoner ever held there.

Paul Brown, steward to **Sir John Paston,** deputy to the **Lord High Admiral.**

Princess Mary Tudor, Sister of **Henry VIII.** Later, wife and widow of **Louis XII, King of France.** Abruptly married **Sir Charles Brandon** thereafter, to the consternation of **Henry VIII.**

Prince Henry Tudor, first and only son born alive to **Queen Katherine** and **King Henry VIII.** He lived 53 days.

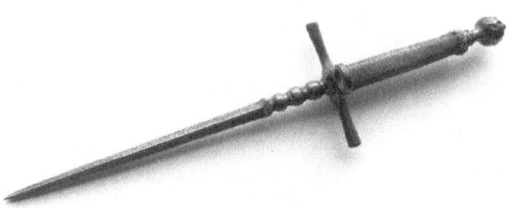

Renaissance-era Italian boot stiletto

PROLOGUE: FUTURE THREATS

A storeroom in Greenwich Palace
Mid-December 1510

Muttering under his breath, King Henry turned and stalked toward the storeroom door, his magnificent gold attire incongruous in the dusty surroundings where he'd cornered Nicola. Before she could relax he spun towards her again, his face still scarlet with rage.

"You thwart my desires at your peril, Lady Greensleeves," he said, through gritted teeth. "You dare pull a dagger on a king? Did you murder my men and steal my cannons? You will prove your innocence, or...or..."

Her stomach lurched as she grasped his threat. "You want me to prove I had nothing to do with these murders? I was with the Queen the whole time. So I am guiltless, unless your lady wife betrayed you too. And how am I supposed to prove it? I am a woman, and a foreigner. I speak almost no English."

Henry's face lost its angry color when she mentioned his Queen, and his expression changed. Was it remorse for his adulterous intentions? Had he just realized her innocence?

"That is not what I want from you and you know it," he muttered.

Fear kept Nicola's anger in check. To calm herself she breathed as deeply as her bodice allowed, wondering how best to fend off this predatory monarch. She curtseyed, still watching him, her dagger pointed at the floor. "I am happy to help find the cannons and the murderers. When my other duties to you allow."

Henry reddened again. "You would rather hunt killers than pleasure a king?" he hissed.

Though he was young and handsome, King Henry was also very dangerous. "I love my betrothed!" she shouted. "And I came here to perform a job. Not to...Not to..."

King Henry snarled at her and turned away, fists clenched. "As you wish. But bear in mind—you are as good as dead if I accuse you of collusion with the killers."

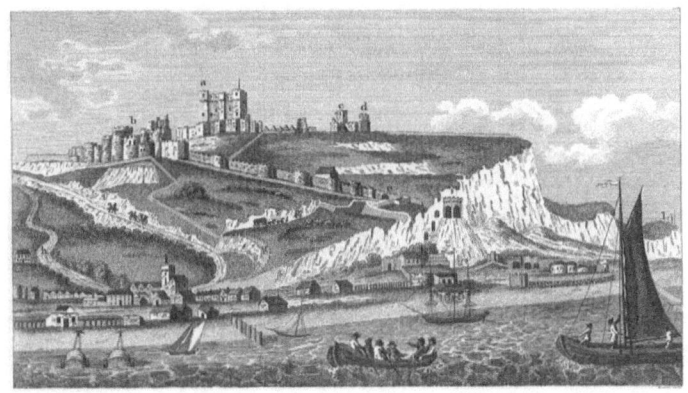

Dover Castle atop the white cliffs, engraving c. 1780

CHAPTER 1: NICOLA COMES TO DOVER CASTLE

Off Dover, England
Earlier in December 1510

"Are all the soils of England white?" Astonished, Nicola Machiavelli pointed at the shore beyond the ship's rail, glinting in the morning sun above a choppy gray-green sea. Gulls soared overhead, the first she had seen in days. She inhaled the subtle land scents of rotting seaweed and wood smoke in the offshore breeze, grateful that her feet would soon feel solid earth again.

Sir Charles Brandon leaned against the rail to peer at the shore, then laughed. "Those are the Cliffs of Dover. White rock, not soil. Above is Dover Castle, where some of your cannons will go. And do you see the flags?" He pointed at the castle. "Those are King Henry's flags. It means he is in residence. He probably came to see his new cannons. We must dress for court."

Nicola realized how unsuitable she looked, and wondered how she smelled after so many days at sea. "Dress for court? Is there even time to wash?"

"Barely. William, could you get some hot water for Lady Nicola from the galley?"

Nicola hurried to the brig, converted to her private quarters as the only woman aboard the Romulus. She hoisted her skirts to her knees and took the ladders two rungs at a time, confidently modest: the entire crew was aloft, shortening sail for docking. Feeling grateful that she would soon escape the below-decks stink of

7

seawater and sewage, she unlocked her tiny "cabin" with its one barred porthole, then slammed the door behind her.

As she washed and dressed she thought about Sir Charles, who treated Sir William like a servant, though both were knights. Charles had repeatedly trying to wheedle his way into her cabin during their weeks of travel from Italy, as if his friendship with Henry VIII excused his adulterous intentions. He thought himself handsome—and perhaps he would have been, without the bushy black beard and the arrogant attitude. She found him repulsive. Only Sir William could have tempted her to open the door, though he too was married. And she herself was betrothed to Raphael, and much in love with him and his art. She missed him, just thinking about him.

Newly-crowned Henry VIII had sent Sir Charles and Sir William to Italy, to fetch the armaments the King had purchased from its finest armory, and to decide whether Nicola could carry out the armory's contract. The English knights told her frankly during negotiations that the King doubted a mere woman could perform the armory's obligations. They had been even more frank during the voyage: Nicola would be held hostage if she could not do the job, until her family's firm made things right. That threat and rougher seas had made her queasy with worry since they left the Mediterranean.

"I have your hot water," William said from outside her door. His eyes widened when she opened it to him.

"Thank you. I already used cold water, as best I could." She turned her back to him. "Would you help me to tighten this _busto_? How do you say it in English?"

She heard him put the water down, and clear his throat. "It's called a stomacher, I believe."

 Nicola could sense his embarrassment. For a knight, he was surprisingly timid. "Please, William. Surely you have done this for your wife. It is nearly impossible to do myself. And we don't have much time."

He sighed, then tugged at the back laces while she adjusted her breasts in front.

"Too tight!" she gasped. "Ah. Better. Is it tied? Now tie my sleeves, *per piacere*."

She pulled them on and extended her arms. He spoke—in Latin, as they always did—as he tied the laces at her shoulders. "What a beautiful gown, my lady. What the English ladies would call a kirtle."

"Kirtle," Nicola repeated. Memorizing English words was easy, but sometimes they were very hard to pronounce.

"The deep maroon suits you, and those are magnificent sleeves. My wife would be envious. So that's what was in those chests."

Nicola turned, and saw him gazing at the finery she had pulled from her wooden chests and strewn across the hammock suspended above them. "The latest Italian fashions. My "Aunt" Caterina insisted. She says if I am to impress, I must dress the part."

He pointed at the pile of brightly-colored silks and brocades. "Your Aunt Caterina does not dress like this."

"She would like to—but she must wear black to show she is a widow, running her late husband's armory. Men in Italy will not deal with women unless they are widows. No one would want our cannons, though they are the best you can buy."

He chuckled. "Makes sense. She is the best-dressed widow I ever met. Your necklace is very fine, too. Did your betrothed give it to you?"

Nicola smiled, remembering the night Raphael gave her the ruby necklace. "Si. *Grazie*, I can manage now. Go get ready."

Shouts and thuds told her the ship was docking while she finished repacking and locking her chests. When she joined the crew on deck, she realized they were all gawking at her first appearance in the bright colors and tight revealing bodice of a lady. Some stared with their mouths hanging open. Embarrassed, she hurried to the rail, twisting to shout "Arrivederci" as she disappeared over the side in the bosun's chair, lowered by two grinning sailors. Crew members shouted farewells, a chorus of "*bella bella bella bella*" and several marriage proposals, until Captain Tedesco roared at them to stop.

As her chair reached the quay, Sir Charles appeared to help her to her feet. She extended a hand, and he took it, and kissed it, and used it to pull her into his arms. Before she understood what was happening he kissed her, thrusting his tongue into her mouth—simply because he could, she realized, with no one to see them against the hull of the ship.

Rage bubbled up inside her. With all that had passed between them, he knew perfectly well that his kiss was unwelcome. She shoved him away and slapped his face, hard. He laughed, which made her want to slap him even harder. Instead, cheeks burning, she hurried to stand next to Sir William, her veil fluttering in the breeze. Together they watched warhorses thundering downhill towards them from the castle, raising clouds of dust.

When Sir Charles joined them, she stepped away from him, still as angry as a half-drowned cat. Why had "Aunt" Caterina believed these men would protect her? And why had she been foolish enough to believe Caterina?

Sir Charles pointed, as if the kiss had not happened. "King Henry is on the lead horse."

Broad-shouldered and a head taller than all the guards and courtiers who followed, Henry VIII's red-gold hair bounced beneath a cockaded cap. He galloped along the quay until frighteningly close, then reined in his caparisoned warhorse, leaped from the saddle and strode towards them, with the grace of a much smaller man. The gold brocades of his garments seemed to glow in the morning sun.

As the King approached, his eyes dwelt on the tops of Nicola's breasts rather than her face. Embarrassed, she curtseyed—but not before seeing the open sores on his chin, not yet hidden by the new growth of reddish beard. To hide her shock she bent her head. She'd seen the French Disease many times, nursing poor prostitutes in the convent that raised her. The pox, the English called it. The King had surely not gotten it from his Queen, who was reportedly very religious. Poor woman—he had undoubtedly infected her. And poor England. The French Disease was fatal, though sometimes death took many years.

Still in curtsey, Nicola lowered her chin to avoid looking at the King's enormous jeweled codpiece, which was only a foot from her nose. He looked like a Greek god: handsome, athletic, and in radiant good health, as if he could stave off the French Disease by sheer force of will. She knew better, from her years of nursing. But perhaps he would live a long time before it finally took him.

"You may rise," King Henry said, extending a gloved hand to assist her. "How was your voyage?"

Nicola realized he had spoken in slow, oddly-accented Italian. "Fine, except at the end," she answered in the same language. She shot Sir Charles an angry look. "Now that we are here, I'm sure things will be better."

King Henry raised an eyebrow at Sir Charles. Then he ignored her, instead chatting and laughing with both knights in English, a language she had only begun to learn. Occasional words popped out at her: "quiet voyage" and "aunt" and "beautiful" and "sisters." She realized they were discussing whether she was as beautiful as her "Aunt" Caterina, as if she were not there. Sir Charles rubbed his cheek, and glanced at her. Evidently he was talking about the slap, too. He and King Henry both laughed.

Nicola winced, wondering if manhandling a woman and sticking a tongue in her mouth was acceptable behavior in this kingdom. She looked up through her lashes at the sores under King Henry's beard stubble while the men chatted. Definitely the French Disease. She was glad the King was wearing gloves when he helped her to her feet. Sometimes the open oozing sores of the French Disease appeared on the palms of the hands.

Sir Charles asked a question that the King answered with a shake of the head and a slashing forefinger across the royal throat. Both men laughed, Henry's high tenor cackle reminding Nicola of a barking dog. Sir William stared at them, round-eyed. Nicola had learned the English word for "head"—The King had ordered people beheaded, she realized. Evidently, Sir Charles and the King found this as comic as her slap to Charles' face. She shivered.

"Does she speak Latin as well as her aunt claims?" King Henry asked, in Latin.

"Your Highness, I speak better Latin than they do," Nicola responded in the same tongue.

"Have you learned any English?"

Nicola nodded and began reciting, "Cannon. Blast furnace. Muzzle. Fuse. Swab out the guns. Watch out. Stay back. Gun powder..."

The king barked his tenor laugh and gestured for her to stop. "I understand from your Aunt Caterina that you sing and read music?" he continued in Latin.

"My aunt told you that?" Nicola blurted. Her "aunt" was secretly her mother, and the respectable widow of an armorer who never knew that Nicola was his wife's bastard child.

"In our correspondence she told us that, and much more. Did she speak true?"

What else had her "aunt" claimed? They had fought before Nicola left Rome, because Caterina wanted her to leave Raphael and find a rich Englishman. "You want me to be a king's mistress, and out of your way," Nicola had shouted at her. "Better than an artist's mistress," Caterina had shouted back.

"I do read music and I can sing. But I am here to deliver cannons and arquebuses, and to show your armorers how best to make them. It seems an odd thing for my aunt to tell you."

"She was explaining your education in a convent, and how you learned about gun manufacture. The Queen wanted to know your background."

"How is the Queen's health, Highness?" Sir Charles asked.

"She is well. And she is here. Her belly is big and the babe's kicking makes her miserable," Henry answered, his voice pleased more than concerned. "But she refused to stay behind. She came in a litter. I watch over her to ensure her comfort."

"When will she give birth?" Sir Charles asked.

"In late January, she thinks."

"A blessed New Year, then."

The King turned to Nicola. "The Queen is eager for a lady who can converse in Latin. And she wants to practice her Italian with you as well. Come, she awaits us."

"A thousand pardons, your Highness, but I cannot come instantly. To fulfill my duties to you, I must first see to the offloading of the cannons destined for this castle," Nicola responded.

"I will assist her," Sir William said. "The wagons are just arriving."

"Excellent," said the King. "Charles, I have a horse for you. Come. The Queen awaits."

Portrait of a Spanish Infanta, possibly Katherine of Aragon,
by Juan de Flandes, c1496

CHAPTER 2: THE QUEEN IS JEALOUS

Dover Castle, the same evening

Hands folded across her pregnant belly, Queen Katherine sat in a wooden gallery above the smallest "great hall" she had ever seen, listening to the singers performing the Credo Henry had just composed. The "great hall" would easily have fit into one of the smaller courtyards in the Alhambra Palace in Spain, where she was raised. The grey stone walls, hung with moth-eaten tapestries, seemed to emanate cold and damp. She pulled her fur-lined mantle closer. The courtiers crowded around the hall's perimeter seemed content enough, but they were used to English winters. Would she ever be?

 Auburn-haired, petite and pretty when she was not pregnant, Katherine now felt swollen and ugly. Her back hurt, despite the feather pillows lining her makeshift throne. She wondered how her mother, Queen Isabella, had managed to rule her kingdom and crisscross it on horseback while pregnant. She had so many daughters that Katherine, as the youngest, had been relegated to this backwater to marry its future king.

Uncouth English ideas about pregnancy now trapped her in this gallery, away from her place at Henry's side. She would soon be in "confinement," an odd English custom that had disastrous consequences the last time she was pregnant.

However, from here she could at least see what Henry was doing. Her observations proved that traveling with him was the right decision.

 Henry was eyeing the new Italian girl as he sang, in the same hungry way he had looked at Lady Anne Stafford when Katherine was pregnant the first time. Katherine had dismissed that look when she saw it with Anne. She knew better now. Nicola was a head shorter than Henry and the nine bearded monks who joined him in singing his new composition. Yet her lovely soprano voice soared above all the others. She looked and sang like an angel. Everyone in the room seemed entranced, Henry most of all.

Katherine stiffened, stifling an urge to sob. She loved Henry with all her heart, but he had been unfaithful to her, all the while declaring his undying love. She had only just begun to believe him again—and there he was, transfixed by another pretty woman. How was she to bear it?

She hugged her pregnant belly, remembering that Henry's flagrant adultery with Anne Stafford had killed their stillborn daughter. Or rather, that her violent jealousy had done so—or so she believed. Henry had blamed his adultery on the abstinence forced by her first pregnancy, and begged her forgiveness. After much uproar and Anne's banishment to a nunnery, she'd pronounced him forgiven. Whether God forgave him was another matter.

Breathing deeply, she avoided tears—but not bitterness, which settled into her chest like a bad cold. She should have learned from her own family. Her sister Juana's angry public jealousy had alienated King Philip the Handsome, who declared his wife a madwoman and continued to flaunt his mistresses. Now she was known as "Juana la Loca"—"Joanna the Mad"—and locked in a tower in Spain. At the other extreme their mother, Queen Isabella, had ignored King Ferdinand's infidelities except in her prayers, which encouraged him to sin frequently and brazenly. Her mother's submissiveness meant that one of her father's bastards might succeed to the throne of Castile instead of Juana, its rightful queen.

In her passion for Henry, she was more unfortunately more like Juana than their mother—Juana, so distraught when Philip died that she refused to allow him to be buried, so that she could visit and caress his corpse. She, Katherine, would never do such a thing. But like Juana, she loved deeply. And felt it cruelly when Henry wronged her.

As the Queen ruminated, Nicola's voice rose above the others, singing *sedet ad dexteram Patris,* "seated at the right hand of God." Henry had obviously worked hard on this counterpoint. He viewed himself as God's anointed—little wonder his Mass would emphasize that phrase. Nicola sang it exquisitely.

The girl was convent-raised and betrothed, according to her aunt. An innocent, married in the eyes of God. And she was important to Henry and England not for her singing, but for her knowledge of Italian gun manufacture.

How could she win Henry back? And protect him from mortal sin and their unborn child from the effects of her jealous rage? And this innocent young betrothed Italian girl? And England, which needed Italian skills to make the best guns in Europe? So many problems. She prayed, and the answer came to her quickly. Guile. She needed to use guile, the sly cunning she had once scorned as suited only to fawning underlings, to whom it was second nature. That was the sin of pride. She now needed guile more than they did.

"Thank you, Father in Heaven," she breathed, convinced by its suddenness that she had received a divine message. She needed to keep Nicola so close that Henry would not be alone with her, yet out of Henry's sight so he would not be tempted by her. These were contradictory goals but, using guile, she would manage them somehow.

With a wave of her hand she summoned one of the ladies seated behind her, and ordered her to fetch Nicola. When the singing was over, the Queen watched a page summon the Italian girl to the gallery. Nicola appeared confused when she saw the row of seated, staring ladies behind the Queen, but made a proper curtsey. As Katherine had anticipated, she was a dark-eyed beauty with perfectly-arched brows, a shapely mouth, and a tiny waist. She had watched Henry eye such women before.

Katherine pointed Nicola to a stool next to her throne, and greeted her in Latin.

"We are pleased with your singing. And also, to have a new woman in court who speaks both Latin and Italian, and was educated by the Church. Have you been assigned a place to sleep?"

"I don't think so, Your Highness. Knowing so little English, I cannot be sure. The knights who brought me here seem to have disappeared."

"I will have a pallet prepared for you to sleep with my other my ladies. And your chests will be brought to my chambers. This old castle is drafty and primitive, but we have plenty of pallets and blankets."

"Thank you, Your Highness. I am very relieved. Sir Charles Brandon was. . . very forward in his attentions towards me, on board the ship. I am happy he is not the one showing me to my resting place."

Katherine's simmering anger at Henry's adultery found new fuel, and threatened to boil over. "Sir Charles is notorious," she snapped. "His wife is pregnant, which excuses much bad behavior by the men of this nation." She breathed deeply, remembering her baby and hoping to calm herself. "Unfortunately, he has been Henry's close companion since they were boys together. You will be safe with my ladies and me, however."

The Italian girl smiled, her teeth so perfect that Katherine felt another stab of jealousy. "I am deeply grateful, Your Highness," she said "May I ask a boon? I hope to write to my aunt and my betrothed, to let them know I am safe. May I entrust letters to the King's couriers who deliver to the Pope? Both my aunt and my betrothed work for Pope Julius. I don't know how else to get word to them."

"You are in luck," the Queen said. "Tomorrow and the next day we spend with the Archbishop of Canterbury. I'm sure he would be happy to send your letters with his couriers, if I ask him."

Nicola bowed her head. "A thousand thanks for your kindness, Your Highness."

The girl was not just distressingly pretty. She was also well-spoken, the Queen realized, again feeling threatened. "I am sure you will return the favor. When your other duties allow, you will help me learn Italian, which I read—slowly—but can't pronounce very well."

Nicola nodded. "I am happy to help you with whatever you wish, when my duties to the King allow."

"His Highness requires Lady Nicola for the singing," a page announced from the doorway.

"And I require her back when the singing is finished," Queen Katherine responded. King Henry was gazing up at them from below, a puzzled look on his face. She waved to him, and smiled her sweetest smile.

Henry VIII's gold-embellished peacock-blue tonlet (skirted) armor,
created for the King to wear in foot-combat at The Field of Cloth of Gold, 1520.

CHAPTER 3: THE KING TESTS HIS CANNONS

Dover Castle, the next morning

In the morning, local knights and members of Henry's court crowded the grounds of Dover Castle when Nicola arrived at the stone steps to the battlements. All eyes gazed up at the King, resplendent in embossed armor and a gold crown. He waved at the crowd and swaggered from cannon to cannon, chatting with the gunners and patting each weapon as if it were a favorite dog.

Conscious that many eyes turned to her, Nicola climbed the steps with head held high, trying not to show her fear. Cannons did not explode as often as they had when first invented, but they still blew up occasionally. Armorers blamed the blasts on progressively more powerful gunpowder, or on poor maintenance. Gunners blamed armorers. Her family's armories made the best cannons in Europe, but they were not foolproof. She worried about the effects of salt or rust on cannons crammed for weeks in the hull of a ship.

The old cannons—simple cylinders of welded iron rods encircled with iron rings, like a barrel—had been piled aside, with the stone shot they were built to fire. Nicola's cannons were small bronze muzzle-loaders, which the British gunners called "demi-culverins," intended for use on ships and in battle. Though shorter than a man and relatively easy to move, they fired deadly iron shot a far greater distance than their precursors.

Each new cannon was now awkwardly lashed to an ill-fitting old gun carriage. Nicola feared that the new cannons would crush the old wooden carriages, or topple and crack on the stone battlements. Even more worrisome: the gunners intended to reload for a second round. Without wheeled carriages to retract the guns, loading through the muzzles would be difficult. Earlier, using pantomime and broken English, she had tried to ensure that Henry's gunners knew how to swab out the barrel of the cannons after each shot. They'd looked at her as if she were a madwoman. Had she insulted them, by trying to teach them what they already knew? She would soon find out. She was ready to step in, if need be.

When all four cannons were ready, Sir Charles Brandon handed Henry a burning torch. The king lit the first fuse, then stepped well back to watch. The court musicians blew a brief trumpet fanfare, conducted by the lead monk to time with the explosion, which rocked the gun carriage. Henry laughed as he strode from cannon to cannon, firing them in succession, trumpets blaring; gun carriages swaying. To Nicola's relief, each shot streaked toward the English Channel, straight and true. Did King Henry understand how advanced these cannons were; how much further their iron shot flew? If he didn't, the gunners certainly did. Nicola could not understand most of their words, but she read their gestures.

While they struggled to swab out and reload the cannons, King Henry moved on to the handheld arquebuses: one with a wheelock, invented by Nicola's friend and mentor, Leonardo da Vinci;[1] one with a matchlock. King Henry refused to use the "arque," the hook designed to steady the long slender barrel of the gun, instead demonstrating his tremendous physical strength by shouldering it himself. Once wound and released, the wheelock whirled and sparked the powder, discharging the round to the fanfare of trumpets and cheers of the court.

Sir Charles then lit the matchlock fuse of the second gun, handing it to Henry to shoulder and point. The fuse sputtered, then re-ignited. Eventually the flame reached the powder and the trumpets blared with the explosion. This time Henry hit a target below the battlement, to raucous applause.

---

[1] Read about it in Da Vinci Detects

Nicola had been watching the gunners, relieved to see they knew their jobs. At her quiet suggestion each gunner knelt to steady a gun carriage. Henry went back and fired a second round from each of the cannons, cackling with laughter. The trumpets blared again, and again every shot flew true.

"Our thanks to Lady Greensleeves here, who brought us these weapons all the way from Italy," the King shouted, gesturing towards Nicola, who was weak with relief. The crowd cheered and whistled.

Nicola felt herself blushing, knowing that she was conspicuous. She wore an emerald green brocade kirtle and matching sleeveless surcoat that displayed her elaborate bell-shaped sleeves, also emerald green, slashed with gold. Very showy—but what better time to wear them, she had decided that morning, with help from the Queen's ladies. The heavy brocade was perfect for a cold day. Also, green and white were the colors of the King's liveried servants. She was now in the King's service, at least temporarily. Why not show it?

After admiring all her finery, the Queen's ladies had insisted on braiding and rolling Nicola's dark hair into an elaborate chignon held by jeweled combs, which they also used to anchor her white veil. The queen herself loaned Nicola an emerald necklace.

After their brief cheer for her, the crowd headed toward the tournament yard, which had been set up for jousting. As she followed them, Nicola heard a familiar voice behind her. "The demonstration was well done," said Sir William Burgoyne.

She turned to see him dressed as he was when they first met in Rome, when she thought him the handsomest man she had ever seen. He was blond and blue-eyed, a rare and dazzling thing in Italy. He now wore the same skirted red doublet and tight white hosen, showing off shapely legs. Today, he had tamed his curly gold locks under a black cockaded cap similar to King Henry's, and added a leather jerkin for warmth. She wished she could give him a handsomer sword from her family's armory. The plain one he wore was a decent weapon but not an ornament.

"I did little but encourage the gunners," she responded.

"You supplied those most excellent cannon!"

"Their excellence is why you purchased them."

"*I* did nothing. The King purchased them."

Nicola smiled. "Let's give King Henry all the credit, shall we?"

William extended his arm to her. "An excellent plan. Will you watch the jousting? The King will be looking for you."

Nicola took his arm. "Why would he look for me?"

"Haven't you noticed he has an eye on you? You outshine every lady here. The green suits you perfectly. Like a woodland nymph."

 Nicola felt herself blushing. "You are too kind. Will the King joust? And will he win?"

"Yes and yes."

"But will he deserve to win?"

William stopped to consider. "Usually. He is a fine athlete."

They watched as Henry, now on horseback ahead of them on the jousting grounds, ceremoniously received a scarf from Queen Katherine and tucked it into his armor, above his heart. Behind him, other knights mounted their armored horses and accepted lances from their pages. Some were checking the tips, to ensure the protective coronal was in place. More pages were erecting the cloth fence, painted with heraldic shields, that would separate two jousters hurtling towards each other, once the contest began.

"Who is the knight on the white charger?" Nicola asked.

"The Duke of Buckingham, Edward Stafford. A member of King Henry's council, and one of the richest men in England."

"It shows. Look at the embossing on his armor. *Magnifico.* Better even than the King's."

William laughed. "He loves to upstage Henry. He carried the crown at Henry's coronation, wearing robes so expensive and showy that they outshone what Henry was wearing. A mistake, perhaps. Henry has never forgiven him."

"I wonder who made that armor for him. I would love to take a closer look."

"Maybe you'll have a chance. The Queen is gesturing to you."

Her Royal Highness was seated on the platform erected for honored guests, bundled in a heavy woolen cloak and headscarf, surrounded by pillows and her ladies. After catching Nicola's eye, she gestured for her to come to the viewing platform, then pointed her out to a page, waved, and sent the boy scurrying to find her.

"I suppose I must go," Nicola said to William, wishing she could stay with him instead.

"I will escort you to the Queen."

A new thought occurred to her. "Who is to escort the cannons that are being sent overland?" she asked, as they made their way through the crowd of spectators, her hand still on his arm.

"I, for one."

"I will see you in the morning, then. I understand the King is impatient to get back to London."

"The court has been here several days already, waiting for the arrival of the cannons. Until tomorrow, then."

He kissed her hand before he left her. To her shock it tingled, as if he had kissed her lips.

Self-portrait of Raphael, c. 1506-08

CHAPTER 4: GOSSIP IN THE QUEEN'S LITTER

Dawn the next morning

As the court assembled to begin the day's journey to Canterbury, Nicola and Sir William stood amongst many wagons, some open and some with high barred windows, all loaded with food, finery and other supplies.

"Rest easy, Lady Nicola," William said. "All is in order."

"I hope so." She decided to re-check the two open wagons, the first destined for Rochester Castle and the second for Windsor Castle, each loaded with four cannons and yoked to two pairs of large draft horses.

The wooden boxes that each held two cannons were still nailed shut, and showed no damage from more than a fortnight in the hull of the *Romulus*. The remaining cannons were still on board the *Romulus*, on their way to the Thames River and hence to London.

"Her Highness requests Lady Nicola's presence," a voice said beside her.

Nicola recognized the page. She had not expected this, and was not dressed for it. "I must go," she told William, trying to sound more confident than she felt.

"Indeed you must. I hope she is well."

Nicola hopped down from Sir William's wagon and followed the page. They made their way from the back of the procession, past soldiers loading wagons with supplies, courtiers reining in restless horses, bearded monks rehearsing a tune to the jingle of tambourines, jesters tumbling and juggling, the king's hunting dogs barking from the cages of their special wagon, chattering ladies seated on silk cushions in wagons with scarlet canopies, and a scattering of knights in armor, mounted or mounting their horses.

Near the front of the procession, the page moved aside the scarlet curtain of a brightly-painted litter sitting on the ground.

"*Misericordia*, I hardly recognized you," said Queen Katherine, peering up from inside. "You look like a nun."

"I almost was one. And will seek refuge in a convent, if I do not feel comfortable in court," Nicola replied. "I dressed this way because I thought I was riding with the wagons carrying the cannons. If my appearance does not offend you, I would be honored to accompany you. Surely though one of your ladies—"

"Never mind them. Help her in," the Queen told the page.

"My ladies are nearly all spies or schemers, and I am sick of them," she said, after the litter rose and began to move forward. "My one remaining Spanish lady is a spy for King Ferdinand—my father—and the English ones are either spies for Henry, or hoping to replace me in his bed. Or both. Even the men carrying this litter are probably spies for one of the old barons who resent my power with Henry. But as commoners they don't speak Latin. Nor do most of my ladies—it isn't the fashion here. You and Lady Margaret Pole and Maria are the only ones I can talk to without the entire court listening."

Nicola was astonished by the Queen's frankness. Searching for something inoffensive to say, she remembered the older lady who helped with her veil the day before. "Lady Margaret seems very kind," she ventured.

"Margaret *is* kind. But I am spying on *her*. Some believe her family has a better claim to the throne than Henry. Once, there was even talk of her ruling as queen. So Henry has charged me to keep an eye on her. We can never be true friends."

Nicola remembered what her Aunt Caterina had said about King Henry: "Two ancient families have battled for the English throne for decades. The new king is descended from both, but from bastards on both sides. So neither family views him as legitimate. His father fought off several rebellions to keep his crown. The son may have to, as well."

"Enough about spies," the Queen said. "I want to know about you." She began peppering Nicola with personal questions, in fluent Latin.

 Nicola told the story she and Aunt Caterina had agreed upon, which was mostly true. "I am named for my father, Niccolò Machiavelli, who is second-in-command of the Republic of Florence, and its chief diplomat. My mother was the daughter of a famous Florentine judge. She died when I was very young."

Nicola crossed herself, her quick penance whenever she lied about her mother dying. Some people reacted with pity. The Queen merely nodded, so she continued her story. "After my mother's death, my father took me to a convent in Rome where the daughters of the rich and powerful are educated."

"San Sisto—I have heard of it. What did the nuns teach?"

"The usual trivium and quadrivium, and double-entry bookkeeping—which had just been invented—as part of mathematics. In Latin, of course. Italian, naturally. Greek was taught by the granddaughter of the last Byzantine Emperor, but it was modern Geek."

"Greek from the granddaughter of an Emperor? Impressive. Were there others of royal birth there?"

Dare she jest a little? "Not unless you count Lucrezia Borgia and her older half-sister, who was one of the nuns," Nicola responded.[2]

---

[2] Learn the history of the Borgia family in <u>A Borgia Daughter Dies</u>

The Queen gasped. "I do *not* count Lucrezia Borgia. Or any of the Borgia pope's bastards."

No more attempts at humor, Nicola decided. Nor did she dare tell the Queen that most of the girls were bastards, deposited at San Sisto by the cardinals and *signorotti* who fathered them.

"People said terrible things about Lucrezia and his other children. But I knew her—I attended her first wedding—and I don't believe what they say about her. She is now called "the Good Duchess" and has founded several convents. A very smart, gentle lady. Her Latin was excellent. Once we learned Latin, we had free access to the convent library, which was a large one."

The Queen raised an eyebrow and changed the subject. "What else did you study?"

"I learned nursing and pharmacy by working in the convent *infermeria.*"

The Queen turned to stare at her. "You learned nursing? Have you assisted with childbirth?"

"Of poor women, yes. Several times."

"Did they give birth to boys, or girls?"

Nicola considered. "Boys is what I remember. Some of the nuns were scandalized to have even infant boys in their presence. Others just wanted to see the male parts."

The Queen laughed—so perhaps she did have a sense of humor. "Having birth attendants who brought boys into the world is said to guarantee a male birth. I will insist that you be with me for my confinement. Most of my ladies cannot bear the thought of witnessing a birth. I am afraid they will faint. Or flee."

Nicola felt uncomfortable with this new role. "Surely there is a royal midwife."

"Of course. But there must be witnesses to a royal birth. Many of them, and all female. You will be one. I'm curious though—why didn't you become a nun?"

"My aunt came to Rome with her husband and then was widowed, almost immediately. They'd been hired to open an armory to make cannons for Cesare Borgia, who led the papal armies for his father. She needed help managing her sudden inheritance. So rather than take vows, I left the convent to assist. We saw to the cannons, and kept the account, and now make guns and armor for Pope Julius."

"How lucky you are, to live in the Eternal City," the Queen responded.

Their conversation turned to religion, and became lively. Once she mastered Latin, Nicola had read every book in the convent library, including the Bible. She loved the stories of the Old Testament—though she didn't find them particularly holy—and had memorized her favorite psalms, the Gospels, and most of the letters of St. Paul.

Queen Katherine had read theological treatises and knew her breviary by heart, but was less familiar with the Bible. They both had read and loved *The Imitation of Christ* and St. Augustine's *Confessions*. St. Thomas Aquinas they found boring.

As a self-taught reader of the Bible, Nicola had developed some religious ideas she knew to be unorthodox. She was careful not to admit this to the Queen, who was obviously devout, and quite conventional in her beliefs.

The clatter of hooves alerted them to a horseman beside them. "How is my beloved Queen?" boomed the King's voice. "And how is our son? And who is with you? Give me your hand."

Queen Katherine rolled her eyes at Nicola, and pushed her hand up through the curtains of the litter. "My back hurts," she responded in Latin. "But otherwise all is well. The Italian lady Nicola is with me. As you predicted, she is very entertaining."

"Lady Greensleeves! Have her teach you some love words in Italian."

"Shame on you, Henry. She is an innocent. You are pulling too hard on my arm."

"*Mea Culpa.* I will leave you then." A riding crop cracked, and hoofbeats trotted away.

The queen retracted her arm, wincing.

"Is there something I can do?" Nicola asked, smiling at the Queen's assumption that she was a virgin. "Here, let me put this under your back," she continued, pulling at the shawl that covered their feet.

"No, no," said the Queen. "I am fine. Tell me about your fiancé. Is he handsome?"

"Very handsome," Nicola responded, glad to be able to distract her. "We met in Florence before he became a famous artist."

"A love match, then," the Queen responded happily. "Henry and I were a love match, of sorts. It is a gift, to be able to marry the person you love. Why did your fiancé let you come here?"

"Let me come here?" Nicola repeated, realizing that even queens were ruled by men. How to summarize something complicated? "Because he wants to keep my aunt happy," she finally said. Which was true enough. "She has great influence with my father, who has not yet paid my dowry."

"*Misericordia,*" Queen Katherine said. "How I hate dowries. My father and Henry's father had endless disputes over my dowry. My ladies and I had no money for food for a while, because my father would not pay it. I was dressing in rags. Even in a love match, there must be a dowry? Perhaps I will get Henry to pay it for you."

Nicola rubbed the necklace Raphael gave her, hidden next to her skin. As much as she wanted to marry him, this was not a good idea. "Your Highness, please don't request the King to pay anything, other than what is in our written agreement. I do not want him thinking that I pressed for extra compensation."

"You do not leap to accept a gift from a Queen, then? That suggests you are trustworthy. Excellent. You will be wealthy enough to support your Raphael, once you finish your work for Henry. Even without my help."

Nicola grinned. "True. But he has become wealthy enough working for Pope Julius, that he does not need my support."

Nicola and Queen Katherine spent the rest of afternoon exchanging stories of how the world had changed, in part thanks to Katherine's parents, Ferdinand and Isabella.

Nicola reminded her that Cristoforo Colombo, their vassal, was born an Italian. As was Amerigo Vespucci, for whom the New World was named. In friendly manner, Queen Katherine claimed both explorers for Spain.

Both recognized that they had found a true friend

Canterbury Cathedral, south side, etching by Wenceslaus Hollar (1607-77)

CHAPTER 5: AN ADULTEROUS ROMANCE

At Canterbury Cathedral, the same day.

They reached Canterbury late in the afternoon. The Queen and her ladies, including Nicola, went immediately to the Archbishop's Palace, so the Queen could rest. While she did, she gave the ladies permission to visit the cathedral and shrine of St. Thomas à Beckett.

Canterbury Cathedral reminded Nicola of the one in Milan, the only other she had ever seen in the French style. Slender stone pillars separated the church into a high nave and lower side aisles, then curved into ribbed arches crisscrossing a ceiling that seemed as far away as the heavens. There was but one small stained glass window in all of Rome's churches, which she and Raphael had admired. But Canterbury cathedral had scores of them, each as tall as twenty men. Those facing the setting sun blazed with reds and blues, and every saint's face was different, and expressive.

"*Magnifico,*" Nicola breathed. "Beautiful," she said in English. "Yes?"

The English ladies, who had otherwise ignored her, nodded. Along with other pilgrims, they were shown the spot where Saint Thomas à Beckett was murdered, and then his tomb. They left their offerings and some, including Nicola, remained to pray.

How did the current King Henry feel about a saint whose murder was the fault of a much earlier King Henry? Nicola wondered, but did not know enough English to ask the other ladies. Nor did she dare. She remembered Henry's gesture on the dock at Dover: he had just ordered people beheaded, and thought it amusing. Queen Katherine had said that some of these standoffish ladies were his "spies." Best to avoid too much curiosity about the King.

When Nicola returned to the Archbishop's Palace, Queen Katherine beckoned to her from a seat by the fire in the Archbishop's magnificent library. Its three walls of floor-to-ceiling books, all smelling of leather and candle wax, surrounded comfortable chairs and long tables for copying manuscripts. Leaded glass windows –a row of them on the eastern wall and rose windows at either end of the room—provided light.

"You must write to your aunt and your betrothed," Queen Katherine told her. "The Archbishop is happy to send your letters with a papal envoy, who leaves in the morning. Writing supplies are over there."

Nicola curtseyed, then hurried to a writing desk. As she sat, mentally composing her first letter, she could hear the Queen whispering to her ladies—probably explaining why a papal envoy would carry messages to Nicola's aunt and betrothed. Some of the Queen's ladies already seemed jealous that she had traveled alone with the Queen by litter. Nicola feared this new special treatment would make their jealousy worse.

Not knowing what to do about it, Nicola tried to concentrate on her writing. She poured out her heart to Raphael, quickly filling several pages with descriptions of the beautiful stained glass in Canterbury Cathedral, how much she missed him, and how she already longed to return home. "If all goes well, I will be back early in the new year," she promised him, signing herself, "with all my love, from your loving and faithful Nicola."

The letter to Caterina was more difficult, because Nicola was still angry about being sent to England. "I am well, and safe,' she began. "Captain Napolitano gave me a locked cabin and protection from his sailors, as he promised. But Sir Charles

Brandon was no gentleman. You were wrong to send me on a long sea voyage, with no protection other than a dagger."

Perhaps this was unfair, she reflected, knowing that Caterina would worry. "Fortunately, he only forced a kiss on me once, and I gave him a good slap for it. Queen Katherine has taken me into her protection," she added. "I should be fine. The cannons for Dover have been installed and successfully tested. I also examined the crates going by wagon to castles nearby. None were damaged."

What else to say? "The Queen's ladies have been very impressed by my Italian finery," she added. "If I can, I will write again.". She signed it "N," and sealed both letters with candle wax and her signet ring, which was embossed with two crossed cannons.

The smell of cooked fish made Nicola aware that a large library table behind her was being set up for dining. One of the Queen's ladies was sampling each platter, apparently tasting its contents for poison.

Nicola placed her letters on a table beside the Queen, then curtseyed. Her Highness held two books in her lap: her breviary, and something larger, and beautifully bound in tooled leather.

"The Archbishop has loaned me this," she said to Nicola. "It's Dante's *Inferno*. I thought you could read it to me, so I can hear the sound of the Italian. And translate for me what I do not understand."

"I love Dante. A very holy man, and such a poet! Shall I start at the beginning?"

"Absolutely. But not this evening. We are called to supper." The Queen beckoned for a servant to take Nicola's letters, then accepted help to her feet from two of her ladies. She beckoned to Nicola to follow. "The Archbishop has created a temporary women's quarters here, with separate meals for us. Eat what you wish. I am exempt from the Advent fast because I am pregnant, so we have a few delicacies that are not being served to the court. I need to save some for Henry. He does not believe that God requires him to fast."

The Queen's black maidservant pointed Nicola to a seat at the opposite end of the table from the Queen. Nicola and most of the other ladies observed Advent fast, though a few grumbled. The fish was delicious; the bread and vegetables less so— but still better than the fare onboard the *Romulus*. Afterwards, Nicola was very comfortable sleeping in a monk's cell, which reminded her of the convent where she was raised.

The following morning Nicola prowled the library, searching for texts in English that would help her learn the language. The Queen and several of her ladies joined King Henry, who was holding court with the Archbishop and the Duke of Buckingham, among other members of his Council. The remaining ladies embroidered, played cards, or stared at Nicola, who wondered how to overcome their hostility.

Margaret Pole crossed the room to speak to her. She was older and thin, with a long face and deep worry lines around her mouth and between her brows. Her attire was the plainest amongst the Queen's ladies—an unadorned grey muslin kirtle with a triangular headdress. Not a beauty, but her brown eyes were kind. "What are you reading?" she asked.

"I am so happy you speak Latin," Nicola said. "I am reading the book of the Psalms, translated into English. Since I know the Latin versions well, I am hoping that studying them will help me learn your language."

Margaret glanced at the other ladies, then smiled at Nicola. "We all wonder about you and your betrothed. And how you know how to make cannons."

Nicola gave Lady Margaret an abbreviated version of the story she had given the Queen. "Feel free to tell the others," she added, nodding and smiling at the ladies playing cards on the opposite side of the room. Who were staring at her, again, and did not return her smile.

Nicola and the Queen spent part of the next two days by the fire in this comfortable place, reading and discussing Dante, joined by the ladies patient enough to wait for the Queen's translations. Queen Katherine seemed particularly struck that the adulterous romance of Paolo and Francesca, whose spirits were buffeted around the First Circle of Hell by winds, but not punished with eternal pain.

"'Thou shalt not commit adultery' is the Seventh Commandment, but Dante treats it as the least of sins," the Queen complained. "Why did he put adulterers in the First Circle, next to the virtuous pagans in Limbo? I understand that the winds keep the adulterous lovers apart, but that is hardly punishment. It feels wrong."

"Dante was a married man, in love with Beatrice, who was married herself.' Nicola responded. "Perhaps he felt buffeted by his passions, like Paolo and Francesca."

The Queen frowned "You mean Beatrice was real? I had no idea. How dare he paint her as an angel?"

"Supposedly he never actually met her," Nicola responded. "Just saw her across a room. She died very young, but he continued to write poetry idealizing her. So in the Divine Comedy she became his guiding angel."

The Queen gazed out a window, scowling. "The religious poet was a married lecher who fell in love with a married woman," she pronounced. "I wish I were surprised." Her angry gaze swept across her ladies, who stirred from their frozen poses in succession, as if a strong wind had just blown through the room.

"We can't blame Beatrice that a man fell in love with her from across a room," Nicola said, feeling very uncomfortable.

Queen Katherine smiled at Nicola, to her immense relief. "Of course not. But I'm sure his wife suffered." She switched to English. "It's always the wives who suffer. Don't you think so, Lady Elizabeth?"

Lady Elizabeth Boleyn looked flustered. A tall, black-haired beauty, she looked too young to have marriageable children—but Lady Margaret had mentioned her two daughters, whom she hoped to bring to court. She rivaled the Queen in sumptuous dress.

Lady Elizabeth froze for a moment, then nodded forcefully. "Wives do suffer," she agreed.

The bells of the cathedral outside the library window rang for Mass. The Queen rose and took Nicola's arm. The two of them led the rest of the ladies, followed by the King's guards.

"I would love to stay here longer," the Queen told Nicola as they walked. She seemed calm now, her eyes fixed on the magnificent cathedral ahead of them. "The Archbishop is a friend and it is very comfortable, compared to where we go next. But Henry loves merriment, which is difficult here. His companions and followers are scattered all over the city, since the Archbishop's Palace is so small. And Henry hates fasting, which the Archbishop requires. The hunting is indifferent and the weather grows colder. So we leave tomorrow. I'm going to ask the Archbishop to lend me this volume of Dante, though."

"Could I also borrow the English translation of the Psalms I have been reading?" Nicola asked. "It is helping me learn English more quickly. All the important words are in the Psalms."

"Reading helped me greatly when I was learning English," the Queen responded. "I'll ask."

Thomas Wolsey, after Hans Holbein the Younger,
line engraving, probably 18th century

Chapter 6: Cannons are Missing

The Road to Rochester Castle, the following morning

At dawn, Nicola arose, dressed, and found her way to the palace courtyard, looking for the wagons with her cannons among those assembling for the trip to Rochester Castle. She located them by spotting Sir William Burgoyne's tall figure. He waved to her when he saw her, picking her way through the chaos.

"I am to accompany the Queen again," she told him. "So I cannot be with you."

"Which explains why you are in court dress," he remarked. "And as beautiful as ever."

This time, Nicola was in blue—Virgin Mary blue, Raphael called it. Over her kirtle she wore Caterina's black wool cloak, since the day was cold. "You are too kind," she said, feeling the blood rushing to her cheeks. "I see that everything is in order. Is there anything further I can do to assist?"

"Nothing. Sir Charles will join me soon. I will see you at Rochester Castle. It looks like we are almost ready to leave. You had best go," he responded.

Happy to avoid Sir Charles, Nicola followed the snaking procession that was rapidly forming, weaving through the supply wagons, musicians, jesters, knights and ladies, to the queen's brightly-painted litter near the front.

41

The Queen was already inside, a soft blue blanket spread over her pregnant belly. When the procession began to move they opened the Divine Comedy, and spent a happy morning working their way through the lesser sins that doomed the dead to the upper circles of Hell.

"Do you think I condone gluttony, by letting Henry eat the delicacies they serve me because I need not fast?" the Queen asked Nicola.

Nicola felt uncomfortable discussing the King's sins. "Perhaps you should ask your confessor that question," she responded. At Canterbury, the Queen had confessed daily and spent hours in personal prayer, evidently her habit.

"My confessor does not like to consider Henry's sins, which I understand. He chides me when I confess them, in fact. I wonder why Dante considered gluttony a worse sin than adultery."

Nicola wondered what King Henry had done, to make his wife react so strongly every time she thought about adultery. "Likely he considered gluttony worse than adultery because he was a man, but probably not a glutton. Every portrait I have ever seen of Dante shows a thin man with a nose like a raven's beak."

The Queen laughed at this. "It is easy to disapprove of things we don't do ourselves," she said. "I think my Italian is improving, don't you?"

Nicola was relieved the subject had changed. "Very quickly," she agreed. "You just needed to hear it. My English is improving, too. Being forced to listen and speak helps."

"I will try to speak English to you about simple matters," the Queen promised. The litter stopped. "Hold on," she said, as it lurched to the ground. The curtain next to her was thrust aside, and Lady Margaret Pole's face appeared. Solicitous hands helped the Queen to her feet.

The four squat men who carried the litter were not permitted to touch the Queen, but more than happy to help Nicola to her feet. She thanked them in halting English. A smiling page offered all of them bread and cheese. Nicola took hers, and decided to seek the wagons carrying her cannons.

On her way, a handsome man with straw-colored hair and a falcon on his wrist stopped her, saying something she did not understand. Nicola had a rehearsed response. "I am sorry. I don't speak English."

He gestured at the falcon on his wrist, and spoke again more slowly. "Bird" was all she understood. "No thank you," she responded, and moved on, hoping to find Sir William, and avoid seeing Sir Charles.

She found only Sir Charles, sitting on a log, devouring a meat pie. "Where is the other wagon? And Sir William?" she asked him.

He swallowed, and wiped his beard with his forearm. "Behind us somewhere. Must have had a problem."

"Unguarded?" Nicola said, looking around them. They were at the end of the straggling procession, with no armed men in sight.

"I suppose so," Sir Charles said.

"Shouldn't we go back and look for them? With some of these soldiers? I hear these woods are full of outlaws."

"They are. But who is going to steal cannons?"

A priest was standing nearby. Tall and thin, he had Italian coloring and chiseled features, reminding Nicola of Cardinal Giulio de' Medici, whom she had once suspected of murder.[3] "I also noticed the missing wagon," the priest said. "The horses are well worth stealing. You will need a second wagon with tools, in case of a broken wheel or axle. I will arrange for it, and for some guards."

"Who was that?" Nicola asked Sir Charles, as they watched the priest stride away.

"His name is Wolsey—one of the king's almoners."

"You mean he gives out alms to the poor?" Nicola said.

---

[3] Read about it in Martin Luther and Murder

"Yes. But he is also very clever and completely trustworthy. The King relies on him increasingly. He must be watching over the supply wagons."

"I will be back as soon as I tell one of the Queen's ladies that I must locate my cannons," Nicola said.

"You need not concern yourself with this, Lady Nicola."

"I have yet to receive the next payment, Sir Charles. Of course I must concern myself. I can drive the wagon."

Would Sir Charles get the wrong idea from this offer? Nicola decided not to risk it. She looked him in the eye, to be sure he was listening. He smiled at her, as if she were flirting with him. "But under no circumstances will I ride with you," she snapped, infuriated at his expression. "And if you touch me again without my consent, I will put a dagger in you. If my betrothed were here, he would use a sword."

He looked so dumbfounded that she had to suppress the urge to slap him again. After all that had passed between them, he still thought she might find him attractive? Sitting on a log with his ugly black beard covered in crumbs? She stormed away to look for the Queen's servants, irked that she felt obliged to go.

The wagon was ready to depart when Nicola returned. But a soldier drove it instead of her, at a speed that made her teeth chatter. Even then, they had trouble keeping up with Sir Charles and the others trotting ahead of them on horses. Clutching the bouncing wagon, Nicola scanned the road and the huge trees on either side of it. Some were leafless; others still showed the remains of fall color. The king's entourage had scarred the road with horse droppings and wheel ruts. Here and there, she saw debris from the court's passage amongst the fallen leaves—a handkerchief, a ribbon, a shoe.

"Stop," she shouted in English, when she saw something else. She shook the arm of the guardsman beside her, her heart sinking. "Stop."

When the wagon stopped, she jumped off and ran back to look at a darker expanse of dirt dotted with a perfect circle of fallen leaves. She ran a finger across a red and yellow leaf, then tasted her fingertip.

"Blood." she told Sir Charles, who had ridden back to join them. "You can smell it, too." He dismounted to inspect himself.

While the men poked at the wet earth, Nicola peered into the woods around them, feeling increasingly fearful. Could they be surrounded by outlaws, who were hiding amongst those giant, gnarled trees, waiting for hapless travelers? Perhaps outlaws thought the gun crates contained something they could sell. What had happened?

And above all, where was Sir William? Dear God, she thought, let that be the blood of a wild animal, killed by hunters. A deer perhaps, or a boar. Don't let it be human blood. But she smelled no animal presence, even as she ventured further into the woods.

There, she saw what she feared. "Oh, no," she gasped, feeling as if her heart were summersaulting in her chest. She waved to the soldiers, and pointed. "Do you see the cowhides? The cannons were wrapped in cowhides. And the pine branches, nowhere near a pine? And the flies?"

Sir Charles spoke to the guards in English, gesturing. They stepped into the woods and threw aside the pine branches, revealing two wooden crates.

"We have found them!" Sir Charles said. "What a relief."

"We have not found them," Nicola said shakily, feeling as if her chest were about to explode. "Cannons don't bleed."

Flies clustered on the dark red stains at the base of each box. Sir Charles exclaimed, then said something to the guardsmen in rapid English. Two of them used their swords to pry open the first box, held only by bent, damaged nails.

Sir William Burgoyne's face stared out, white as a winding sheet and frozen in a look of surprise. He had been cleanly beheaded; his head placed atop his belly. His legs had been hacked off and shoved under his body, feet wedged against the bottom of the box, which was too short for a full grown man. He looked like a surprised pygmy, holding his own head and ready to hop out of his coffin, spotted with blood.

Nicola gagged, and turned to vomit into the greenery. Memories of other grotesque corpses forced themselves into her brain: Caterina's husband, his face contorted by poison; the naked cardinal she and Martin Luther stumbled over; [4] the mother who bled out in childbirth; the drowned prostitute with the mark of a garrote around her neck. She willed them all out of her mind. When her stomach was empty she continued to kneel until her breathing calmed and she could control her tears.

When she stood, the men had already opened the second box. "It's the man who drove the wagon," Sir Charles said. "Don't look."

"I have seen plenty of blood in my life," Nicola responded, willing her voice to remain steady. They stared in silence at a much bloodier headless corpse. Nicola pointed, her hand trembling. "This man saw his death coming," she cried. "See the horror on his face? And his wounds? The sword hacked at his raised arm, there, and took off his hand. You can see he fought back. Sir William has no defensive wounds. He was left to bleed out on the road while they killed the wagon driver."

 She swallowed hard, tasting the vomit that rose again to her throat, and pointed again at Sir William's corpse. "And Sir Charles – this was treason. Someone in the court was plotting while we were in Canterbury. Who else would have known about the cannons, or when they would reach this spot? And William trusted his attacker, or he would have fought back. Do you see that his neck has been cut cleanly through? With one stroke? To reach him, it had to be someone tall and very strong, with a heavy, sharp sword, standing close by."

---

[4] Read about the murder of Caterina's husband in <u>A Borgia Daughter Dies</u> and the cardinal's in <u>Martin Luther and Murder,</u>

Gingerly, she walked to the corpse, and pulled the sword still strapped to William's waist from its scabbard. "It's clean. He never drew it."

"Maybe he was surprised from behind?"

Nicola glared at Sir Charles. "By a strong man with a sword who climbed over the back of a wagon? Not possible."

Sir Charles swore again, and turned to address the guardsmen, who were muttering among themselves in English. They then spoke all at once, gesturing and pointing, until he gave them some kind of an order. They stood at attention and nodded.

He turned back to Nicola, who was still shaking. "I told them no one must know of this, because it may be treason. They agree. I said I will take them with me to the King to hear their stories but for now—silence. But I know Henry well. He hates treason, and tries to deal with it secretly. He will not want this bruited about."

He glanced at the guardsmen, put his finger to his lips, and pointed at Nicola. "That goes for you, too, Lady Nicola," he continued. "You must say nothing."

"Even to Queen Katherine?" she asked.

Charles frowned. "If she asks, tell her she must talk to Henry. Ordinarily he keeps no secrets from her, but she is about to give birth. She does not need more worries."

Nicola nodded. "I don't speak," she announced to the guardsmen, in English, making the gesture of a key, locking her mouth.

"Good!" said one of them.

Sir Charles spoke sharply to them and gestured towards the crates containing the bodies. Another animated discussion followed, which Nicola could not follow. At the end, the guardsmen retrieved tools from the wagon, and began nailing the crates shut again, their gruesome cargo still inside.

"We'll cover the crates with those cow hides and take them back with us," Sir Charles told Nicola.

"Was there a disagreement about something?" she asked.

"Whether we should try to find the cannons now. I told them it would be dangerous and probably useless. We don't know how many traitors we are up against. And, we will be lucky to catch up with the court before dark."

Nicola nodded, relieved. "We just passed a major crossroad. Where does it go?"

"That's just it. To coastal towns, either on the Channel or the south coast. The cannons could be loaded on ships by now."

"We should at least try to determine which road they took, while it is light. They have stolen four cannons. The wagon ruts will be deep."

Nicola and Sir Charles replaced the pine branches while the guardsmen loaded the crates into the wagon they had brought with them. "Sir Charles, who will tell Sir William's wife?" she asked. "And what will she be told? He had *children*."

"The wagon driver had a family too—a baby and her brother who can scarce walk yet, according to one of the guards. The king will provide for all of them, believe me. And he will decide the story to tell. Wolsey will find coffins somehow—he always comes through."

Detail from *Judita* by Vinceno Catena c. 1520-25,
Showing woman dressed in an Italian renaissance-era camicia

CHAPTER 7: THE KING'S DESIRE

Rochester Castle, later that night

A hand shook Nicola from a deep sleep. "The Queen wants to see you."

Nicola sat up, confused to find herself lying on a pallet in a darkened room full of them, some occupied by sleeping women.

"The Queen is awake and wants to see you."

It was Lena, the Queen's dark-skinned maid, speaking English with a heavy Spanish accent. Stunned by sleep, Nicola did not understand at first. Lena gestured and pointed.

"I wear only my *camicia*," Nicola said.

"Wrap a blanket around yourself. Blanket. *Cobija*. Here. Put it around you." Nicola groaned, pulled the blanket around her shoulders, and followed Lena to the Queen's bedroom, remembering gruesome nightmares and wondering how she had slept through the raucous laughter and singing emanating from the castle banquet hall.

King Henry stood beside the Queen's bed, bent over her, with his hand on her belly. Their faces, framed in candlelight, radiated happiness.

"Our son is kicking," the Queen said. "Henry came to look in on me, but I was not asleep."

"Too much noise?" Henry asked, eyes locked on hers. "I shall order silence this instant." Roars of laughter rose from the banquet hall as spoke.

"No, no," Katherine, clutching his hand. "It's the baby. Not the noise."

They exchanged a look of such loving intimacy that it embarrassed Nicola to intrude on it. And made her ache for Raphael, and the times he had looked at her like that. She blinked away a tear, and turned to watch Lena poke the fire into a bright blaze.

"Leave us, Lena," the Queen said. "And close the door."

When Nicola turned, she realized that Henry, now standing upright, was ogling her bare calves. And that Katherine, lying amongst her pillows, could not see them. Or the way Henry was leering at them.

Nicola stepped towards the foot of the bed to hide her naked skin. Even from a distance, the King reeked of wine. "How may I assist you, Your Highness?" she asked the Queen.

"Henry has told me about the murders you saw today, and that Sir Charles swore you to silence."

"You need not keep silence with the Queen," Henry said.

"Exactly. I need to hear your whole story, so I can help Henry decide what to do. But not now. Tomorrow you will ride in my litter again. We will talk then."

"One thing," the King said. "Charles said the wagon with the cannons was headed towards the Channel. Do you agree?"

"If that is to the east, yes. The deepest wagon ruts went in that direction."

"As you feared," the Queen said to Henry. "Where is Richard de la Pole these days?"

"In France, say my spies. Trying to persuade King Louis to declare him king of England and give him an army. Don't fret, though, my love. Louis is not that foolish."

"There was something else important I wanted to tell you," Nicola said. "Give me a moment. It's about the cannons." Still half sleep, she adjusted the blanket wrapped around her shoulders, and noticed Henry ogling her again as she did it.

"I remember now," she said. "If there is a plot to overthrow you—which Sir Charles and I suspect—someone may also try to steal the cannons that are coming to London by river. Who will greet the ship and guard them if it reaches Greenwich Palace before we do? And what has happened to the wagon with four cannons destined for Windsor Castle? Was it properly guarded? The stolen cannons were not."

The King bent for a whispered conference with his Queen, then addressed Nicola. "We passed the road to Windsor Castle this afternoon, while you were with Sir Charles. So the second wagonload of cannons is on its way there. I don't know if they were properly guarded. Charles would have seen to it, but he was with you."

He scowled. "I will send a rider to ensure those cannons arrive safely. And another to Greenwich, to see to the security of the others, if the ship arrives before we do."

"More than one guard should be sent to Windsor, considering what happened to Sir William," Nicola said. "Also, Sir Charles told me that most of the river shipment will be stored in the Tower of London, until the ships you are building are ready to be outfitted. And that the Tower is a very strong place where Your Highness keeps traitors." Her voice trailed off. Her tone was not respectful enough.

She paused to adjust the blanket that had again slipped from her shoulder as she pondered how best to sound servile. Henry reacted with a crooked smile and a raised brow, inspiring her to pull the blanket even closer. "Your pardon, Highnesses," she said, "but is it wise to keep traitors and enough guns and cannons for an army in the same place? If you do, you should keep the only key."

The King flushed and grimaced. She had said too much. "The Tower is extremely safe," he snapped. "Armaments and traitors have been kept there simultaneously for hundreds of years."

"Now, go back to your rest," said the Queen. "You have earned it."

Nicola left as quickly as she could, trailing her blanket to hide her bare legs, and wishing she had not seen the lust in the King's eyes.

Sedan chair or litter, 16th century

Chapter 8: The Conspiracy Grows

The road to Greenwich Palace, the next morning

The next morning, Nicola told Queen Katherine about the murders as they rode in the Queen's curtained litter, reclining against newly-stuffed embroidered cushions that smelled of rose petals and fresh rosemary. She kept her voice low, though it was unlikely that the litter-bearers spoke Latin.

"It sounds like Wolsey saved the day," the Queen observed when Nicola concluded her tale. "He always appears whenever the King needs him. Explain to me again why these murders were treason, and not just outlaws in the woods? Henry thinks it was outlaws."

"First, William Burgoyne had no defensive wounds. He died with his sword in its hilt. It means he likely knew his killer, because he did not feel threatened by him. Second, it was an ambuscade near a crossroad. No one except members of the King's court knew precisely where those cannons were, and when they would arrive at that place. So someone who is part of the court likely planned the ambuscade. Unless you suspect the Archbishop of Canterbury or someone who works for him—and how likely is that?"

"Not likely at all. The Archbishop of Canterbury is a holy man and a trusted friend." She sighed. "I will make Henry understand. He is very intelligent, but also very young—only nineteen, five years younger than me. Young, and not raised to be king. He was brought up to fight battles for his older brother Arthur, who died. Which is why Henry commissioned a navy and ordered cannons from your aunt, as soon as he was crowned. He loves thinking about battles and war and ships. But he does not love consulting his Council, or holding court." The Queen lapsed into silence.

"I'm sorry," Nicola said. "You were married to Arthur, *si*?'

"Briefly, but only in name. Arthur was very ill when I arrived from Spain, and lived only a few months. It was God's will that Henry be king when his father died, and I his queen. For now, though, Henry prefers to let others—including me—do most of the mundane work of ruling the realm, while he thinks about future glory in battle. Mind you, I am not complaining. My mother—Queen Isabella—was a ruling queen, and raised me to be one, too."

She pulled a curtain aside, allowing a glimpse of the surrounding forest. "But this treason—possible treason—has gotten Henry's attention. He will not rest until he can punish whoever stole those cannons and killed Sir William."

"Is Lady Margaret safe?" Nicola asked. "You spoke last night of a traitor named Richard de la Pole, who must be related to her somehow?"

The Queen settled back into her cushions. "When he was first crowned, Henry sought the love of his people by showing mercy to many who had opposed his father, who was a hard man. But not to the de la Pole brothers. He couldn't. Their father tried repeatedly to seize the crown from Henry's father, and they have tried to do the same from Henry. That is why two of them are in the Tower of London while Richard tries to raise an army of invasion in France."

As if suddenly chilled, the Queen pulled her blanket around her. "The brothers in the Tower are lucky. So far. Henry has had two of his father's chief councilors beheaded."

"They weren't related to Lady Margaret, were they?"

"The ones who were beheaded? No. And those men were hated for completely different reasons. Margaret had nothing to do with her cousins' rebellions.

Besides which she is not a man, so she is not viewed as threatening. At least I hope not."

Nicola longed to ask what the executed men had done, besides being "hated." But she did not dare.

Queen Katherine seemed to sense her question. "Sometimes a monarch has to do things for the good of the realm," she mused. "My mother would get down on her knees and beg God's forgiveness, when she had blood on her hands. Henry thinks he's doing God's will when he orders an execution. And he seems to relish it, which concerns me. I have been a pacifying influence on him. But if I were to die in childbirth—"

"You are not going to die in childbirth," Nicola assured her, hoping to change the subject. The Queen's confidences made Nicola uncomfortable—but who else did the unfortunate woman have to talk to? She'd made it plain that she trusted no one around her—not even her royal husband. "You are young and strong," Nicola assured her. "You will recover quickly from the birth, and live to see your grandchildren. Shall we read more Dante?"

"You read aloud, please. I will tell you if I don't understand."

Reading Italian poetry was pleasant, even though it was about Hell. Dante led them through the Circle of the wrathful, who scratched and bit each other in deep mud, then into the Circle of heretics, who lay in tombs of eternal fire.

At midday they stopped to eat in a field of stubble dotted with haystacks, on the bank of the Thames. Pages distributed crescent-shaped meat pies that they called "pasties," and poured weak beer from flagons into pewter cups. Most of the court, including Nicola, ate while standing.

As Nicola finished her pasty, she watched the King and Queen, seated in gilded chairs, laughing and talking with Sir Charles, the Duke of Buckingham, and other members of the inner court. A messenger arrived and whispered something to the King, who in turn murmured to Katherine, whose eyes widened before she gestured to him to lean closer, and spoke at length in his ear. The King then rose, his face solemn. "On to Greenwich Palace," he shouted. "We are almost home."

Nicola returned to the litter, and was eventually joined by the Queen, who motioned a page to help them in. When they were moving again, the Queen whispered, "You were right. The cannons that were headed to Windsor have been stolen. And everyone who was with them is dead."

Nicola was not surprised. "How were they killed?"

The Queen hugged her pregnant belly, as if to protect her unborn child. "We don't know yet. We did not want to acknowledge a problem in front of the entire court. The man who discovered this is waiting to speak to us at Greenwich Palace."

Nicola nodded. "I'm very sorry, Your Highness. Soon your armorers will be able to make English cannons to replace the ones that were stolen."

"The cannons are the least of Henry's worries, as I'm sure you understand."

"Of course. I will do what I can to help. For now, would you like to read some more from Dante?"

"I don't think I could concentrate. Do you hear the cheers?" She peeked through the curtain. "We must be getting close to Greenwich. The forests have turned into fields and the serfs who live in this village have come out to greet us."

Peering past the Queen, Nicola caught a glimpse of hooded men and women in drab garb, their faces red from the cold, waving at the litter and shouting "God save her! God save the Queen!"

Katherine waved back, then let the curtain fall and settled back in the litter, smiling. "The people do seem to like me."

"I can hear them cheering for King Henry as well."

"I must try to sleep a little," the Queen announced, when it became quiet again. "I slept poorly last night and will get little rest when we arrive. I often read Henry's correspondence for him. There will be a pile of it."

While the Queen dozed, Nicola berated herself for the lie she had inadvertently told earlier, when trying to comfort the Queen's fears of dying in childbirth. This Queen would likely not live to see her grandchildren. The French Disease would eventually kill her and King Henry both, if something else didn't do it sooner.

Should she tell the Queen? It would do the poor woman no good, and possibly great harm. Making that announcement would be like blowing up a large keg of gunpowder in the royal Presence Room. And she herself would be the likeliest victim of the explosion, because no one would want to believe her. Other people surely had guessed this truth, but none dared say anything. Wisely. It was obvious that Henry's subjects feared him for good reason. He was a powerful sovereign— a gesture across his throat meant a beheading. He had apparently had prominent men beheaded recently, simply for being hated.

Nicola shivered, and vowed to hold her tongue.

View of Greenwich Palace, 1630

CHAPTER 9: WHERE IS THE SHIP?

At Greenwich Palace, the same day

Nicola eased herself out of the litter next to the walls of Greenwich Palace. "The Queen sleeps," she said quietly in English to the bearer who helped her out. "Tell her I go to look for the ship."

"The sheep?" he said, his face puzzled.

"Ship. The ship with the cannons. Boat. There," she pointed.

His face broke into a smile, and he nodded.

She wove her way back through the King's entourage, looking for the *Romulus* among the many vessels, large and small, docked alongside the palace and busily disgorging goods into wagons and onto the backs of porters. When the Duke of Buckingham passed, leading his company of knights, she paused long enough to memorize the pattern embossed on his magnificent suit of armor, and his unremarkable chubby face.

The *Romulus* was nowhere to be seen. But a group of guards, dressed in the King's colors, was lounging on a dock, looking downstream. Nicola approached them. "Do you wait for the *Romulus?* From Italy?" she asked, in English.

"You must be the Italian lady. Yes, we wait for the *Romulus*," said one of them.

Nicola was relieved. "You know when she is coming?"

They all talked at once, and she could not understand them. But it had something to do with wind, and a toe.

She was puzzled. "Toe?" she asked, pointing at her foot.

They laughed. One of them made motions, as if he were pulling a rope. A second made rowing motions. She still did not understand, and was tempted to laugh at their antics. A third then pointed towards the middle of the Thames, where a ship, sails flapping, was being pulled slowly upstream by a rowboat with eight men at the oars, who were working very hard.

"I see," she said. "Bad wind." They laughed uproariously at this, which she did not understand. "I must know when *Romulus* comes," she continued. "Immediately. Fast, fast. Can you do this for me? I stay with the Queen. You tell the Queen's ladies and I will know."

They nodded, grinning at her, and their captain said something about Wolsey. "He is coming too?" she said. "Good. Please you tell him and Captain Napolitano to wait for me. Please? Thank you."

Turning to watch the court procession, she saw that Greenwich Palace stretched along the waterfront for a quarter mile or more. Built of red brick and studded with leaded glass windows, its low wall fronted directly on the river road. At its main entrance, the broad central tower was four stories tall. Most of the court had disappeared into the main gates by the time she managed to rejoin it near the end of the procession, between bearded monks, singing and marching three by three, and the King's barking greyhounds, caged in their specially-made cart.

A page approached her at the entrance. "The Queen is worried about you," he said. "Come, I will take you to her."

Grateful for the guidance, she followed him up flights of stairs, through a maze of rooms, and along an exterior arcade that looked out over a tiltyard, where knights on horseback practiced with their lances, while others on foot practiced with wooden swords.

Chaos reigned in the Queen's quarters when they arrived. The Presence Chamber—where the Queen received distinguished guests—was magnificent, the interior walls covered with bright tapestries depicting a queen in Roman armor, opposite a wall of leaded glass windows punctuated with window seats, overlooking the Thames and the setting sun. Floor tiles emblazoned with red and white Tudor roses were dotted with Turkish carpets, and the high coffered ceilings painted with banners and heraldic shields. But everywhere were crates, bundles, wooden chests, cloaks, shawls, and even half-eaten loaves and meat pies. Pages and ladies trotted in and out with more bundles, chattering loudly. Fires had been lit but the space was cold, and smelled musty.

Queen Katherine sat next to an enormous marble fireplace in front of a crackling fire, hands folded over her pregnant belly and feet on an embroidered footstool. Her nap had evidently done her good—color had returned to her checks, and her eyes were less bruised-looking. She smiled when she saw Nicola. "Has the ship arrived?" she called out.

"Not yet. I do not see my belongings, Your Highness, and I am worried." Nicola said. "I will need access to my inventory as soon as the ship arrives."

"Some things have gone to storerooms, I'm afraid. Ask a page to help you."

Renaissance-era Italian boot stiletto

CHAPTER 10: THE KING'S THREATS

A storage room in Greenwich Palace, the same day

Nicola and one of the pages went from room to room, looking for her chests. To Nicola's surprise, the castle's "garderobes"—"clothing keepers" in Italian—were actually interior privies, their wooden seats surrounded by stacked chests and hanging garments.

"Why do they do this?" she asked the page.

"The smell keeps away moths, of course," he told her.

"I don't understand."

He made a face and pinched his nose. She wondered what "moths" were, and whether the English wanted smelly clothes. Surely not.

She was thankful that her belongings were not in any of the garderobes. Rather, they were in a small storeroom piled with stacks of ornate wooden chests, most painted with coats of arms. The page helped Nicola extract the chest that contained her cannon inventory and related documents, then went to fetch help to move all her belongings the Queen's quarters.

She was looking at her inventory by the window when the door opened, then closed again.

"Finding you alone is not easy," said King Henry.

She gasped. Heart pounding, she looked up to see him striding rapidly toward her, dressed in glittering gold, arms extended as if to embrace her, a triumphant look on his face. Without thinking, she drew her dagger from her boot—and pointed it at her own throat, instantly realizing that the Yeomen Guards, who accompanied the King everywhere, would kill her if she threatened him.

"Stay away," she shouted in English, so that the guards outside the door would hear. "Stay away!"

Henry stopped short when he saw the dagger, a shocked look on his face. "Come, come, my lady," he murmured. "I know you are betrothed, but there is no harm in a kiss."

"There is harm. *Malum!*" she repeated loudly, realizing that the Yeoman Guards would hear loud voices and know that Latin word, from reciting the Mass. She backed further from Henry as he continued to approach her, which seemed to surprise him even more.

"The harm in a kiss comes from those sores on your face," she said quietly, in Latin. "That is how the French Disease—the pox—is spread."

Henry's hand touched his cheek, and his face turned scarlet, and contorted with rage. "How dare you even imply....if you ever repeat such an accusation to anyone—especially the Queen...."

The King was threatening her, in perfect Latin. Nicola felt the dagger quiver in her hands, and realized her whole body was shaking. "Stay away from me, and I won't," she promised, her voice shaking too. "It's too late to help your Queen. But I will defend my honor."

Her back was now to the wall. When he took another step towards her, she pricked the top of her throat with the dagger, and felt the blood trickle down her neck.

Eyes wide, he stepped back again. "I have never taken a woman by force," he said. But his tone was tentative, as if he were considering the possibility for the first time. He looked her up and down. Was he trying to decide whether to rape her?

He was twice her size. His guards would not intervene to help her, even if she cried out. Should she fight? Wound herself? Was it better to die fighting than from French Disease?

"And I have no disease," he added more firmly.

"Godly men do not do such things. Stay away!" she screamed in English, her dagger shaking in her hand.

His angry red face sagged into a different expression. Fear? Guilt? Frustration? Muttering under his breath, he turned and stalked toward the storeroom door, his magnificent gold attire incongruous in the dusty surroundings where he'd cornered her. Then he spun towards Nicola, his face still scarlet with rage.

"You thwart my desires at your peril, Lady Greensleeves," he seethed, through gritted teeth. "You dare pull a dagger on a king? Did you murder my men and steal my cannons? You will prove your innocence, or...or..."

"Or give my body to you?" she shouted in English. "I am not for sale."

She realized he had threatened her again. Her stomach lurched, and her English failed her. "You want me to prove I did not do these murders? I was with the Queen the whole time. So I am guiltless, unless your lady wife betrayed you too. And how am I supposed to prove my innocence? I am a woman, and a foreigner. I speak almost no English."

Henry's face lost its angry color when she mentioned his Queen, and his expression changed. "That's not what I want from you and you know it," he muttered.

Fear kept Nicola's anger in check. To calm herself she breathed as deeply as her bodice allowed, wondering how best to fend off this predatory monarch. She curtseyed slowly, watching him, her dagger pointed at the floor. He seemed less angry. Was he feeling guilty for his adulterous intentions? Did he recognize that she had done no wrong?

"I am happy to help find the cannons and the murderers. When my other duties to you allow," she said.

Henry reddened again, and clenched his teeth. "You would rather hunt killers than pleasure a king? How can this be?"

Henry was very handsome, but he was also very dangerous. And a carrier of deadly disease. "I love my betrothed!" she screamed in English. "And I came here to perform a job. Not to... Not to..."

King Henry snarled at her and turned away, fists clenched. "As you wish. But bear in mind—you are as good as dead if I accuse you of collusion with the killers." With that, he stomped out and slammed the door.

*****

Queen Katherine, still seated in her Presence Chamber, beckoned to Nicola when she reappeared. It was obvious that the Italian girl had been crying.

"Pull that stool close to me, and sit," she told Nicola, gesturing towards an embroidered ottoman next to the one where her own feet were propped, near the crackling blaze in the room's principal fireplace. "Now. What has happened? And why is there blood at your throat?"

Nicola looked not only miserable, but frightened. She glanced around at the ladies and servants still bustling to set the Queen's chambers in order after the day's journey, some obviously hoping to listen. "This should be for your ears only, Your Highness," she whispered.

It was about Henry, then. He had done something. And Katherine had a good idea what it was likely to be. She froze her expression to mask her anger, then shooed her other retainers away with a flick of her wrist. "Lean towards me, and tell me."

Nicola pulled her stool closer. "The King tried to kiss me. But I told him no, I was betrothed," she whispered. "Then he accused me of collusion in the murders and theft of the cannons. Said I have to prove my innocence. And that I was as good as *dead* if he accused me publicly. The blood is because I pricked my own throat with my dagger, to keep him away from me."

This was shocking, even for Henry. That he tried to kiss Nicola angered Katherine, without surprising her. But threatening her with death? "He accused you of stealing your own cannons?" Katherine whispered back. "And of murdering knights twice your size? That makes no sense. Besides, you were with me the whole time."

"Exactly what I told him. That seemed to calm him somewhat. He was very angry that I refused him, Your Highness. So perhaps he did not mean what he said."

"He will not accuse you of murder," the Queen promised, though she had private doubts. "Henry is hot-tempered and sometimes says impulsive and illogical things. But his temper cools quickly. And once it does, he is honorable, and reasonable. And at heart he is God-fearing."

Nicola nodded slowly, as if she doubted what she was hearing. The poor girl was trying to clean the blood at her throat, using a handkerchief wet with her own tears. "I know you love him, Your Highness," she said, sounding sincere to the Queen's ears. "I am happy to help find my cannons, and William Burgoyne's killers. William was always courteous and kind to me. I have helped find murderers in the past 5 and for his sake, I would do it again."

Nicola stopped herself, cocked her head, and frowned. "Provided I can complete my other work *pronto* and get home soon to my Raphael. But I speak almost no English. And in any event, I will need help."

"You certainly will. Let me think a moment." Katherine settled back into the pillows her ladies had placed behind her back, fighting exhaustion after the long day's journey. She knew it was a sin to curse her own husband, so she didn't. But she wanted to. She loved him so much. How could he do this to her, after swearing his eternal devotion?

She had to get Nicola away from him, for the sake of their marriage and their unborn child and the girl herself. Her stratagem had been to keep Nicola so close that it would be impossible for Henry to do what he had just done anyway. Truth

---

5 See the Nicola mystery series, all available here

was, he could do whatever he wanted, and right now he was angry and threatening. She sensed an ugly confrontation coming, if Nicola stayed with the court.

Should she send Nicola to a nunnery, like Anne Stafford? That would infuriate Henry. Besides, she liked Nicola. Nicola was now her friend, and she had very few of them. She didn't want to send her away.

Then, there was the problem of these murders, and this conspiracy. Henry was rash; he could easily lash out against a scapegoat. She needed to help him protect the realm from this new threat. But how could she possibly do such a thing, when she was about to enter her confinement? She would need eyes and ears outside the palace.

At a loss, she decided to pray for guidance. Closing her eyes, she fingered her rosary, and asked God's help. In the midst of prayer, she suddenly knew what to do. A calm resolve settled over her.

After giving thanks, she opened her eyes and focused on Nicola, who was staring at the fire. "How good a rider are you?" she asked.

Nicola sat up and looked at her. "Passable. I can ride hard, and astride. I brought a split skirt with me for that very purpose."

"Then wear it tomorrow, and be at the stables before dawn. I'll have Lena wake and take you. Sir Charles Brandon and Sir Henry Marney–the Captain of the Yeoman Guard—will ride out with a small company of soldiers and Father Wolsey, to view and bury the men who were killed when the cannons headed to Windsor were stolen. I will have my strongest horse saddled for you and notify Sir Charles that you will go with them, as my eyes and ears. They will not dare oppose me."

She paused to scrutinize Nicola's expression. "Will you do that for me? I trust you to keep me informed. Perhaps you will see things they do not. If nothing else, it will get you away from Henry while he calms down."

Nicola's tear-streaked face twitched into a smile. "With all my heart. But what will you tell the King? I am afraid of him. I want to stay away from him."

Katherine's simmering anger against Henry boiled a bit hotter as she considered this. *Guile,* she reminded herself. *Now is the time for guile.*

"Henry and I are already doing a kind of dance around you," she said. "I know he is attracted to you, and he knows I know. And he also knows that I love him with all my heart and soul, and that my jealousy could harm our baby. So he is doing his best to hide what he is up to—whatever that may be. He may well be abusing some scullery maid, since we must be chaste until after the birth. But at least I don't know about it."

She made a sudden decision. "I will tell him the truth—that I have chosen you as my eyes and ears in this matter because I trust your judgment, based on your observations from the first murders. And besides, the cannons are yours until we pay for them. You have a personal stake in this."

She reached out and patted Nicola's hand. "I will not let on that I know what he did to you. Or rather, tried to do," she said, feeling her spirits rise as she realized the power over Henry this would give her. "I'll leave him wondering about that. To keep peace, he will not dare object. And since you are acting as my eyes and ears, he will think twice about trying to kiss you again. Please don't cry."

Nicola had been swallowing sobs while the Queen spoke. She mopped her eyes with her bloodstained handkerchief. "I'm sorry, Your Highness. Hearing that he might abuse a scullery maid scared me again. A long hard ride that takes me far away from him will do me good."

"Another excellent reason to go, then." A page was hovering just out of hearing range, his face frightened. "What is it? she snapped at him.

"Your Highness. The King is back from the hunt. He invites you to sup with him in his Privy Chamber."

"I'll be there directly," she promised. To Nicola she whispered, "I am relying on you. I will see that you are escorted straight to me when you return."

"I will do my best, your Highness. I hope you believe me—truly, truly, I did not want your husband to come anywhere near me—"

Katherine believed her. "I know. Lean closer for a moment, and give me that handkerchief."

The Queen used the wettest part to wipe a last smear of blood from Nicola's throat, and a little from around her eyes. "Now smile. And go back to your English psalms."

A Soldier on Horseback
by Anthony van Dyck 1616

CHAPTER 11: MORE CORPSES

Dawn the next day

When Nicola reached the palace stables before dawn the next morning, her mare was saddled and ready. As a stable boy helped her up, she realized that the soldiers assigned to bury their murdered confederates were staring at her from their own mounts. One of them laughed outright as she adjusted her cloak and split skirt. Nicola realized she must look like a nun with her legs spread in the practical garb she had chosen, left over from her time in the convent. She was glad that her white wimple—which she wore under her heavy nun's veil for warmth—helped hide her blush.

It was so cold that the ground was tinged with frost, and the full moon showed the horses' breath. As soon as she mounted, Sir Charles and two knights in full armor led at a canter through the palace gates, followed closely by Father Wolsey, the four soldiers from Henry's Yeoman Guard, and finally, Nicola. They rode hard toward the moon, retracing the path the court had followed the day before. Nicola was soon left behind, though not out of sight.

As she galloped, hearing nothing but pounding hooves and her own breath, Nicola wondered if the ghosts of the murdered men lurked in the harvested stubble that stuck up around her like dead fingers, stiff with frost. In the distance, a low mist obscured everything but the tops of haystacks, white-tinged in the moonlight and round like skulls.

The fields gave way to dense forest soon after sunup. The riders swung right on a well-traveled road that the court had passed the day before. Soon they halted ahead of her and disappeared on foot into the woods, leaving one man with the horses.

Nicola halted a stone's throw behind them, and tied her horse to a tree. While listening to the shouts in the woods ahead, she examined the damp sandy soil of the roadbed, which was pockmarked here and there by the passage of horses and men.

When Sir Charles Brandon emerged from the woods, she motioned for him to join her. "Just like before," he said, when he reached her side. "Both beheaded. One without defending himself. And no sign of the wagon."

Nicola responded by pointing. "Look here. I think I have found where they were killed. Look at these tracks. A heavily-loaded wagon stopped here. And it looks like someone walked up to it and held the horses. A man stood in front of it, there."

She stepped forward, careful to avoid the footprints. "Another man stood here, facing the mounted man's horse," she continued, pointing. "Probably, he was holding it. A third stood next to the horse. He was a big man. See the size of those boot marks? Yours, back there, are smaller—and you are not a small man. Opposite, there, is where the horseman fell. Here." She bent, and scooped up a bit of dark, wet soil. "You can smell the blood."

Sir Charles backed away. "I smell it now."

"You can see where the bodies were dragged, there. And here's the most important thing," Nicola said. "See the wagon tracks? The deep ones? They turned the wagon, and went back the way they came. There."

Sir Charles eyed the wagon tracks, then the footprints, then his own boot prints. Finally, he nodded. "Would you stay here? I will bring the others in a moment."

A loud discussion that Nicola could not understand followed Sir Charles' return to the woods. The two knights who had led them from the palace emerged and strode rapidly toward her, with Sir Charles trailing behind. The grim-faced older man wore full ceremonial armor. Surely this was the leader the Queen had mentioned: Sir Henry Marney, the Captain of the Yeoman Guard.

"Show me the tracks," he ordered Nicola. She did, repeating what she had just explained to Sir Charles.

"Did you see these tracks?" Sir Henry barked at his subordinate.

"No, Sir Henry."

"How did you find the dead men, if you didn't see the tracks?" Nicola asked him.

"There was blood in that rivulet that crosses the road up there," he told her, pointing to where the horses were drinking. "If we hadn't known about the first killings, though, I would never have noticed."

Captain Marney glared at him, then at Sir Charles. "Brandon, will you kindly explain what this woman is doing here, and why she knows things she shouldn't, that the rest of us don't?"

"She is here because the Queen ordered it. And she knows so much because she was there when we found the first dead men."

"The Queen trusts me to be a good observer," Nicola added. "I can make a picture of the tracks for you, if you like. I have a good memory for such things."

The Captain ignored her, continuing to stare at Charles Brandon. "And why was she with you when you found the first dead men, for the love of God?"

Sir Charles, mouth agape, appeared to struggle for words. "I own the stolen cannons until I am paid," Nicola interjected. "That's why. Now I am the Queen's eyes and ears as well."

"So the Queen's note to me said," Sir Charles added.

"She owns the *cannons*?" Nicola watched Sir Henry's deeply-lined face struggle with emotion, quickly mastered. He looked at Nicola, as if noticing her for the first time. "You're the Italian woman," he said, as if it explained everything.

"I am the Italian woman, yes. And I hear..." she made the motion of a shovel, not knowing the English word. "I want to see the murdered men, before they are put in the earth."

The Captain scowled at her. "It is not a sight for a lady. Much less for a nun."

"I am not a nun. But I lived among them, nursing the poor. So I am used to blood. I will stay out of the way." She tucked her hands in her sleeves, and walked towards the woods with short steps, as a nun would. It had always amazed her, how people stepped aside when she wore nuns' garb and mimicked their movements. She was also surprised that she'd understood much of the English she was hearing, and was able to speak it in a basic way. She was learning quickly.

The forest of huge mossy trees was silent, except for the sound of shovels. She picked her way across a carpet of brown fallen leaves, followed by Sir Charles and Sir Henry. Together, they stared at the two headless, bloody corpses, smelling of blood and excrement, that were neatly laid out next to the graves the soldiers were digging for them. Father Wolsey stood to one side, rosary in hand, head bent in prayer.

"Where did you find the bodies?" she asked.

One of the men pointed. "In those rocks by the stream there, covered with leaves and branches."

"Did you check that one's sword?" she asked Sir Charles, gesturing at the dead soldier.

"Still in its scabbard. And clean."

"Looks like the soldier lost his head with one...." Not knowing the English word, she swung an arm like a sword. "The wagon driver, more than one. But the only defensive wounds are on the wagon driver's hands and arms. Where are the heads?"

"Over there. We covered them—no one wanted to look. You should not look, either."

Nicola swallowed hard as she tossed the branches aside, praying for God's help. The dead guard, still wearing his helmet, stared from a chalky-white face with sightless eyes, his mouth open as if in surprise. The cart driver's contorted face seemed to scream at the guard. Slow-moving flies buzzed and landed where blood had stained the pasty-white faces and necks.

After a moment, Nicola swallowed the vomit that rose to her throat. She swayed a bit, and Sir Charles grabbed her arm. Furious, she brushed him away.

"Lady Nicola, I should not have kissed you against your will. And I apologize," he said, in Latin. "But you are carrying this to extremes. Come, sit over here."

He had been joined by Father Wolsey, the priest who had sent them to find the first missing wagon the day before. Both men helped her move away from the severed heads. She gratefully inhaled gulps of fresh forest air to compose herself. Charles insisted she sit on a boulder.

"I have seen worse, nursing the dying," she said, when she felt less wobbly. "From his expression, it looks like the soldier was surprised. He certainly didn't defend himself. Just like the other one. Do you agree?"

"Yes. And I fault myself," Father Wolsey said. "I should have sent more guards with the second wagon, once the first one went missing."

Nicola shook her head. "Don't be hard on yourself, Reverend Father. You did no wrong. You sent help, as soon as the first wagon went missing. Why would you suspect murder, when it was far more likely a problem with the heavy load? If not for you, none of the corpses would have been discovered for a long time. Maybe never. The murderers think they are safe, which makes them easier to catch. You will say a Mass for these poor *infortunati, si?*"

Wolsey smiled at her. "I wish we could bring the bodies back with us, but the King does not want these murders known, for the reason you just gave—to catch murderers who do not know they have been discovered." He sighed. "I have done what I could for their victims—given them last rites, in hopes that their souls lingered where they were slain. I will say a requiem Mass for them before I leave, and sanctify their graves, as we do for soldiers who must be buried in the field during war."

"If the murderers drove the horses hard all night, could they be at the coast by now?" she asked.

"The coast—no. But the Thames River, easily. And near its mouth," Sir Charles answered, his face grim.

"And there by boat—"

"To anywhere."

Three Singers, by Angelica Kauffmann c. 1759

CHAPTER 12: THE QUEEN INTERVENES

That evening

Queen Katherine, seated by the fire in her Presence Room, watched Nicola move slowly towards her, as if it hurt her to walk. Little wonder—the poor girl had ridden hard for most of the day. And was probably still upset at the King for threatening her the day before.

"Take Lady Nicola's cloak, Lena, and bring her something to eat," the Queen called to her body servant. "Come sit by the fire, Nicola. Right next to me, here. You looked chilled and exhausted. The court has already had supper, but I made sure they saved something for you. Leave us," she told her ladies. "You, too, Lena."

"Tell me what I need to know about the murders," she murmured to Nicola, when they were alone.

"It was as we feared," Nicola responded, her voice sounding tired. "The guard knew his attacker. Or at least, was not afraid of him, because he allowed the man to stand next to him and hold his horse. He was killed without drawing his sword. Just like Sir William, the day before. They killed the wagon driver afterwards, like the one the day before—he had defensive wounds but no weapon to fight back. The wagons did not travel far after leaving the court procession. Meaning that members of the court could have been the attackers. The tracks showed there were at least three of them."

"It could have been outlaws from the woods, who set up an ambuscade when they saw the court go by," Queen Katherine suggested, though her intuition was telling her otherwise. The men had followed the same plan for all the killings. It had to be the same killers.

"If the guards had defended themselves, I would agree that it could be outlaws. But their actions suggest they knew their killers. And why would ordinary thieves steal cannons? I fear a conspiracy against His Highness. Whoever did this, it was carefully planned."

Queen Katherine nodded, one hand on her belly as she felt the baby move. She did not want to believe Nicola's answer, but it seemed logical. "What comes next?"

"The soldiers are trying to track the cart with the stolen cannons. Sir Charles and I stayed for the requiem Mass that Reverend Father Wolsey said for the murdered men. On our way back, though, we saw that the cannon tracks were headed towards the Thames."

Katherine clutched her belly. Was her baby trying to do summersaults? "So we will know more in a day or two," she said. "Thank God those men received a decent Christian burial. If the thieves reach the Thames, and put the cannons on a boat…"

"They could be far away by now. And not only that. Coordinating with a boat requires planning. Which again suggests a conspiracy."

Katherine saw the logic, but did not want to believe it. "I wonder if Henry will see it that way."

"I hope so, for his sake. Sir Henry and Sir Charles are probably with him now, trying to convince him. Perhaps you can help him."

The Queen felt a burst of anger, at Henry. There was no logic to when these feelings arose, though she had plenty to be angry about at present. She knew God required her to help her husband, however angry she felt. And that she must banish angry thoughts, so as not to harm their baby. She patted her belly, and tried to set her feelings aside.

"I will try to make Henry understand. Now, I need to tell you about the gossip in court today. Because you were the subject. Henry knows nothing of what is being bruited about. Can I trust you to keep silence from him about this?"

Nicola looked her straight in the eyes, something few people dared do. "Of course. I do not gossip. And as you know I want to stay as far away from him as possible."

"So you told me, and I believed you. And today's gossip confirms you. You are now famous, as the only woman ever to say "no" to King Henry. I am hoping you have taught him a lesson that he will convey to others in the court. There are many ladies here who feel the same way."

Nicola's jaw dropped. "Famous? What are people saying?"

"That he pursued you into a storeroom, and tried to kiss you. You told him that there is harm, even in a kiss. To stay away. That you are betrothed and not for sale."

Nicola nodded, and her face relaxed. "All true."

"Heaven will reward you for your virtue. Which is more than I can say for some of the other women in this court." The Queen felt her anger spike again, and she willed it away again. "Now—enough cannons to do great harm are missing, and four good men are dead. We need to find the killers. There may be a conspiracy against the King. You are my eyes and ears. What do you need to help us destroy this conspiracy?"

Nicola did not hesitate. "I have been thinking about this. First, I need maps. I want maps that show me the castles of the rich and powerful close to the English Channel. At least, the ones who are potential enemies of King Henry. Is there such a thing?"

"There should be. English kings have long worried about invasions from across the Channel. Henry, in fact, is planning more fortifications to strengthen our defenses there. There are surely maps with the location of all castles and manor houses. I will inquire. Anything else?"

Nicola hesitated a moment, staring down at her hands. "My aunt said that there had been various rebellions against King Henry and his father, that they managed to quell," she finally said. "If that is true, I think I need to hear the stories of those rebellions. Of the families and rebels involved, the locations, and so on."

"Lady Margaret can tell you that," the Queen responded. "Her family was in the middle of most of them. I will speak to her for you."

"Have you said anything to the King? About me, I mean. I am afraid of him. I want to stay away from him."

"Just what I told you earlier—that you are my eyes and ears." She smiled. "That took him aback, but he made no objection. In fact he said, 'The more, the better I suppose.' He has had time to calm down about you."

Nicola looked down at her hands. "But...he told me in Dover that he wants me to sing in the revels coming up after Christ's Mass. I just want to complete my work and go home."

Katherine thought about this new problem. "Christ's Mass is when the court will move to Richmond Palace, which is being prepared for my confinement," she mused. "Once I enter confinement, I will want you with me the entire time. I am to spend it in a darkened room, attended only by women, with no access to fresh air or light. No Christmas revels for me."

Nicola grimaced. "What a horrible custom. Why do they do this?"

"Supposedly for my health. Though I think it has more to do with Henry's grandmother, who actually wrote a book on how queens' confinements should be conducted. She wanted to control his mother, who was the daughter of a king. And she was very successful at it."

Nicola gazed at the fire, scowling. "And I hear this confinement is to last an entire month? *Misericordia*."

The Queen smiled, glad for the sympathy from a fellow foreigner, who thought the custom as strange as she did. "Depends on when I give birth. At any rate, I will release you for brief periods to do your work, and see that you are never alone. I will send trusted ladies with you, always, with instructions to protect you. Is that satisfactory?"

Nicola raised her brows and cocked her head as she paused to consider her response. "Here is the problem," she said. "I will need access to the armory in the Tower to do my work."

"You will travel back and forth on the Thames by wherry, attended by one or more of my ladies. And stay in the royal residence there, if necessary. For the caroling, you will be attended by my ladies who sing. Which, happily, includes the ones I most trust. They will sing with you during the revels, and you will all return to me immediately afterwards. It will give me a window into what goes on in the court during my confinement. And you can sing to me, too!" The Queen sat up, feeling excited. "Oh, I like this idea."

Nicola grinned. "I would love that."

"Good. Then we have a plan." Katherine was suddenly happy. She was learning to use guile to avoid confrontation with Henry. Her plan would keep Nicola from being alone with him, make him merry during the twelve days of celebration that follow Christ's Mass, and protect their unborn child from the stress of her jealousy. All at the same time. Her mother, Queen Isabella, would have been proud.

Tower of London. Etching by Wenceslaus Hollar (1607-1677)

CHAPTER 13: VOYAGE TO LONDON

The following morning

The following morning, in the pleasant chamber where the Queen's ladies took their leisure when not needed, Nicola was interrupted as she studied her English book of psalms. "The ship is here," the Queen's body servant told her. "The *Romulus*."

Nicola peered out at the River Thames through the leaded glass window above her cushioned seat. She could just see the prow of the *Romulus*. "Thank you, Lena. Find my cloak, please?"

By the time Lena reappeared, Nicola had gathered the documents she needed, folded the most precious one into a small square, and pushed it deep into her bodice. "Come," Lena said, "I will show you the way."

People stared at Nicola as she swept through the palace hallways, following the Queen's trusted servant. The Queen herself had suggested that Nicola wear her showy green kirtle and sleeves, to demonstrate that Lady Greensleeves was not afraid of the King. Though she *was* afraid, she walked gracefully, head held high. Fortunately the King did not appear.

Once she emerged from the palace gates, the *Romulus* loomed large and obvious at dockside. As Nicola hurried toward it, she saw familiar sailors, waving at her from the mastheads. She waved back, happy to see friendly faces.

Captain Napolitano stood on deck, supervising the men who were lowering crates of cannons to the dock with block and tackle. *"Buon giorno, Capitano! How was the rest of your voyage?"* she called out, glad to be speaking Italian again.

He turned to look at her, and his eyes widened. Then he grinned. "Sorry we took so long," he yelled back. "How beautiful you look, *Madonna!* It's good you didn't dress like that on my ship. My sailors would have lost their minds. As soon as we unload the rest of your cannons at the Tower, they get shore leave. For the first time in many weeks."

Hearing this, several sailors cheered and whistled, and those not busy lowering crates waved at Nicola again. This inspired the English soldiers who had awaited the ship to wave and cheer themselves.

A familiar voice behind her snapped, "I have porters waiting. Can we begin the inspection, please?"

Nicola turned and looked up to see the frowning face of Father Wolsey, who was holding a copy of the cannon inventory. He had been sympathetic in his priestly role, the day before. Now he was businesslike, and a little intimidating. Much more reminiscent of the unpleasant Giulio de' Medici, whom she knew from Rome, and whom he resembled.

"I'm sorry, Reverend Father," she said. "The Captain is a friend, from our long voyage together."

"The Captain wants to be on his way, I assure you. Most of the delivery to Greenwich Palace has already been unloaded. Let's start."

Wolsey had inspected the cannons ordered for Greenwich Palace on shipboard, and had them loaded directly onto horse carts. Nicola nodded to the Yeomen Guards flanking the wagons, counted the crates, and checked off her own inventory.

"Are you ready to ride the ship to the Tower of London?" Wolsey said, when she was finished. "The wind and tides are fair, and the Captain is eager to cast off."

"I think all is in order. The crates are undamaged. You will sign the acceptance?"

Wolsey did so. "Here."

Nicola took it, feeling relieved, and grinned at the sailors who had already lowered the bosun's chair for her. "I'm ready. *Sono pronto*," she called to them.

Nicola realized she had a large audience for her slow ascent up the side of the ship. She waved at one of the Queen's ladies standing on the shore road. A motley assortment, from beggars to courtiers, waved back. Some whistled and cheered. Was she quelling rumors that she had run away from the King's amorous advances, or creating new rumors that she was escaping by ship? Or neither? Maybe these people had nothing better to do than wave at ships.

Strong hands helped her to the deck as sailors scurried to cast off and raise sails, in response to bellowed orders from Captain Napolitano. Father Wolsey, who had used the ship's ladder to board, gestured to her to join him at the opposite rail.

They stood in silence as the ship moved sedately upstream, past harvested fields dotted with haystacks and small groves of trees. Periodically, large and beautiful homes looked out over the river, their numerous brick chimneys belching dark smoke that rapidly disappeared in the breeze propelling the ship. Most were two stories and bi-colored, with a lower story of dark brick or wood, and an upper story of white stucco, crisscrossed with large, dark timbers that supported steep slate roofs. All were foreign-looking to Nicola's eyes.

"Our *palazzi* look very different from these," she remarked. "In Florence they have striped buildings, but the stripes are made of stone. And the stripes point in the same direction, not splayed out like these."

"The building style is called 'half-timbered.' Said to have been used by the ancient Romans to build their forts when they conquered England. The timbers point as they do for practical reasons."

"Romans built this way? I am Roman, and our buildings do not look like this."

"But we have endless forests, and you do not."

"True. And cold weather. Does your family live in one of these grand houses?"

Wolsey laughed. "I am the son of a butcher," he said. "I earned my education and positions through hard work. Fortunately for men like me, King Henry—like his father—appreciates talent, and mistrusts the great families with long pedigrees."

"Perhaps with good reason," Nicola responded, remembering what her Aunt Caterina had said about those families' attitudes toward the upstart Tudors.

"Undoubtedly with excellent reason. You are an example of the type of person King Henry likes—though you are certainly the first woman he has hired. He is very taken with you."

"I serve his Queen as well," Nicola said, uncomfortable with the direction the conversation was taking. "I will remain with her through her confinement. Except when I am working with the armory."

"You owe us the plans for the blast furnace. And I suggest you stay away from the construction. The armorers are not going to take supervision from a woman."

"Under our contract I don't owe you the plans for the blast furnace until you pay me for the cannons. And if you want me responsible for the results, I had best keep an eye on the construction."

"We'll see. We can take care of the money, at least, while we are in London. Who does your aunt's firm bank with?"

"We have an account with the Fugger bank."

"Excellent. We can go there after the ship unloads. It's near Bridewell Palace, where I live." Seeing her face, he grinned. "Don't worry. I will send you back with a proper escort, in a fast wherry. Going back downstream, it is a quick trip."

On shore, agricultural fields had given way to a townscape of higgledy-piggledy streets and buildings that stretched out from the river road. Most were in the black and white "half-timbered" style; some as tall as four stories that each jutted out slightly over the one below. The top stories were sometimes so close that occupants on either side of a narrow street could easily shake hands.

Ahead of them loomed a vast, low bridge with squat half-timbered buildings lining its edges. On the downstream side of the bridge were docks—the last ones that tall-masted vessels could reach from the ocean, without negotiating the drawbridge. Behind the docks on her left was the Tower of London.

It really wasn't a tower, Nicola realized, though there were several towers inside and ringing it. It was a formidable castle with high crenellated stone walls surrounding it, one of which rose directly from the Thames.

They docked at the Tower, close to a large gate, barred with iron. For the next several hours, Wolsey and Nicola inspected and supervised the unloading of the remaining cannons and small arms through that gate. Wolsey had arranged for a gaggle of carts pulled by draft horses, and guarded by at least a dozen soldiers.

As crates emerged from the ship's hold, the seamen separated the ones destined for Richmond Palace, which were lowered directly onto a smaller oared vessel. "The passage under London Bridge can be very treacherous, depending on whether rains have flooded the river. And the tides," Wolsey said. "The drawbridge is rarely used."

"I'm here with my carts to move the cannon molds into the armory," said a voice behind them. It belonged to a giant of a man with a wide, weathered face and massive scarred arms, who wore a leather apron covered with burn marks over a brown jerkin and trousers.

"Lady Nicola, this is John Smith, Master of Ordnance," said Father Wolsey.

John Smith strode up to Nicola and stared down at her, if she were a pet dog. "Are the cannon molds emblazoned with the Tudor rose, like we ordered?" he demanded.

"Yes. Of course," she said, moving away from him to watch the wherry carrying her cannons to Richmond Palace negotiate the current under London Bridge.

He followed her. "Can I see them?" he demanded.

She did not like the way he was hanging over her. "They have already been inspected," she responded.

"All is in order," Wolsey said to him. "Take your crates."

When the ship was empty and the gun count correct, Wolsey signed the remaining acceptance, and handed it to Nicola, who put it in the inner pocket of her cloak with the others. "Come. I have to see that these weapons are properly stored," he said. "Then we can see to your money."

They strolled towards a corner of the Tower grounds far from the river, where men were unpacking and transferring cannons into a low stone building, using wooden dollies. Piled next to the building were the animal skins and shipping crates that had just been emptied.

"Those crates and skins go to the armory, correct?" Wolsey asked Nicola.

"Yes. They are used in gun manufacture."

"Used in gun manufacture?" Woolsey repeated, shaking his head. "You will have to explain that to me."

Nicola smiled. "After you pay me." She pointed at a workman, crouching behind the heavy wooden door. "Are you changing out the lock?"

"Yes. King Henry has decided that he should have the only key, since these guns are destined for ships that are still being built."

"A wise idea," Nicola said, remembering that it was her idea.

"Wise indeed. I heard that it came from the Queen." He winked.

"The locksmith is speaking Italian," she said in surprise.

"You Italians are supposedly the most advanced at everything," Wolsey responded. "You aren't the only one that King Henry has brought here, to teach Englishmen the latest techniques. Flemish too, and even a few Frenchmen. The locals are resentful, but they are also learning."

He turned to a soldier seeking his attention, and listened to his question. "I think that the arquebuses can simply be stored in their crates, but I would like to look at them again," he answered. They moved to the interior of the stone storage building, where the soldier opened a crate.

Woolsey peered at the long-barreled guns stacked inside. "Are they very heavy?" he asked Nicola.

"It takes a strong man to lift and point one. That is why they have a hook at the end of the barrel. We are working to build a lighter version that is still safe and accurate."

Wolsey shook his head, and lowered the top of the crate. "I can't imagine it will ever replace the good English longbow. But if King Henry wants new toys, he is certainly entitled to buy them."

"We are finished," said a voice outside the building. "The molds shipped fine." John Smith, the Master of Ordnance, peered inside at the piled cannons, mouth agape. Wolsey stepped out to confer with him, speaking English too rapidly for Nicola to follow. The two men examined their lists and pointed into the once-empty building, now full to the rafters with stacked cannons and crates of arquebuses.

While they did so, Nicola stepped out to chat with the Italian locksmith, who was delighted to hear his native tongue. He was from Milan, knew the Biaggi armory well, and missed his wife. "I have taught these *Inglese* most of what I know," he told Nicola. "I will return home soon."

"*È finito?*" he asked, when the two Englishmen turned to them.

"*Finito*," Wolsey said.

Grinning, the Italian slammed the massive door, locked it, and ceremoniously handed Wolsey an enormous key.

"The transfer is complete," Wolsey said to Nicola. "Come, let's head for your bank, and see to your money."

German banker Jakob Fuggerand his accountant
Matthäus Schwarz, 16th century, artist unknown

CHAPTER 14: THE HISTORY OF BANKING

The same day

Nicola's bank had its London office on Fleet Street, a busy cobbled thoroughfare next to the River Fleet, a stream just as smelly and filthy as the Tiber in Rome. Nicola was relieved to see that the Fugger bank was built entirely of stone, unlike the churches and other half-timbered buildings surrounding it. Tall, plain and ominous, its only windows were at the high roofline, and barred. Swiss guards armed with pikes and dressed in red, blue and yellow stripes, the colors of the Fugger coat of arms, stood on either side of the massive metal door.

They knew Father Wolsey, however. "The lady is with me," he told them. The Swiss guards glanced at them and at the royal guards, easily identified by their green and white livery and the Tudor rose on their shoulders. Then they opened the doors, and waved Wolsey and Nicola in.

They entered a dimly-lit stone anteroom with barred windows far above their heads, and approached an ornamental brass cage behind a marble counter. A Swiss guard stood at either end of the counter, near the twin fireplaces warming the room. A seated man, his back to them, hunched over documents inside the

91

brass cage, beneath the light of two oil lamps. Next to him a brass door led to a room at the rear of the building.

"The Biaggi arms firm, in Italy, has accounts with your bank in Rome," Wolsey said to the banker in Latin, when the man turned to look at them. "The Crown needs to transfer funds to them. Here are the necessary documents."

Nicola turned her back to the men and reached into her bodice to pull out the document she had tucked there that morning. "I also have a deposit, from our Roman account," she said as she placed it on the counter. "I require some English money back, to pay for tips, and wherries, and what-have-you. What amount do you recommend, Father Wolsey? Given the difficulties of getting here."

"We are paying you in sovereigns because they are solid gold—but you can't use them as ordinary coinage. For tips and ordinary purchases you will need pennies and ha'pennies. There are twelve pence—pennies—to a testoon, and twenty testoons to a pound. Perhaps three pounds, in small coins?"

"Double that amount, and give me half in small coins," Nicola said to the banker. "I require the rest of the deposit and the Crown's payment as a bill of exchange. It should be payable by your Roman bank, either to me or to Caterina Biaggi. Who is my aunt, and owner of our firm. And two copies, if possible."

The banker stared at her, then the documents, and gasped. "This is an enormous sum," he said, pointing to what Wolsey had given him.

"Is there a problem?" Nicola asked.

The banker cocked his head, and stared at her again. "I'll need to make sure the King has that much money on deposit with us."

"I'm sure he does. But by all means," Wolsey said. The banker bowed, unlocked the metal door behind him, and disappeared behind it.

Nicola was hoping Wolsey would do her a personal favor. So far, they had gotten along well—but a little flattery might help. "Reverend Father, I know you are a very important churchman," she began. "My aunt is Pope Julius' armorer, and my betrothed is the Vatican's chief artist and architect. It would promote good relations if you would kindly ask a papal courier to carry a copy of the bill of exchange to my aunt, in care of the Vatican. With letters for both of them, if possible. If the bill of exchange gets there, it will get to her. By now they both will be worried about me. And what if something happens to me, on the long sea voyage home? Or to her? That's why I asked for two copies."

"If the King approves, I can do that. Yes."

"What if the Queen approves?"

He smiled. "Currently, that is the same thing. I'm sure it will not be a problem."

The banker soon returned with a bag of coins and a receipt for Nicola. "Here is money from your deposit," he said. "A question: does our branch in Rome know your aunt?"

Nicola gave him her best smile. "They know her very well."

"From what I hear, she is an older version of this lady here. Just as lovely, and the best-dressed widow in Rome," Wolsey added.

"They know both of you then, by appearance. That helps," the banker said. "I can give you two copies of the bill of exchange. Each will acknowledge that there is a copy, and allow only one of you to withdraw the money. Once I give out these documents, the King no longer has access to these funds. You do understand that?" he asked, gazing at Wolsey.

"Of course," Wolsey said. The banker nodded, bowed, and sat down with quill and ink at the desk inside the barred space, writing busily.

"Your aunt actually sells weapons to Pope Julius?" Wolsey said to Nicola, who was trying to sort her coins.

"Weapons and armor. He is called 'the warrior pope.' Had you not heard? Currently he is warring against the French and Venice. Probably besieging Mirandola."

Wolsey raised an eyebrow. "So I heard—yesterday. How is it you know more about current happenings in Italy than I do?"

"Pope Julius shouts constantly, and hides nothing.[6] He has been shouting for months about besieging Mirandola." While they talked, Nicola grouped like coins on the counter. "Will you help me with these coins, please? I have separated them by appearance. Please tell me what each is called, and what they are worth. How much to tip a servant, for example."

"These are groats and pennies. One groat to four pennies," Wolsey responded. "And as you can see, the pennies are cut into halves and quarters. The big ones are testoons." Working together, they confirmed that the banker's coin count was correct, while chatting about English tipping.

The banker interrupted them by clearing his throat. "I have a receipt for you, Reverend Father, and identical bills of exchange for the lady, with her receipt. Would you like to look at them before I affix the ribbons and seals?"

Nicola examined hers. "This is not the amount agreed upon," she told Wolsey, suppressing an urge to snap at him. "I have no authority to re-negotiate. Do you want the plans for the blast furnace or not?

He looked down at his feet, and sighed. "At the King's insistence, I subtracted a *pro rata* amount for the eight missing cannons. The look in his eye told me he would brook no argument, so I gave him none. I will do my best to see that you receive the full amount when the contract is completed and the final payment is due."

What could she say? She put her hands on her hips and glared at him. "I promised the Queen I would help find the missing cannons, and I will do my best. But it is not an easy task, and it is certainly not my fault, or my armory's fault, that they were stolen." She paused, purely for effect. "Since you have given your word to provide the full amount at the end of the contract, however, this amount will be satisfactory for the present."

In truth, the amount was more than satisfactory. She was well aware that the King's initial payment for the cannons—in gold, and already safe in Rome—had

---

[6] Read about "warrior" Pope Julius n Martin Luther and Murder

already covered the armory's costs. She and Caterina had fought bitterly after that payment—Caterina insisting she had to go to England; Nicola refusing, and in tears. "I never thought the King would accept my offer but he did, no questions asked," Caterina told her. "Our reputation is at stake. I can't go because I don't speak Latin, or oversee the production process. But you do."

Even without payment for the missing cannons, this bill of exchange meant that Nicola and her aunt were amply compensated and enormously rich—assuming Nicola could get the bill of exchange back to Italy.

"Leave one of my copies without the ribbons and seals," she told the banker. She folded that copy carefully, turned to the wall, and stuffed it between her breasts. She placed the beribboned, sealed copy into the inner pocket of her cloak with her other documents, strapped the bag of English coins to her waist, and hid it under her cloak.

Wolsey began walking as soon as she was ready. "The Archbishop of Canterbury has envoys returning to Italy soon. I'll get them to take one copy of your bill of exchange, and any letters you wish to send with it."

"Thank you, Reverend Father. And thanks to you as well," she called to the banker over her shoulder. Wolsey was already holding the door for her.

"They charge an enormous sum for those bills of exchange," he remarked as the royal guards helped them mount their horses.

"But they are worth it," Nicola responded as she adjusted her skirts. Sidesaddle was awkward, but she was growing used to it. "Transporting huge sums in coin would have been impossible for my aunt and me. Foreign trade must have been terribly difficult before we invented bills of exchange."

Following the yeoman guards, they rode side-by-side into the crowded streets. "By 'we,' you mean Italian bankers, I assume. Banks have helped enormously. Though sovereign kings with armed men at their disposal had little difficulty in times gone by."

The sun was low in the sky as they picked their way through the carts and people clogging London's narrow cobbled streets. Around them, shop owners closed their shutters and peddlers shouted "only a penny" for wares sold at tuppence an hour before, as citizens scurried for home ahead of the sunset. The horses' hooves stirred up intense odors of horse droppings and emptied commodes, stenches at their foulest in the hours before the night soil carts emerged to clean.

"We still have to deal with the drawings for the blast furnace," Wolsey said, when their horses drew close enough to speak. "Do you have them with you?"

"Yes. I should probably be there, to explain them to the armorers."

"I agree. So I will arrange for you to stay in the royal apartments in the Tower for the night, because it is later than I hoped. I will join you there in the morning, so we can work with the armorers together."

Nicola's heart thudded in her chest. "I am afraid," she blurted out, loudly enough that a rag seller trudging next to her horse gave her a startled look.

Wolsey's eyes widened. "Afraid of what? Of staying in a royal residence inside the Tower? There is no safer place in England."

"Of being alone. Of the King, and Sir Charles Brandon," she confessed, hoping that this powerful priest—who had heard Sir Charles apologize for kissing her against her will—would protect her. "They have both. . . behaved improperly towards me. Can't I please go back and sleep with the Queen's ladies?"

Wolsey studied his horse's mane, in a way that made Nicola wonder if he were praying. "The Queen herself suggested you stay in the royal apartments in the Tower as necessary," he finally said. "I think I now understand why. I can promise you—neither the King nor Sir Charles will be at the Tower this evening. I am quite sure of it. The Queen knew this as well."

"But she is expecting me," Nicola protested.

"I will have the guards bring her word. We are nearing my residence. The guards will see you safely housed in the royal residence. And I promise, you will be treated like royalty. You and your coins will be safe. If it makes you feel better, you can ask several female attendants to sleep on your floor. I will send word that you are to be obeyed."

The sun was low over Bridewell Palace when they reached it. Nicola saw a woman with blue eyes and wheat-colored hair waiting next to the gate, calming a fretful baby in her arms and looking as lovely as the golden-haired Madonnas in Raphael's paintings. Father Wolsey dismounted and kissed her cheek, then made cooing noises at the baby. After handing off his horse to the guard at the gate, he escorted the woman and her baby inside, a hand on her back.

"And him a priest," said one of the soldiers accompanying Nicola, as they continued towards the river.

"Many priests are like that," she responded, in careful English, remembering several in Italy who had tried to seduce her. "Will we reach the Tower before dark?"

A Tudor-era bedroom

CHAPTER 15: KING HENRY INVENTS THE BRITISH NAVY

The following morning

Nicola slept poorly, startled by the calls of guards on the Tower walls outside her window and the strange cries of animals in the Tower menagerie. The cries worked their way into intermittent dreams that something terrifying was chasing her. Near dawn, she finally dozed.

She awoke to a bright morning, and a servant shaking her.

"Father Wolsey is waiting for you in the armory," said the woman, one of the two who had slept on her floor because she requested it out of fear. "We sponged the mud off your kirtle and sleeves. And we made the *tisane* you asked for last night. Come dress by the fire."

Nicola gulped down her *tisane*, redolent of mint, as the servants helped dress her. She had never before slept in a bed so enormous, or a bedroom so large and elaborately furnished. But the bed curtains and tapestries looked old and faded, and the chair and table by the window even older. The room also smelled musty, despite competing aromas of mint *tisane* and woodsmoke.

Bread, dried fruit and cheese lay on a linen napkin on the table. She tied the food in the napkin, and told the servant to lead her to the Tower armory.

They headed across a grassy yard, tinged with frost, toward a tall rectangular building at the center of the castle grounds with a square tower at each corner, which the servant called the White Tower. "Oldest building here," she said. As they neared it, Nicola could hear the sound of blacksmiths' hammers behind it. There, a burly worker was shoeing a warhorse.

Inside the ground floor, and blessedly warm, she saw a large space with a brick forge glowing with coals at its center. Several men were finishing a suit of armor next to the forge, using small hammers designed for delicate work. It could have been any of her aunt's armories in Italy. For the first time since leaving there, Nicola felt at home.

Father Wolsey and John Smith, the huge man Nicola had met the day before, stood talking beside a large table. Since they were ignoring her, Nicola spread the blast furnace drawings on the table, where drawings of ships were already laid out.

"Here they are. You see?" Woolsey said to Smith, who bent to examine the drawings.

"They explain themselves, I think," Nicola said to him, in English. "Start here. This is inside, this is outside. These are the bellows. Here is where the metal pours out. This is the crucible. I brought several—I see them over there. I can answer questions, if you speak slowly."

The armorer jabbed a finger at the schematic of the blast furnace interior. "You didn't draw these yourself, did you?"

"No. Our draftsmen did. We had help from Leonardo da Vinci, who is a famous engineer.[7] Have you heard of him?"

"No. But he can draw," John Smith said. He turned his back to her, and summoned his men to look at the drawings. They talked excitedly, and far too rapidly for Nicola to understand.

---

[7] Read about Leonardo's history as an engineer in <u>Da Vinci Detects</u>

Nicola examined the other drawings on the table while she and Wolsey waited to see if the armorers had questions. "I have never seen ships this big," she said to him. "They are many times bigger than the *Romulus*. Or any other ship I have ever seen. And I saw many on my voyage from Italy."

She pointed at one of the drawings when Wolsey joined her. "I see that the lowest guns will be very close to the water. The portholes can be closed, but water can still penetrate. The designers of these ships were not concerned about this?"

He frowned. " I know they wanted the cannons to be low, to act as ballast. I'm sure they must have thought of that."

"What is ballast?"

"Weight. Needs to be low, to keep the ship steady."

"I see. But I know from my voyage, that ships sometimes lean with the wind. And suppose the portholes are open, during a battle—"

Wolsey smiled and held up his palms, to end the discussion. "It's beyond our control, my lady. The hulls of these ships have already been built. They are finishing the upper desks and waiting for the masts to bring them here for fitting out. One is to be called "The Mary Rose," and the other, the "Peter Pomegranate." The "rose" is for the Tudor rose, and the pomegranate, for Queen Katherine. It is the symbol of her Castilian family."

Nicola ran her finger over the three tiers of guns on the drawing, and made a rapid calculation. "It looks like the Mary Rose will carry forty-five cannons on each side. And more fore and aft? *Dio Mio,* they could destroy a small city with that many cannons."

"Somewhere around that number. The specifics keep shifting. That's why the armorers have these drawings."

John Smith moved to Nicola's side. "The drawings are excellent. Very clear. We can build this."

He was speaking over Nicola's head to Wolsey, which irritated her.

"You have no questions?" she asked, keeping her voice polite.

"Not for you. The materials list is in Latin. We'll need Father Wolsey to translate it."

If she was going to work with these men, they needed to respect her. "I wrote that list, and read Latin. And I know the materials. I have made cannons myself. With Leonardo da Vinci," she added, hoping da Vinci's fame would give her credibility.

Smith glowered down at her. "You made cannons?' he asked, in a tone suggesting she was claiming she had made the moon.

"As I said. And I load and fire and swab them out, too. To be ready for the next shot. Because the Biaggi armory tests its cannons, many times. And I am one of the owners. So I do the testing myself."

"You test them yourself," he repeated, sounding even more doubtful.

Father Wolsey cleared his throat. "Perhaps we should go over the materials together, since my English is better than yours," he said to Nicola. Together, they translated the list. John Smith started out looking only at Wolsey. By the end, Nicola realized he was watching her give the answers.

"Buy the best you can get," she advised. "The strong heat of the blast furnace will make all the metals more pure."

"We know that," he barked. "Do I really have to keep those skins and crates they sent here yesterday?" he added, waving at the neat stack next to the castle wall.

This man did not want to take direction from a woman. He would have to learn. "Yes," she answered firmly. "You must keep them. Unless you want to buy new ones."

Smith glared down at her again, as if she were a misbehaving dog. She looked him straight in the eye, and smiled.

Wolsey also grinned at the scowling armorer. "Let's be off," he said to Nicola.

"Where to?"

"Back to Greenwich Palace."

*****

After a rapid trip by wherry, Wolsey left Nicola with Lady Margaret Pole, whom they met just inside the gates of Greenwich Palace. "I'll get you back to the Queen's apartments," Lady Margaret said. "The passageways are very confusing, until you know them."

Nicola's sense of dread returned as soon as she stepped inside. King Henry had followed her through these hallways, cornered her in a storeroom just ahead, and threatened her with death when she refused his advances, only two days before. She realized that some of the courtiers she and Margaret passed were staring and gesturing at her. The Queen had called her "notorious" as the only woman ever to refuse King Henry. Feeling conspicuous in her showy green kirtle, she wondered if her overnight disappearance had started new gossip about her, and dreaded finding out what it was. Even more, she dreaded seeing the King in the halls, and wished Wolsey were there to accompany her.

The King did not appear. However, Nicola saw two of the bearded monks who served as court musicians walking in front of them. Remembering the Queen's wishes, she hurried ahead of Lady Margaret to catch them.

"Brother Michael," she called out. "Do you have music for any of the carols that are sung after Christ's Mass? The Queen wants me to learn them."

The bigger of the two monks turned to stare at her. He had bushy white brows, like Leonardo da Vinci, and a bushier grey beard. "Music?" he said. "Written out? For carols? No—everyone just knows them."

"We will teach them to you, Lady Nicola," said Lady Margaret. She thanked the monks, and held Nicola back. "The Queen has asked me to share certain stories of English history with you," she murmured. "That is why I was waiting outside for you. These are not matters commonly spoken about in this court."

"I don't want to remain in a hallway, please. The King gave me a bad scare the other day and I would prefer to avoid him. Where can we be private, inside Her Highness' rooms?"

Lady Margaret took Nicola's arm and patted it as they moved towards the Queen's apartments. "I understand. I will arrange for us to remain behind when the other ladies go to Mass with her."

War of the Roses: Red Rose (Lancaster), Pink Rose (Tudor), White Rose (York)

CHAPTER 16: THE WAR OF THE ROSES

Later that day

Nicola watched Lena close the door behind the Queen's ladies as they filed out for Mass. She returned to stoke the fire for Nicola and Margaret, and left a hot *tisane,* redolent of chamomile, for them to drink.

"Where to begin," Margaret said, when they were alone. "Understand, this is the story as told by my family. The York family. Others might tell it differently. Particularly members of the Lancaster family."

Nicola nodded and sipped her *tisane.* She decided to commit everything to memory—a talent she had, when she chose to use it.

"I will try to make this as simple as possible for you," Lady Margaret said. "We had a king called Edward III, who had a son called John of Gaunt, who was Duke of Lancaster. The Lancasters are descended from John of Gaunt. The legitimate line of that family of kings ended with Henry VI, decades ago. Are you following so far?"

"I think so," Nicola responded.

"Henry VII and his son—our present Henry—are descended from one of the bastards born of John of Gaunt's mistress. The Lancasters claim those bastards were later legitimized, when John of Gaunt married his mistress after his wife died. But the Yorks disagree. Henry is also descended from Owen Tudor, a philandering Welsh commoner who secretly married Henry V's widow, even though Parliament forbade any marriage. The Tudors prospered because Henry

VI was kind to his half-brothers. He married one of them to Margaret Beaufort, our Henry's grandmother, the last in the line born of John of Gaunt's mistress."

"Bastards on both sides," Nicola remembered her "aunt" Caterina saying about the Tudor ancestors. So Caterina had been right. Nicola's old shame at her own bastardy pricked her once again. She should stop hoping that her parents would marry when Niccolò Machiavelli's wife died. Niccolò was a bastard in the insulting sense of the word, though Caterina could not admit it. The English—or at least Lady Margaret—did not believe that a later marriage erased the shame of bearing a child out of wedlock. By that logic, the marriage Nicola once prayed for would hurt Caterina, and do her no good at all.

Lady Margaret had paused to sip her *tisane*. "I am of the York family," she continued, after setting aside her cup. "The Yorks are descended from Edward III's second legitimate son, who was Duke of York. Who was actually older than John of Gaunt."

"Older than John of Gaunt? But I thought the eldest son always succeeded—"

"You are correct. But John of Gaunt's grandson overthrew Richard II, last descendant of Edward III"s oldest son. So the Yorkist line was bypassed when John of Gaunt's line took over. And this was not legitimate, in the view of the Yorks, who took over from Henry VI."

Margaret stared into the fire for a moment. "What comes next touches me personally but I've learned to describe it without weeping. The Yorkist line of kings died out with King Edward IV and King Richard III, who were brothers. Or with Edward IV's two young sons, who disappeared into the Tower as children thirty years ago and were never seen again, if you want to count them. Everyone assumes Richard III had the young princes killed, because he took over when his brother died. Though some think Henry VII—our Henry's father—did the evil deed."

Margaret paused to sip her tisane. "For many decades, the Lancasters and Yorks fought, sometimes internally. But always over who should rule," she continued.

The symbol of the Lancaster family was the red rose, and the York family, the white rose. So it came to be called the War of Roses."

"Once those young princes were killed, there were no obvious heirs to the throne?"

Margaret hesitated, turning her cup in her hands. "Essentially," she finally said. "My late brother and I are children of the brother between Edward IV and Richard III in age, so perhaps my brother had a claim. But our father was declared a traitor and executed by Uncle Edward. And my brother was only eight years old when Uncle Richard seized the throne from Edward's sons—those young princes—and locked them in the Tower."

"Seized the throne? I'm sorry," Nicola said, remembering the violent English history Caterina had mentioned. "And your father was executed? That must have been hard for you. And frightening."

Margaret sighed. "It was. My mother was already dead, so my brother and I were bounced around like tennis balls between guardians who were not always kind. At any rate, our present King Henry's father was the last Lancastrian to claim the throne. He defeated and killed Richard III—last of the Yorkist kings—at the Battle of Bosworth. Then he married Elizabeth of York, oldest legitimate child of Edward IV. This united the Lancasters and the Yorks. Henry Tudor became Henry VII, and adopted the red and white Tudor rose as the Tudor symbol. But the wars raged on."

Surprised, Nicola put down her *tisane*. "Why?"

"Money and power. Power and money. Unscrupulous lords and foreigners didn't want Henry VII as king, for a variety of reasons. So they promoted commoners who looked like the missing princes. We call them 'the pretenders.'"

"Are any of those unscrupulous lords and foreigners still around? The ones who promoted the pretenders?" Nicola asked.

Margaret frowned, closed her eyes, and sighed. "Most of them," she said. "But most are beyond Henry's reach. The king of France, Louis XII. Maximilian, Holy

Roman Emperor. Margaret of Burgundy, a sister of Edward IV and Richard III. James IV of Scotland."

"Let's approach the issue another way," Nicola said. "Who is still a threat to Henry's crown?"

"Richard and Edmund de la Pole, definitely. Though the first is in France, and the second is in the Tower."

"Not the men who pretended to be the missing princes?"

Lady Margaret shook her head. "I don't think so. They both admitted they were pretenders, and one was executed. Everyone now believes the missing princes are long dead themselves—it's been nearly thirty years since they were last seen. Edward Stafford, Duke of Buckingham, is descended from the youngest son of Edward III. He is also one of the richest men in England, and supposedly thinks his claim to the throne is better than Henry's. He has reason to hate Henry over something having to do with his sister—I won't get into that, now. In any case, he is a potential threat. Sir Francis Lovell, who fought Henry's father several times, would have been a threat if he hadn't disappeared fighting for one of the pretenders."

"I remember seeing the Duke of Buckingham with the court when we came from Dover," Nicola said. "That places him near the murders. Where is the pretender who is still alive?"

"You have met him. Henry VII recognized he was an innocent, and took him on as a kitchen worker in one of his palaces, so he could keep an eye on him. He is now a grown man, and one of Henry's falconers. I saw him talking to you when we stopped for lunch after Canterbury. A handsome man with a falcon on his arm, named Lambert Simnel."

"I remember him,' Nicola said, surprised. "He was flirting with me, I think, but my English was not good enough to understand. I saw him speak to the Duke of Buckingham as well."

Margaret nodded so violently that her headdress moved. "So did I. So did everyone," she added as she readjusted it, and smoothed her veil.

"In Italy, he would have been secretly garroted, whether he was innocent or not. I'm surprised he's allowed so close to the King. What is the de la Pole claim to the throne?"

"Richard III had no surviving children. John de la Pole was King Richard's brother-in-law, married to one of Richard and Edward's older sisters. Her oldest son—also John—claimed that before King Richard died at Bosworth, he named John the younger as his heir. Both Johns are long dead, but the youngest had three brothers: Edmund, William and Richard. Edmund and Richard are asserting the family's rights."

Nicola thought about what she had just heard. The de la Pole brothers' claim to the throne seemed dubious, but she was hardly going to voice this to Lady Margaret. If she had worked it out right, their mother was Lady Margaret's aunt. So the de la Pole brothers were Margaret's cousins. "What about the third brother, William?" she asked.

Margaret shook her head. "He is actually the second brother. But William was never ambitious. Like me, he prefers a peaceful realm to endless warfare. Anyway, he is also in the Tower—a victim of who his parents were. Like my brother. My brother was thrown in the Tower when he was ten and beheaded by Henry VII at twenty-four, for no worse a sin than being a possible claimant to the throne." Her eyes filled with tears, and she paused to dabble them with an embroidered handkerchief. "I was twelve when they took him away. I had been both sister and mother to him since our parents died—our mother the year after he was born and our father two years later." Choking back tears, she pulled out a handkerchief, rose to her feet, and hurried to the window.

Nicola remembered how devastated she herself was at that age, when she lost her best friend in the convent. And how much she'd longed for a home with two loving parents. She followed Lady Margaret to the window and patted her shoulder. "I'm very sorry Lady Margaret," she said. "To lose both parents and a brother when you were so young must have been very hard." Margaret put her handkerchief over her face and choked back sobs. Nicola kept a hand on her shoulder in silence, while watching the wherries moving along the Thames.

When Margaret was calm, they returned to their seats. Sensing she was near the end of her story, Nicola knew she had to ask a difficult question, or lose the opportunity. She made her voice as gentle as she could. "Could you be queen, if women could rule as queens?"

Margaret shook her head and blew her nose, red-eyed but composed. "England has never had a queen who reigned in her own right—unless you count Mathilda, hundreds of years ago, who was never crowned. There was a civil war around that, which she lost." She paused to sip her tisane. "Our Henry's mother had a far better claim to the throne than mine, if women could be reigning queens. She was older sister to the two princes who died in the Tower. If the crown passed to the oldest legitimate child instead of the oldest legitimate son, she would have been queen. That's why Henry VII married her."

Margaret wiped her eyes again, and tucked her handkerchief in her belt. "The succession is already muddy and complicated, without getting into the female lines. Do we go back to Edward III's first daughter? Unthinkable. Can you see the complications those sisters and widows and dowager queens have already caused? So, no. I could not be queen."

At that, the Queen herself bustled into the room from Mass, trailed by her ladies. All wore bright colors and the triangular headdresses favored by the English, looking together like they had stepped from one of the decks of the cards the ladies favored for their play.

Lady Margaret and Nicola rose, to give the Queen her seat by the fire. "Stay, both of you," the Queen said, waving to them to be seated again. She grinned. "I have something amusing to tell you. Sit there. You will never guess what the latest rumors are about you, Nicola."

Nicola sat, her stomach churning. "Oh, no. What now?"

Katherine smiled at the ladies who were lifting her feet to its stool and tucking her pillows and shawls around her favorite chair. "Half the court thinks you took ship to escape Henry, and some think you actually flew to the ship." She made flying motions with her arms, and laughed, prompting a titter from her ladies. "But the rest say no, you were raised up to the ship in some kind of chair. Others are saying you took vows as a nun to escape Henry, which is why you sometimes dress as one. Though they don't understand why you would do that to your betrothed. Who is handsome and famous and paints naked women in Italy, it is said. But you love him anyway."

Nicola grinned, and realized that the Queen had spoken English, with all of her ladies listening. And she herself had understood most of it. She responded slowly, to be sure she got the English right: "Most of that is true. Except flying. And becoming a nun."

"And everyone wondered where you were last night," the Queen continued. "But then word came that Wolsey had put you in the Tower, in the royal apartments. Which became reports that he locked you in the Tower. To protect you from Henry." Her ladies giggled again.

There was some truth to this, but Nicola thought it better not to say so. "Has His Highness heard this gossip?" she asked.

"I certainly hope not," Katherine said, directing a regal gaze at her ladies, who promptly stopped laughing. "Certainly not from me, or any of my ladies. We all understood that you stayed there because your business at the armory detained you. I hope your stay was comfortable?"

"Very comfortable," Nicola responded.

"And your business there was completed?"

"Yes. This morning."

"Excellent. Leave us, please," the Queen said to the ladies, who curtseyed and left the room. "Stay, Nicola," she said in Latin.

When they were alone, the Queen chuckled. "I shouldn't find it amusing, perhaps. But Henry would be doubly embarrassed if he knew people were gossiping about his failed conquest of Lady Greensleeves. And I take perverse pleasure in that. May God forgive me."

"I am delighted it gives you pleasure. The King is the one who needs forgiving. Should I do anything differently?"

"No. Continue to carry yourself proudly, like the virtuous woman you are. Eventually my ladies will correct any nonsensical gossip. I hope. Anyway, there will be something else to gossip about soon. There always is. Here, sit closer to me."

Nicola took the stool next to the Queen. "How did your talk with Lady Margaret about the War of the Roses go?" Her Highness murmured, her eyes on Lena, who had just entered. "Did she enlighten you?"

"She did," Nicola whispered. "Did you know that one of the 'pretenders' who tried to overthrow Henry's father—named Lambert Simnel—is one of Henry's falconers?"

Queen Katherine's brows rose. "I remember the story of Lambert Simnel working in the kitchens when he was a boy. I had no idea he somehow grew up and became a falconer."

"A very tall, strong one with a big knife on his hip. I met him when we left Canterbury. And saw him speak to the Duke of Buckingham there, as well. Couldn't he be dangerous to King Henry? If spies are still watching him, it might be good to check with them. To see if anything suspicious has happened recently."

The Queen pushed herself to her feet, grimaced, and lumbered to her writing desk, one hand on her enormous belly. There, she took up her quill. "I'm sure this pretender was watched carefully in the early days. But now? I have no idea. But I know who to ask. You will speak to him."

"But I don't know enough English. And I don't even know how to find him," Nicola stammered.

"I am summoning him. We will both speak to him," the Queen said, as she addressed and sealed her note. She glanced toward the doorway. "Lena, what is it?"

The Queen's body servant, who had been standing out of earshot, came forward. "Sir Henry Marney wants to see you," she said to the Queen.

"Show him in, then leave us. Take this note. You stay, Nicola."

Nicola recognized him. Now that he was no longer in full body armor, Sir Henry did not look as intimidating as he had after their long ride together to view the corpses his men had buried in the woods. In dark hosen and a green doublet adorned only with the Tudor rose, he still carried himself like a soldier. But he looked grizzled and old, with a careworn face. He stopped short, staring at Nicola, then swallowing hard.

"Nicola is of my ladies and confidants," the Queen told him. "She is my eyes and ears when it comes to the missing cannons and the murders of the men who guarded them. Is that why you are here?"

"It is," he admitted. "By order of the King."

"Then speak to both of us."

He stared at the Queen for a moment, his face inscrutable. "I remember her. You trust her?"

She raised a brow, somehow managing to appear regal, despite her advanced pregnancy. "Absolutely. And if I am wrong, what harm could she possibly do? A foreign woman, from a country we have no quarrel with, who barely knows English? Speak."

He turned his stony-faced stare on Nicola, who raised a brow herself, and stared back. "Very well," he said, then swallowed and took a wide-legged stance, like a soldier reporting for duty. "We got a dispatch from the men who are looking for the missing cannons. They found the wagons and all but three of the missing horses in a field on the bank of the Thames. They spoke to a cottager who lives there. The night before, he and his wife heard a disturbance in the forest. The area is used by smugglers. The old couple hid in their hut while men—many men, the husband thought—loaded something heavy onto boats going back and forth to a larger vessel. They could hear the men grunting, and the splashes of oars."

"Are you following so far, Nicola?" the Queen asked.

"I think so. The cannons were loaded on a ship," Nicola replied. "Horses are missing."

Sir Henry nodded, frowning, and continued. "In the morning, the cottager got up to discover the remaining horses and both wagons, which he reported to the sheriff. A French ship had been seen on the Thames near there, off and on. The villagers speculate that it was awaiting this shipment."

"The villagers don't know about the cannons, do they?" the Queen asked.

"Not from our men, anyway. They think we are hunting smugglers. The soldiers will try to trace the wagon tracks. The murderers must have had an assembly point somewhere, where they waited for the second wagon and the ship. The woods nearby all belong to the Archbishop of Canterbury, though apparently he has never set foot in them."

"Wasn't that where King Henry and the court hunted, when we were at Canterbury?" the Queen asked.

. "It's a vast area. But yes."

"Did you follow, Nicola?"

"It was a French ship. The Archbishop of Canterbury owns the woods where the wagons met. Your Highness, all this suggests a conspiracy, possibly by members of the court," Nicola responded.

"Does the King understand this is evidence of a conspiracy?" the Queen asked Sir Henry.

"All too well. He is agitated. Your Highness, he hopes you are feeling well enough to join him in his privy chamber for a late supper."

"I will," the Queen promised. "Perhaps it is good, that the boat came from France? Eight cannons in France are less dangerous than eight cannons in the hands of disloyal Englishmen."

Sir Henry shook his head, his face grave. "Only if the cannons did not go to Richard de la Pole, who is reportedly in France, assembling an army to take Henry's throne. Those eight demi-culverins can be placed on wheeled carriages and used by foot soldiers. Load them with grapeshot and they will mow down an entire company of men. They are just what Richard de la Pole needs."

Sheet music, 1551, with solfeggio notation at bottom

CHAPTER 17: OF CAROLS AND FEASTS

The following day

The following morning, Nicola studied English psalms in one of the window seats of the anteroom used by the Queen's ladies, while the Queen met with the King and his Council. Later in the morning, Lady Margaret and another of the Queen's ladies interrupted her study, announcing that Her Highness had directed them to teach her English Christmas carols.

The two of them looked at each other, grinned, then sang something together—a rollicking tune about a boar's head, or perhaps about something the "boar said," Nicola was not sure which. The Queen's Spanish favorite, Maria de Salinas, sang beautifully but spoke poor English. The only words she sang were 'boar's head,' or perhaps "boar said.'" Lady Margaret Pole sang all the words and could carry a tune, but did not have a strong voice.

Nicola was glad for something joyful to distract her from thoughts of cannons and corpses and an amorous king. "Do either of you read music?" Nicola asked them. Both shook their heads "no."

"*Va bene.* I will write these carols down using *solfeggio*, which is easier to learn than reading music," Nicola said. "That will help me learn them. And we will work out harmonies, which I will also write down, so we can sing them in a group. Then you, Lady Margaret, can add the English words. Come, let's go to the Queen's writing table."

"What is *solfeggio*?" asked Maria.

"An Italian invention," Nicola said, as she seated herself and inked a quill. She sang a scale: "'Do Re Mi Fa Sol La Ti Do.' Now I will use the names of the notes to sing the first line of the Boar's Head Carol we are learning." She sang, "Sol Do Do Do Ti Do Sol" in the rhythm of the carol. "It's about the head of a pig, yes?"

Maria, ordinarily solemn, smiled broadly. "A pig, *si*. English is hard. But I can learn this."

They worked for several hours, laughing frequently as they mixed Spanish, English and Latin, to write out the Boar's Head Carol and figure out harmonies. Eventually, the Queen's other ladies left their embroidery and card games to help. Some remembered verses that Margaret did not, or sang a slightly different tune. By early afternoon, all of the Queen's ladies were singing and laughing together.

"King Henry has been out hunting for boars, every morning," Maud Parr said. "He wants to spear the biggest one, so his own kill will be paraded around at the Feast of St. Stephen."

"They parade a boar on St. Stephen's Day?" Nicola asked, feeling happy that she understood the ladies' chatter. "Why?"

"It's the start of the twelve days of feasting between Christ's Mass and the Epiphany. People long for meat, after the long fast during Advent. The entire boar is roasted and eaten," Lady Margaret explained. "They can't fit the whole thing on one platter—it takes two people just to carry the head, if it's a big one. It's an ancient custom."

"Sometimes in Italy the cooked body of an animal will be shown during a *festa*," Nicola responded, in slow English. "A peacock with its feathers put back, maybe. But we don't sing to it."

When the Queen joined them, they sang two verses of the Boar's Head Carol for her, in imperfect but enthusiastic harmony, with Maria and Nicola singing the lower parts. Afterwards, they all applauded, including the Queen.

"Has the King killed a boar yet?" Lady Maud asked.

The Queen smiled. "Not yet." She went to her mirror and adjusted her headdress. "Nicola and Margaret, come with me, please," she said. "The rest of you, stay and sing."

"Where are we going?" Nicola asked as they walked.

"To see Henry and something he wants to show you. Don't worry," she added, when Nicola stopped short. "You will come with me and leave with me. The King won't dare pursue you any further. But he needs you for this."

Detail of map of Dorset coast by Cotton Augustus c. 1539-40

CHAPTER 18: OF MAPS AND MYSTERIES

That afternoon

The Queen worried about Margaret Pole as they walked through the hallways of the palace, preceded and trailed by Yeoman Guards. She was fond of Margaret, despite herself—but Margaret was in trouble now. And nothing she could do would help. She moved with as much dignity as she could muster with her big belly, searching her mind for a way to assist Margaret without angering Henry. Nothing occurred to her. She would do the best she could.

She brought Margaret and Nicola to a small interior room with dark paneled walls, lit by a small fireplace and beeswax candles in a wrought iron chandelier. Leaving the guards in the hall, the Queen herself shut the door.

The King, dressed splendidly in bejeweled red and gold, stood next to a large table, which was covered with hand-drawn maps. Beside him were Father Wolsey, Sir Charles Brandon, Sir Henry Marney, and Henry's Spymaster, a man with a pointed black beard. "It's best you don't know his name," Henry had told her.

The King frowned and cocked an eyebrow when he saw Nicola. "Why dress like a nun, Lady Greensleeves?" he asked.

"If it please Your Highness, a nun's habit is warmer and more comfortable than bare shoulders and a tight stomacher. The Queen permits it," she responded, curtseying.

"I do indeed," Katherine said, forcing herself to smile at her husband. "I told Henry about the maps you requested," she continued, looking at Nicola. "Here they are." She pointed. "These castles, on the coast to the north of us—closer to York—seem to be of most concern."

Margaret Pole took a quick breath, as the King stared fixedly at her. Her face looked drawn, the way it did when she was deeply worried. "Wingfield," she said. "Something is afoot there."

"Tell us," Queen Katherine said, relieved that Margaret was volunteering what the Queen feared she would hide.

Margaret curtseyed. "I recently received a letter. As you probably know, since his mail is always opened," she began. "The letter was from my cousin William de la Pole, who is in the Tower. You will recall, he inherited Wingfield Castle when his older brother was declared a traitor. His lady wife has faithfully sent him regular funds so that he may live comfortably in the Tower. Until recently. She is not answering his letters. She is much older than he, and he is worried about her."

"And of course he wants his money, to live comfortably in the Tower," the King added, venom in his voice. His face was reddening, the way it always did when he was angry.

Margaret flinched. "Of course. I have been weighing what to do. Whether, possibly, to go there for Christ's Mass, and see that his lady wife is well. You'll recall her, Your Highness. She was Lady Cathryn Stourton, before she married him. Very wealthy, and of good family. A nice woman, too."

Being told about a "nice woman" seemed to infuriate Henry. His face turned fiery red and his mouth into a snarl as he turned to glare at Nicola. "Tell us who the greatest sinners are in Dante's *Inferno*, Sister Greensleeves. The ones in the lowest circle of Hell," he said, in a tone that made Margaret quail, and even frightened the Queen a little.

Nicola swallowed hard, looking at Henry as though afraid he would strike her. "Traitors to their lords are the greatest sinners, according to Dante. Like Judas."

Lady Margaret turned white. "My King, I have never. Ever—"

"Worse than murderers," the King said. "Worse than—"

"Adulterers," said Katherine, glaring at Henry. She felt every eye in the room on her as she stared her husband down. Her smoldering anger at his infidelity seemed to ignite when he mistreated other women. He was being very unfair to Lady Margaret. How was it her fault that her cousin's wife was not sending him money?

The king's Spymaster broke the uncomfortable silence by clearing his throat. "We are particularly concerned about that part of the coast because of what is going on across the Channel in Holland right now," he said. "There have been reports that Richard de la Pole is assembling an army there."

"I thought he was in France," the Queen said.

He gave a slight nod. "So did we." As always, his voice betrayed no emotion.

The Queen was alarmed, knowing that the north of England was an old Yorkist stronghold. "Does Emperor Maximillian know about this?"

The Spymaster cocked his head, considering. "Likely he does, and is turning a blind eye. But we don't want to take the matter up with him. Not just yet. It might reveal our spy network, to no good end."

Nicola bent over the map, and put a finger near the Channel. "Is Wingfield Castle really a castle? Meaning, it has walls that could be defended with cannons?" she asked, looking at Lady Margaret.

Margaret raised her head to look at Nicola. "It's both a manor house and a castle. And yes, it has massive battlements that could be defended with cannons."

Nicola circled an area of the map with a forefinger. "Wingfield is here, correct? I know my firm's cannons when I see them," she said. "And I know how to disable them, too. And they do have identifying marks. Under each of the trunnions— that's the crosspieces that stick out of the sides cannon, to allow it to pivot on its carriage—there is a letter 'B.' For the Biaggi arms firm. It's impossible to see without turning the cannon over."

"What is your point?" the King barked.

Nicola bowed her head, then looked up at him. "The Biaggi arms firm has never sold any weapons to England, except to Your Highness. So if Margaret and I went to Wingfield Castle, and I could get close enough to identify Biaggi cannons..."

"We would have our missing cannons, and our traitor," Father Wolsey said. "Or at the very least, know that Wingfield has not turned back into a stronghold for the de la Poles. It would be a logical place to garrison, if we are anticipating an invasion from Holland."

"Splendid," Queen Katherine said. She had to restrain herself from grinning like a jester who has just told a joke. God had given her the answer to two problems at once: how to determine Margaret's loyalty, and how to keep Henry away from Nicola. "You should leave immediately for Wingfield, Lady Margaret," she said. "Nicola, you must go, too. Disguised as a servant."

Margaret swallowed hard and peered at the Queen, like a dog expecting punishment. "May I take my youngest sons, Your Highness? William de la Pole and his lady wife are childless, but my boys have played with the son of the steward there. If it looks like a family visit to celebrate the season of Christ's Mass, whoever holds the castle is less likely to be suspicious."

"Wait," King Henry said, his face no longer red. As quickly as it had erupted, his anger had evidently cooled. "You and your boys will miss all the yuletide festivities if you go now. The boar's head. The yule log. The Lord of Misrule. And Lady Greensleeves here will not be present to sing the carols she has been rehearsing."

"Your pardon, Highness, but I am here to serve you and the Queen," Nicola said. "This is far more important than singing carols at a festival. The Queen's other ladies will do an excellent job at that. And until the armorers finish building the blast furnace, I have little to do in your service."

"I, too, am here to serve Your Highnesses. I, too, am happy to go, even if I can't take my sons," Lady Margaret said. "But it would work better if they were with me."

Queen Katherine looked at Wolsey with a raised brow, hoping he would see the advantages in sending Lady Margaret on this mission, and getting Nicola away from Henry. He acknowledged her with a slight nod. "There are plenty who can sing carols at Christ's Mass," he pronounced. "They should go by ship, and take a company of soldiers with them. Your Highness' good ship *Sovereign* is in port at Gravesend. Soldiers could garrison aboard, waiting for Lady Margaret and Lady Nicola to learn what is needed."

"And my good men can take Wingfield Castle, if need be," Henry added. His face brightened. "Of course this is more important than the revels for Christ's Mass. I will go. And captain my ship. And lead the army!"

The Queen gasped. When would Henry stop playing soldier, instead of acting like a king? "With me so pregnant, and Christ's Mass coming? In the time of storms and snow and cold?" she gasped. "I beg you, Henry. Don't even think of it. Besides, what if you get there, and nothing is wrong? You would look ridiculous. If you attack needlessly, you could start another rebellion."

Henry's face fell. He looked down for a moment, then raised his head and smiled at Katherine. "You are right, my love. As usual. It is best I pretend nothing is awry and rule the kingdom instead. And misrule the kingdom, perhaps—I am thinking I will serve as Lord of Misrule this year. "

Another bad idea, the Queen thought to herself. But now was not the time to address it. "How long will it take to make the arrangements?" she asked.

Wolsey frowned, then conferred in whispers with Sir Henry and the Spymaster. "Give us two days," he said. "Can you have your boys ready by then, Lady Margaret? And you, Lady Nicola?

The two women looked at each other. "Yes," Lady Margaret said. She still looked stricken.

"If we find the stolen cannons, do you want me to disable them?" Nicola asked.

The men looked at each other. "What is entailed?" the King asked.

"It is called 'spiking'—you hammer a piece of metal into the fuse hole. It can be temporary or permanent, depending on whether your armorers can extract it. If you need to take a castle armed with eight cannons, it would be better to disable them. I would need help from your armorers. And plenty of good luck, inside the castle."

"Make it temporary," the King said. "And we will pray you have good luck."

"I can't promise the luck, but I'll see to the armorers," Sir Henry said.

Typical servants' clothing, as shown in "Old Woman Spinning,"
c.1646 to 1648, by Michael Sweerts

CHAPTER 19: A DISGUISE IS NEEDED

The following morning

"The Queen wants to see you. And you, Lady Margaret." said Lena, early the next morning. She led them into the Queen's bedchamber, where Her Highness lay fully clothed on her ornately-carved four-poster bed, head propped on a pillow.

Nicola wondered if the Queen had taken ill. But her eyes were open, and her face showed a healthy color. She smiled at them. "Help me up, Lena. My back hurts a bit," she explained. "I attended Mass with Henry this morning, early, before he left to hunt boars again. The seats in his private chapel are hard and of course we knelt."

Nicola and Lena helped the Queen to her feet. "I will wrap a warm brick to put behind your back by the fire," Lena said.

"In a moment," she said, waving Lena away.

"Let's sit here," she said to Margaret and Nicola, gesturing towards benches with embroidered cushions, arranged in a corner.

"I have another surprise for you, Nicola," she continued, when they were seated. "There are nine monks awaiting you in my Presence Chamber. Along with Maria de Salinas. The King directs you to teach them all *solfeggio*. And whatever harmonies you have created to the carols you were working on yesterday. And you are to help, Margaret.

Their faces must have shown their dismay, because the Queen laughed. "The monks sang so beautifully this morning that I complimented them after Mass," she explained. "And told them and Henry about your caroling, and the *solfeggio*. Henry is full of plans for the twelve nights of celebrations that follow Christ's Mass. Which now include this."

"Your Highness, I barely have time to get ready to leave in two days. I have to make arrangements not only for me, but for my two sons," said Lady Margaret, who looked miserable.

"Lady Margaret's services are unnecessary," Nicola said, wanting to help her. "Brother Michael speaks Latin and the other monks do too, probably. I can communicate with them. They can't learn *solfeggio* in two days, but Maria and I can help them begin. And anyway, Brother Michael knows how to write out music and lyrics. And he said they all know the carols."

"But do you also need this time to get ready to leave for the coast?" the Queen asked her.

"I have little clothing that is suitable for a servant," Nicola said. "I can ready it quickly."

The Queen frowned. "You have no clothing suitable for a servant," she said. "I should have thought of this. You either dress like a lady, or like a nun. Nuns dress like ladies from long ago, not like servants. That's a problem."

She beckoned to her body servant. "Lena, can you help? We must dress the Lady Nicola as Lady Margaret's servant. And tell no one about it."

"Where are you going?" Lena asked Nicola, hands on her hips. "It's cold out, and getting colder. Your cloak is too fine for a servant. And not warm enough."

Nicola pulled out her purse, chiding herself for ignoring this detail. "I had hoped my oldest nun's garments would do, but perhaps not," she said. "I need at least two sets of warm clothing for a servant, and a good warm cloak. And a long wool scarf I can wrap around my head, like the peasants do. And warm gloves. And boots. Nothing tight-fitting or revealing, please. I will pay for everything."

Lady Margaret, the Queen and Lena spoke rapidly in English and Spanish, while Nicola fished for coins. "Is this enough?" she asked.

"Too much," Lena replied, smiling. "I will return some."

"Your Highness, may I be excused now? To attend to my sons?" Lady Margaret asked.

The Queen waved Margaret away. "One more thing for you, Nicola. This afternoon, Henry wants to show you off to his old tutor and his friend Thomas More. And a scholar who tutored them both, called Erasmus."

Nicola's fear of Henry erupted again. His recent irrational anger, though aimed at Lady Margaret, had made her stomach churn the day before. "Show me off?" she gasped. What does that mean?"

The Queen looked pained, whether because her back hurt or because of the question, Nicola could not tell. "These men are probably the foremost scholars in England, Nicola," she snapped. "Henry likes to philosophize with them. He wants to show them that he has hired an Italian cannon expert who is also an educated woman. You are—a novelty. It should not worry you. I will be there. Thomas More is a kindly man."

"I apologize for the question. As long as you will be there, I will be happy to go," Nicola said, feeling relieved.

"No need for apology," the Queen said as she pushed herself to her feet. "But you can't dress like a nun. Henry wants you in the blue kirtle you wore when we left Canterbury."

Nicola's queasiness returned. "The King remembers what I wore at Canterbury? Does he tell you what to wear, or any of the other ladies?" she blurted.

"He often tells me what to wear," the Queen said, her voice icy. "He has dictated everything about my dress during pregnancy. Appearances are important to him. It's a mark of favor."

Nicola hung her head, her cheeks burning. Queen Katherine had many reasons to feel pain and anxiety right now. She did not need Nicola making matters worse. "I apologize again for misunderstanding." she said. "Do I need to change now?"

The Queen flashed Nicola a quick smile as Lena helped her into a more comfortable chair, placed a heated brick behind her back, and propped her feet for her. "Not yet. Take the Lady Nicola to the monks," she directed Lena. "Then find her the servant's clothing."

"I hear them singing," Nicola said to Lena. "I will find them. Please help Her Highness instead."

Nicola followed the sound of the Boar's Head Carol to the Queen's Presence Chamber. She could hear Maria sing each part in succession, and the monks singing it back.

"Where is Lady Greensleeves," the King's voice boomed, from behind the door.

"She is with the Queen," Maria responded loudly.

Would King Henry never leave her alone? Nicola fled back to the Queen's inner rooms, trying to avoid unseemly haste. Katherine looked up from her prayer book when Nicola entered, and raised an eyebrow.

"Pardon, Your Highness," Nicola said. "The King is with the monks, asking for Lady Greensleeves. I would like to avoid him."

The Queen smiled and set aside her breviary. "I'll go with you. And don't worry."

When they entered the Presence Chamber, the King, Maria and the nine monks were all gathered around the table in the center, looking down at the sheets created the day before, and singing the *solfeggio* scale, up and down, over and over.

"My lady Queen," the King boomed, when he noticed her. He strode over to her, grabbed her hands, and kissed them exuberantly, with a grin. "You have found Lady Greensleeves. I thought she was going to teach us *solfeggio*. But Maria has already learned."

Maria smiled, and spoke to the Queen in Spanish. "The King wanted to take Lady Nicola and me back to his rooms. His *rooms*. But I told him I must stay here."

Nicola understood, and was frightened. She looked to the Queen for guidance.

Queen Katherine was staring at her husband, stony-faced. "You seem to be doing very well without Lady Greensleeves," she said, in English. "I could hear the carol, all the way in my sitting room. Come, sing it again for me."

Nicola remained silent as they sang, wondering what would have happened if the King had managed to get her and Maria into his private quarters. Surely he would not have risked the Queen's anger by trying to flirt with her—or worse—in front of one of the Queen's most trusted ladies. Would he? As a king he could do what he liked.

As Nicola worried, she noticed Maria carrying the melody and Henry singing with the tenors. He had a pleasing voice. Though the singing was not yet perfect, it was closer.

"Beautiful," the Queen said, when the singers stopped. "And well done. Please continue your practice."

She turned to her husband. "I require Lady Greensleeves for now, Henry. I will bring her with me, suitably dressed. when we meet with Thomas More. As you know, she has much to do in the next two days."

Anger flashed across Henry's face, and he stood silent for a moment. Then he smiled at Katherine. "As you wish, my lady love. It's all here," he added, tapping the sheet where Nicola had written out a musical scale, with 'do re me fa sol la ti do' underneath the corresponding notes. "Those Italians," he continued, "So clever. I am sure Lady Greensleeves could teach me many things."

Nicola felt herself blush. She could not bear to look at the King but could not politely turn her back to him. So she pulled another sheet from the table and curtseyed low, hiding her blush by looking down at the floor. "This is the *solfeggio* for "Christ was born on Christmas Day," she said, "Maria and I began writing parts for it."

Henry launched into singing "Christ was born on Christmas Day," joined by the monks and the Queen's English

ladies, who had followed the Queen into the room. Nicola looked up at the frowning Queen, who cocked her

head towards the doorway. Relieved, she arose and handed the *solfeggio* sheet to Maria, then hurried out.

Quentin Massys c. 1510 – 1520, Portrait of a Man,
believed to be Thomas More

CHAPTER 20: THOMAS MORE AND ERASMUS

Later in the day

The Queen led Nicola across the palace to meet with Henry and his guests, trailed by four of the Yeoman Guards. Her back hurt, and she was acutely aware that her advanced pregnancy made it impossible to walk regally, as a queen should. The more she tried to avoid it, the more she was convinced that she waddled like a duck—today, a purple duck with a triangular headdress that made her face look even fatter than pregnancy did. She wished she had not let Henry talk her into such showy maternity clothes.

She also did not like his demand that she bring Nicola to meet his scholarly friends, dressed to dazzle. But how could she object? She would be there. Surely Henry would not shame himself by showing his infatuation for Nicola in front of these famous and holy men.

 Nicola looked beautiful, regrettably. The Queen could not help being jealous of her. Elizabeth Boleyn and the other ladies had insisted on tying ribbons on her sleeves that matched her blue brocade kirtle, styling her hair into an elaborate chignon, and tightening her bodice at the waist until she begged for mercy. They tried headdress after headdress on her, until she refused to try any more. She had also refused cosmetics, but Lady Maud had stopped them at the door to redden Nicola's cheeks by pinching them, as if she were a piece of unripe fruit. "Smile,"

Maud said, and Nicola had obeyed, showing her perfect white teeth like a cat who wanted to bite.

Nicola's face had been sullen when they left. As they walked, she began to seem more cheerful. Henry would see the beauty he had demanded. Feeling swollen and ugly, Katherine dreaded his reaction.

"If it pleases you, Your Highness, it might be helpful if I knew something about these men we are meeting," Nicola said.

"Of course. Baron Mountjoy was one of Henry's tutors growing up. He's a prodigious scholar. He married one of my Spanish ladies—so many of them left me, either to marry or to return to Spain."

The Queen paused a moment, suddenly missing Inez, and remembering her wedding. "The other two men are Mountjoy's friends," she continued, as they started to walk again. "Thomas More is a brilliant lawyer, but also a famous scholar—speaks both Latin and Greek and knows all the classics. Erasmus was Baron Mountjoy's tutor—Henry met him as a young boy, and was very impressed with him. He is from somewhere in the Holy Roman Empire, and just joined the faculty at Cambridge. Before that he lived with Thomas More, working on a book."

"What am I to do?" Nicola asked.

"Sit and listen, until you are called. Henry loves talking about classical writings with them. And astronomy, and theology—everything but politics. He gets more than enough of that from his Council."

Nicola nodded, frowning. "What do I do, if I am called?"

"You may not be. You do whatever the King asks. I told Henry that you have memorized large parts of the Bible—he might call upon you to recite. Both Erasmus and Thomas More have strong ties to the Church. More was once a monk, but gave it up for the law. Don't worry. It will be nothing embarrassing or harmful to you. My presence guarantees that. Here we are."

Two pages opened the doors to the King's Privy Chamber. The Queen gestured to Nicola to sit in one of the carved wooden chairs that lined the tapestried walls, then walked slowly to join King Henry on the dais, trying not to waddle. She wondered what the topic of today's discussion would be.

Henry kissed her hand, then helped her make herself comfortable on the throne that had been set up for her, beside his. "Erasmus has just completed a new book, '*In Praise of Folly*,' and is reading parts of it to us," he told her. "I think you will find it most amusing." He nodded at Erasmus, who continued reading from the thick manuscript in his hand, in Latin so heavily-accented that Katherine had difficulty understanding him. But Henry was right—Folly praising herself made all of them laugh, Henry loudest of all. It was a joy to be with him at such a moment.

Nicola's musical laugh rang out in the background. Henry turned to look at her, his eyes widening. "Here is my Roman gunmaker—just as I told you, Thomas. Is she not a beauty? Come here, Lady Greensleeves."

Nicola walked gracefully to the dais, and curtseyed. "Your Highness. Thank you for allowing me to listen to Professor Erasmus," she said. She turned to him. "I will look forward to buying your book when it is published."

Erasmus stared at Nicola, open-mouthed. "You understood me?"

"I knew a young monk from the north who spoke with your accent," Nicola said. "I had trouble understanding him at first. He is also a professor, at one of your universities. Martin Luther.[8] Do you know him?"

Erasmus nodded. "A scholar of the Bible. I know of him. You are from Rome? What do you think of our 'warrior pope' Julius?" He smiled at her, a twinkle in his eye.

Nicola hesitated, then smiled back. "I think he is an excellent judge of cannons. He is the best customer of my aunt's firm."

---

[8] FN Read about it in Martin Luther and Murder

"Diplomatically stated," Erasmus said, grinning.

Henry turned to Katherine, who had been watching him, and missing his attention. "Katherine and Lady Nicola are reading Dante's *Inferno* together. In Italian of course."

"I did not know you had mastered Italian, Your Highness," said Thomas More to Katherine, with a courtly nod of approval.

He was flattering her, Katherine knew, but she enjoyed it. "My classical education was every bit as good as Henry's," she responded, smiling. "My mother saw to that."

Henry was not listening, she realized. He was staring at Nicola. "She also sings," he said. "Sing something for us, Lady Nicola."

Nicola's blush made her prettier than ever. For a moment, the Queen hated her. "I am not used to singing by myself in front of people," she said.

"Come, come. You sang in front of people at Dover," the King responded.

"That was with a group, singing a Mass. I am used to that, from the convent."

Nicola was charming these men, leaving Katherine feeling fat, puffy, pregnant and ignored. "There are only four of us, Nicola," she snapped. "Choose something familiar."

Nicola looked down for a moment, then raised her head and began singing a "Credo" from the Mass. Katherine watched Henry's eyes widen and his jaw drop, then realized what was surprising him: Nicola was singing the Credo that Henry himself had written, and singing it beautifully. His face wore the same expression she saw when he first heard Nicola singing in Dover, the night she arrived. He was entranced with her. He desired her. Katherine had feared his expression then, and it frightened her even more now.

"I wrote that. It is part of a Mass I am composing," he told his guests when Nicola reached the "Amen." While they praised Henry's Credo, Nicola looked at

Katherine, and gestured with her head towards the door. Nicola wanted badly to leave, the Queen realized. She had understood Henry's look, too.

"You remembered my Mass, note for note," Henry said to Nicola, with a caress in his tone that made Katherine wince.

Nicola frowned. "I had to memorize it, in order to sing it. There is never enough music to go around. That is what I do."

"You have memorized entire Masses, as well as large parts of the Bible?" the King asked. Nicola nodded. "That is remarkable."

"How did you learn these feats of memorization?" Erasmus asked.

"I didn't learn them. I just do it, sometimes without knowing it," Nicola responded.

"You are the first woman I have met with such a talent," Thomas More said.

Nicola had enchanted them all, without even trying. The Queen felt ignored and did not like it. "Your singing is lovely, as always," she said to Nicola. "Henry, I am afraid we must leave you now. I did not sleep well. I need to rest."

"Leave Lady Greensleeves here," Henry said, without looking at her. "I will see that she gets back to you."

Nicola looked at her, eyes begging to leave. "I require her assistance now, Henry," the Queen responded. "Help me up."

He did, again without looking at her. "Stay," he said to Nicola, in a tone that sounded more like a lover pleading than a king commanding.

She curtseyed deeply, then stood and looked Henry in the eye. "Your pardon, Your Highness, but I have a terrible headache. The Queen needs help her to her rest, and I require rest, as well. I pray you excuse me." She turned abruptly, then strode rapidly to the door, opening it herself. The guards on either side of it, though wide-eyed, remained stiff as statues while she exited.

Katherine followed her as quickly as she could, stopping only to glare at the guards until they held the doors for her, and fell into step behind her. Nicola was already halfway down the long hallway.

"Wait, Nicola," the Queen called out, slowing to see if anyone else would follow from the Privy Chamber. No one did. She was furious with Henry for being so blatant about his desires, and grateful to Nicola for resisting them. The poor girl could not help her beauty.

"You did well," she told Nicola when she caught up with her, resisting the urge to pat her shoulder.

Nicola's face was still angry. "I can't wait to leave for the north with Lady Margaret," she responded. "I want to get away from him. I want to go home."

The Two Princes Edward and Richard in the Tower, 1483
by Sir John Everett Millais, 1878

CHAPTER 21: THE PRETENDER

The following day

The Queen, seated on her throne the next morning, was surprised to see that Lambert Simnel was a middle-aged man when the Yeoman Guards brought him into her Presence Chamber. She should have realized he could not be perpetually eleven years old. She had learned his story as a young Spanish bride—but even then it was an old story, from early in Henry VII's reign.

Now, Lambert Simnel's face was lined and his blond hairline receding. Still, he was tall, broad-shouldered and handsome, with a proud carriage despite the green and white livery that marked him as a servant. On the rare occasions that commoners walked into her Presence Chamber, they generally gawked at the tapestries and the elaborate coffered ceilings. Simnel took his surroundings in stride, moving like a king in commoner's clothing. Yet his tight-lipped face looked worried, perhaps even fearful. He approached, knelt gracefully, then prostrated himself in front of her, in complete silence.

She beckoned to King Henry's Spymaster, gesturing for him to stand close to her. "Are there any suspicious reports about him?" she whispered.

"None," he whispered back. "But you were right. He has not been watched carefully in recent years."

She nodded and waved the Spymaster away. "You may rise," she told Simnel. He did, and made courtly bows to her and to Nicola, the only other person in the room beside the guards. The Spymaster had not wanted Nicola present, but the Queen had insisted, in part to ensure that Henry stayed away from her. She was seated below the dais in nuns' garb, her head down. Simnel did not appear to recognize her.

"I understand you are Lambert Simnel, and that you now hunt with my husband?" the Queen said.

"At times, yes, Your Highness," he responded, his eyes respectfully cast down. "For the main part, I simply train and care for the royal falcons."

"When I heard this, I was concerned for Henry, who is not always cognizant of his own safety. Especially when it comes to the sports he enjoys, like jousting and hunting. I realize the last rebellion occurred before he was born. Nonetheless, as the Queen and his wife, I worry."

"I am his most loyal subject, Your Highness," Simnel exclaimed, looking up at her. "I would protect him with my life."

"Nonetheless, out of the love you bear us, I ask that you take that knife off your belt and hand it to the guard beside you. And from now on, as a favor to me—no more knives when you are hunting with the King."

Simnel's eyebrows rose. "There are times I need a knife when we hunt, Your Highness."

"I am sure there are. And I am equally sure that one of the Yeoman Guards would be happy to lend you one, when it is necessary. Am I not right?"

The guard next to Simnel nodded and held out a hand. Simnel handed him his knife, hilt first, then patted his own thighs, as if to assure himself that he was still wearing clothing. He opened his mouth as if to say something, then pressed his lips together again and swallowed, looking like he had just forced down rotten food.

The Queen could not tell if he was angry, fearful or both. She smiled, hoping it would reassure him. "Tell me the story of how you went from being a boy turning a spit in the palace kitchen to becoming one of King Henry's falconers."

Simnel nodded, and again swallowed hard. "When everything started, I was ten years old or thereabouts. In the previous two years, I had gone from being an orphaned street beggar to being the pupil of an Oxford priest who taught me reading and manners—who was probably my father, though he never said so. He thrust us among nobility who taught me courtly skills: to ride a horse, speak properly, dance—and hunt. I was a quick study, but I found all of it tiresome. Except the horses and the hunting. I especially liked falconry." He patted his left wrist, where a falcon would sit.

"Go on," the Queen said.

"I didn't really understand what it was all about. At that age, you know, you just accept what comes to you. During the years I was on the streets, many odd things happened. This just seemed more of the same. Then suddenly I was in Ireland, with a crown on my head in a Dublin church. All because I looked like a prince who had been locked in the Tower of London, who everybody thought was dead. It was clear to me that I would never actually be a king, but I had to learn how to act like one. And then I was in the middle of a war, but always kept away from it."

A page entered with a note for the Queen. She took it and waved the boy away. "Continue," she said to Simnel.

"Then I was actually in front of the King—King Henry's father—and terrified. He questioned me for a long time, and I answered honestly. Next I knew, I was in the royal kitchens, turning a spit. That is hot, heavy work for a boy. Especially one used to being treated as a nobleman. My arms and back ached so much I cried. King Henry had agreed I was an innocent—and I was—but it felt like I was being punished."

He frowned and stared down at the brightly-tiled floor. Then he looked up and smiled, a charming smile. "But whenever I had a chance, I went to visit the horses and the falcons, and begged to handle them. I occasionally got to exercise horses, and actually showed talent with the falcons. By the time I grew too tall to stand inside the hearth, I was strong as an ox. There was talking of putting me to work as a porter, but I begged to be outside with the animals. I started as a stable hand, shoveling manure. The rest you know."

"You are content?" the Queen asked.

"Yes, Your Highness. I have a job I like, good food in my belly, and a wife and child. For someone who spent years as a beggar, what more could I ask?"

"No one has approached you, asking you to pretend you are a prince again?"

Simnel shook his head. "No, Your Highness. If they did, I would run to the Yeoman Guard, to turn them in. I have said over and over again—there is not a drop of royal blood in me. Why would I pretend otherwise now?"

The Queen smiled. "Why indeed. How often are you alone with the King?"

"Almost never. Falconry is an activity for groups, in open meadows. Where you can see the birds fly. When the King is off hunting in the woods he doesn't take the falcons with him."

"What about when he was hunting in Canterbury? Were you the only falconer with the court?"

"I was. We hunted one day with the birds. Brought down very little. The rest of the time the King was off in the woods with his closest companions and the dogs."

"Was the Duke of Buckingham with him?"

Simnel stopped to consider. "He was with us for the falconry. I'm not sure about the rest of the time—but probably. He's a great one for the hunt."

"And where were you, when the King and his closest companions were hunting in the Archbishop's woods?"

"With the birds, in their wagon."

The Queen stared down at him for a long moment, wondering if there were other questions she needed to ask. She could think of none. Simnel looked increasingly nervous. "Be aware, you are being watched. You may go," she told him.

 Simnel bowed deeply, backed away so as not to turn his back to her, and exited. "You stay," the Queen said to the Spymaster, in Latin. She gestured to Nicola to join them.

"Could you understand, Nicola? And what did you think? The Queen asked, when they were alone.

"I understood most of it," Nicola reported. "And I watched his face, and the way he held his body. He moves like a nobleman. I think he hated King Henry's father, for putting him in such a hard job. But he didn't seem hostile to King Henry. Still, he is a big strong man with a big knife, and he was in the woods where the wagons carrying the stolen cannons assembled, before they were loaded onto the French ship. He could be one of our killers."

Queen Katherine looked at the Spymaster. "Is there any way to check whether he was actually in the wagon with his birds, the whole time the court was at Canterbury?"

He stroked his beard, frowning. "Even if I found the man who drove it, he would be unlikely to know whether Simnel was always inside it. Likely he wasn't. He doesn't seem the type to stay cooped up in a wagon when he could be outdoors."

"I don't trust the Duke of Buckingham, who was in those woods with Henry," the Queen declared.

"Nor do we. But as yet he has done nothing to arouse suspicion."

She felt her anger spiking. "The Duke of Buckingham is the last direct male descendant of Edward III," she pointed out, in her most regal voice. "Some think his claim to the throne better than Henry's. And you don't think his sister's behavior when she was my lady-in-waiting suspicious?"

The Spymaster blinked—the only hint of emotion she had ever seen on his face. "You neutralized the threat from his sister very effectively yourself, Your Highness," he noted.

She suppressed a smile. Was this flattery or a genuine compliment? The Spymaster did not seem the type to flatter, but doubtless he had hidden talents. "I hope you are watching the Duke," she said pointedly. It was an order, not a request.

"We are and we will," he assured her, his face expressionless.

"And you will see that Lambert Simnel is watched now as well."

He bowed. "I will indeed." He turned to Nicola. "Are you ready for your trip north, Lady Nicola?"

"Lena has your servant's clothes for you," the Queen said to her. "Go try them on."

Wingfield Castle, Suffolk, by John Carr, 1776

CHAPTER 22: MENACE AT WINGFIELD CASTLE

Several days later, outside Wingfield Castle, Suffolk

Nicola stood at the edge of the forest with Lady Margaret, her sons, and seven soldiers, hidden among the trees. Four shiny cannons pointed out from the top of the massive curtain wall surrounding Wingfield Castle.

"Are those your cannons?" Sir Bartholomew asked. A tall, broad-shouldered man with flaming red hair, he was a good friend of King Henry, and the leader of the expedition. Nicola had found him intelligent, thoughtful and trustworthy.

"Too far away to know. But they could be," she answered, willing her voice to stay steady.

As much as she wanted to find the cannons, she had hoped they would not face this nightmare. If these were Biaggi cannons, it meant that Wingfield Castle was occupied by traitors to the Crown. And she had thoughtlessly volunteered to disable their defenses.

"Please, let's arrive before sunset," Lady Margaret said. She clasped her sons' shoulders. "You know the plan, boys?" They nodded.

"I will hope to see you on the righthand lookout, soon," Sir Bartholomew told Nicola.

"Pray God I can get up there. If you see me, those are Biaggi cannons." She took a deep breath. "Let's go."

Sir Bartholomew and five soldiers faded into the forest, while the remaining two helped Lady Margaret and Nicola remount, and handed a boy up to each of them. Nicola held the youngest around his waist. His hair smelled of the sea.

They had left Greenwich Palace quietly before dawn three days earlier, boarded ship at Gravesend, and made a fast voyage, careening up the coast of the English Channel on Henry's new ship *Sovereign*.

Though the offshore wind had left relatively calm seas near the coast, Lady Margaret had been violently seasick. She spent most of the trip draped over the leeward rail, leaving Nicola to chase her sons around the decks.

"Are young boys always like this?" Nicola had asked the sailor who helped her tug Geoffrey away from the ship's wheel, which he was trying to steer despite the pilot's efforts to keep it steady.

"How old are they?"

"Reginald is ten. Geoffrey is nine."

The sailor, who had a struggling Geoffrey under one arm, dumped him on the foredeck. "They're all pretty much like this. It gets worse," he added, as the boy glared at him.

Geoffrey jumped up and scampered away, rubbing his buttocks. Sighing, Nicola hurried after him.

They had rested in a sheltered harbor, to allow Lady Margaret to recover and send a message to Wingfield Castle, announcing her visit. There they made their plans, while the company of soldiers sent with them polished their armor and sharpened their weapons.

Now it was time to follow the plan. Nicola felt strangely calm. She had been given a big role to play, but it was manageable and well-defined. And surely easier than avoiding King Henry in Greenwich Palace. With luck, it would work. Without luck—well, hadn't she always been lucky?

As daylight began to fade, they rode silently through cleared fields, then through open gates in an outer wooden palisade. Between the palisade and the stone curtain walls of the castle they followed a long causeway between two large fish ponds. The tips of the bronze cannons mounted on the curtain wall ahead of them gleamed in the setting sun.

The entire castle was moated, but the drawbridge was down. Behind it, a heavy wooden gate still barred the way. As they waited on the drawbridge, one of their guards dismounted and banged on the gate.

Nothing happened.

Reginald slithered off the horse, and kicked the gate "Michael," he yelled. "Michael, it's me, Reginald. Let us in!"

"Reginald," came a child's shout from inside. "Let them in. Let them *in*."

Nicola and Lady Margaret dismounted and looked at each other and at her boys, who were both kicking at the bottom of the gate. It swung slowly inward, and the boys ran inside.

"I am Lady Margaret de La Pole, cousin to William de la Pole. I wrote to say I would be arriving with my sons," she told the guard who admitted them.

He nodded stiffly as he ushered them in. "We just heard."

While Lady Margaret continued towards an approaching lady, Nicola watched the three boys clasp shoulders and jump up and down. "Let's see the cannons," Reginald said. All three ran to the narrow stairs that led to the top of the curtain wall.

"See to them, Nicola," Margaret ordered. She then turned her back to address the well-dressed woman who had emerged to greet her.

"Yes, my lady." Nicola hurried up the stairs, feeling triumphant. Reginald had played his part admirably. Their plan was working.

The cannons were Biaggi cannons, unmistakably.

There were only four of them, but four were enough to establish that the hereditary castle of the de la Pole family was again involved in a treasonous plot against the Tudors.

"Careful, boys," Nicola said to them. They were taking turns riding one of the cannons like a horse, which seemed harmless enough. Piled next to each Biaggi cannon were stone shot and pieces of rock and chain—not good ammunition for distance damage, but devastating to soldiers approaching the walls.

Nicola strode quickly to the lookout where Sir Bartholomew hoped to see her, and mounted the stairs. At the top, she climbed and stood on a squat stone buttress, to be as high as possible. The sun had not yet set. Surely the soldiers hiding in the woods would be able to see her.

"May I help you, Mistress?" said a male voice behind her.

"I wanted to see the sea," Nicola responded, emphasizing her Italian accent. "Where is it? Is it there?" She pointed.

"The sea is hidden by the forest. Come down, please."

Nicola decided to linger a moment longer, to be sure her message was understood. "Oh, but I can see the sunset. And it is *magnifico.*"

"Quite nice," he agreed, as the sky lit up in shades of pink an orange. "But see the dark clouds coming in? Snow, is my bet."

"Snow? I have never seen a big snow. When will it come?" Nicola wondered whether snow would complicate their plan, though she had always wanted to see the world, covered in white.

"Sometime after sunset. Do I need to help you down?" the guard asked. "I would like to." He had a big, leering grin on his face, and terrible teeth.

Nicola found him repulsive. "No. I can get myself down, thank you," she said. Nonetheless, he hurried up the steps and grabbed her around the waist, lifting her off her feet. She crossed her arms, to keep his face away from hers, and wriggled to loosen his grip. His breath was terrible.

She backed quickly away from him when he put her down. "I'm on duty until midnight," he said, still grinning. "If you'd like to come up and watch the snow with me. There will be a fire over there, where it's sheltered from the wind. And hot wassail to drink."

She glared at him, gritting her teeth. Did the men of this country not understand what "no" meant? Or was Italy the same, and she unaware because she'd always had a servant to make her appear respectable, and protect her? Now all she had was a dagger. And to make matters worse, her dagger did not fit easily into these English boots. She would need to fix that.

"Leave me alone," she snapped, hearing the fury in her voice. His expression did not change, which infuriated her even more.

"Boys. Nicola. It is time to go in," Lady Margaret called from below.

"Lovely meeting you," the guard said. "Is that your name? Nicola?"

She was tempted to throw Italian insults at him—she had learned some choice ones from the sailors on the *Romulus*—but that would draw attention. Instead she ignored him, helped Geoffrey off the nearest cannon, and followed the boys as they galloped down the narrow stone steps to the castle yard below.

"Careful," Lady Margaret called to them. "Slow down."

They ran to her side. "We're hungry. Michael is going to take us to the kitchens to get something to eat," Reginald announced.

"May I, mother?" Michael said to the heavyset woman standing next to Lady Margaret. Nicola curtseyed to her, knowing from Margaret that Michael's mother was Alice Fitzpole, wife of the castle steward. In a showy maroon kirtle and matching necklace, she looked more like a lady, though she wore a large ring of keys at the waist. Alice smiled at her son and waved the boys away.

Margaret, walking beside Alice Fitzpole, stood taller and moved with more confidence than she did as a lady in waiting to the Queen. She was now Lady Margaret de la Pole, cousin to the owner of the estate and niece to kings, and her posture showed it. "Come, Nicola. We're going to see Lady Cathryn."

Nicola bowed her head and fell in step behind them, still angry about being manhandled by the guard. But good servants were inconspicuous. To perform her role for King Henry she needed to be not merely inconspicuous, but invisible. She would do her best.

Alice led them through a series of hallways to a large, pleasant room with leaded glass windows looking out at the sunset. A white-haired woman dressed in black sat next to the fire. Behind her stood a servant of similar age.

"Here is Lady Margaret, come to visit," Alice said loudly. "Finished your drink?"

"Not yet," the old woman said. She was clutching a cup. "Who are you?" she asked Margaret.

"Lady Margaret de la Pole, your husband's cousin. Leave us, Mistress Fitzpole. See to our sons."

Alice Fitzpole hesitated, as if she did not want to leave. "We'll be fine," the old servant assured her. Lady Margaret stared Alice down, again showing a regal demeanor that Nicola had not seen before this day. Alice seemed to wilt, as Margaret seemed to grow. Finally Alice bowed, and left.

Lady Margaret turned to the servant. "Agnes, isn't it? I remember you from last time we were here. Agnes, I have not eaten. Kindly fetch me something from the kitchen. Bread and cheese, perhaps." Then she turned to Nicola. "Were they what you thought?"

Nicola realized she meant the cannons. "They were, my lady," she replied.

When Agnes was gone, they turned to Lady Cathryn, who appeared to be falling asleep. Margaret pulled the cup away from her, none too gently, and handed it to Nicola. Then she rubbed the old woman's wrists. "Lady Cathryn, Lady Cathryn, Lady Cathryn," she said loudly, until the old woman looked at her. "I come from your husband William. He is in the Tower. He is *worried* about you," she announced.

"He is dead," Lady Cathryn said, her eyes fluttering as though she were about to fall asleep again.

Margaret squeezed both her hands. "He is not dead, I assure you. I have a recent letter from him that I can show you. He is concerned about you."

Lady Cathryn opened her eyes wide and sat up. "Not dead? Peter told me he was dead."

"Peter Fitzpole, your steward, told you that?" Margaret's voice was shrill. She checked over her shoulder. "He was wrong," she continued more quietly. "Sir William is worried about you, and needs the money you send him to live comfortably in the Tower."

Lady Cathryn stared at her. "There is nothing wrong with me. Except I am sleepy. Or was, until you told me this." She shook herself free from Margaret's hands. "You have a letter from him? Show me."

While Lady Cathryn read her husband's letter, rocking back and forth in her chair, Nicola showed Lady Margaret the cup the old woman had given her. "I know why she is sleepy," she whispered. "This posset she is drinking is laced with valerian and poppy. I can tell from the smell, and those seeds you see. Whoever makes it is sedating her."

Margaret gasped. "Sedating her. Are you sure?"

"I worked in the *infermeria* in the convent where I was raised, where we made the medicines. We were famous for them. Even Pope Julius used them.[9] Yes, I am sure."

Agnes bustled in with a plate of bread and cheese. "Where would you like this, my lady?"

---

[99] Read about it in Martin Luther and Murder

Margaret stood tall and took a deep breath. "On the table there, if you please," she directed, waving her hand the way the Queen did when she wanted something done. "Agnes, you have been here since Sir Williams time, haven't you? Who prepares this posset for your mistress?"

"Thank you for remembering me, my lady. Mistress Alice prepares the posset. But I am to make sure my lady drinks it."

"Agnes. Do you remember this woman?" Lady Cathryn said to her. The slackness of sleep had left her face, which now looked anxious. The rolled up letter from her husband was clutched tightly in one hand.

"And her children, yes, my lady. They were here for Christ's Mass, a few years ago. Don't you remember? It was a happy time. And now it's almost Christ's Mass, and she's here again, with two of her sons. They're playing with Michael in the kitchen. Isn't that wonderful? A blessing for you."

Lady Cathryn peered at Margaret. "Of course. I remember you now. Come, Lady Margaret. Help me up, and hand me my cane. Let's walk by the window. It will help me wake up. You, bring me my posset."

Nicola, holding the cup, followed them to the other side of the room. "You must not drink this posset anymore, Lady Cathryn," Margaret whispered to her. "It is laced with valerian and poppy. You are being sedated."

Lady Cathryn swayed and grabbed Margaret's arm as her cane clattered to the floor. "Mother of God, no wonder I am so sleepy," she whispered back. She shook her head violently, as if to clear the cobwebs. "Thank God I only drank part of it. I never did trust that wife of his. Let's walk faster."

Nicola handed her the cane. "Where can I throw this out?" she asked quietly, gesturing with the posset.

"The garderobe is just outside the door. Lady Margaret, you and I have much to discuss. Did Agnes say it is almost Christ's Mass?"

When she returned from the garderobe, Nicola joined Agnes and watched the goings-on from across the room, as a good servant would. Lady Cathryn clutched

Margaret with one arm, and occasionally used her cane to gesture as they walked. They kept their heads together, and spoke too softly to be overheard.

"Something wrong with the posset?" Agnes asked.

"She decided she didn't want it," Nicola said. As they watched, Lady Margaret helped Lady Cathryn sit at a writing table, where she took up quill and paper. Lady Margaret found a candle and lit it for her.

"What's it like, working for the Fitzpoles?" Nicola asked.

"Well I don't, you know. I work for Lady Cathryn. Always have. I have wondered about that posset—seems to make her sleepy. But then, you know, she is old. So who am I to say anything? But here we are, the day before Christ's Mass, and nothing has been done to get ready for it. In the old days, Lady Cathryn would organize a feast for the tenants and there would be singing and dancing and merriment. Now there's plenty of food in the larder—enough to feed an army— but no visitors."

"Enough food to feed an army," Nicola repeated.

"Aye. Hams and cheese and flour and lard and salted meats. Sugar, too. Raisins. Spices. Enough to make bread and cakes for an army. And the steward just collects the rents and squirrels it all away. Maybe he's afraid to order a feast because Lady Cathryn is too sleepy to tell him to. I don't know. But it isn't like the old days. She's plenty rich. We need some joy back in this house."

"Did you hear that her husband died?"

"Aye. Of course. Odd that no one went to the funeral. Odd that his body wasn't returned here, to be buried with his ancestors. But who am I to say? He was in the Tower, and things aren't the way they used to be."

"So many changes. Your mistress was grieved? When her husband died?"

"Of course. Still is. Sits and stares, when she's awake. He was a good master. We all were grieved. Except maybe Peter Fitzpole, his bastard. They never did get along. When Lady Cathryn dies this castle goes to someone else, and he's out a job."

"Peter Fitzpole is Sir William's bastard?"

"Aye. We don't talk about it, but Lady Cathryn knows. Everyone knows—it's right there, the "fitz" in his name. Lady Cathryn loves Michael—his son—but not him. Or his wife. Bit stuck up, that one. Dresses like her betters."

As she listened, Nicola watched the two ladies across the room. Lady Cathryn blotted and folded a letter, sealed it with wax from the candle and the signet ring on her finger, and handed it to Margaret, who quickly shoved it deep into the leather satchel she was carrying. Meanwhile Lady Cathryn was at work on a second letter.

Nicola wondered if she could assist somehow. "Would you like your bread and cheese now, my lady? You are looking pale," she called to Lady Margaret.

Lady Margaret looked not only pale, but frightened. "Please."

Nicola put the plate on the edge of the desk, wondering why Margaret looked so anxious, and was promptly waved away, like the menial she was pretending to be. Re-joining Agnes, she watched Lady Cathryn seal and hand a second document to Margaret, who stuffed it in her bag.

"Most lively I've seen her in months," Agnes said. "Wonder what they're up to?"

"Who knows? It's almost dark now. Should we light more candles?" Nicola asked.

"The steward hates to waste candles, but why not?" Agnes said. "They don't seem to want anything. I'd stir the fire, but I don't want to interrupt them."

The two ladies had returned to the fireplace, their heads bent in conversation. Agnes and Nicola busied themselves lighting candles, until Alice Fitzpole arrived, and saw them. "What are you doing?" she barked at Agnes.

"Lighting candles, my lady," Agnes said, her face frightened.

"I requested it, Alice," said Lady Cathryn. "Is dinner almost ready? Come, Lady Margaret."

"You don't want your dinner here?" Alice said.

"Of course not. We have a guest. By the way, have you ordered the feast for Christ's Mass yet?"

Alice looked from Lady Cathryn to Lady Margaret, and swallowed. "I didn't think you wanted one this year, my lady. Since you are in mourning for your husband."

"You were mistaken," Lady Cathryn said. "But no matter. I will take care of it. Agnes, give me your arm. We are going to the kitchen. Alice, take Lady Margaret to the sitting room, and make her comfortable. When will your husband be back?"

Alice looked as if she had seen a ghost. "I'm not sure, my lady," she stammered.

"No matter. We'll see him at dinner."

Saint Andrew's church, Wingfield, Suffolk, built c. 1362

CHAPTER 23: CAN THEY ESCAPE ALIVE?

Same time, elsewhere in the castle

Alice Fitzpole seated Lady Margaret in front of the fire in a pleasant sitting room and left her there. Nicola, who had followed silently, joined her immediately from the corner she had chosen to avoid being noticed.

"Finally, we can talk," she said. "I signaled the soldiers that the cannons were the stolen ones. What did Lady Cathryn say?"

Lady Margaret looked around, as if fearful they would be overheard. Her face was drawn and worried, with lines in it Nicola had never noticed before. "She is frightened of her steward, who is cousin William's bastard son," she whispered. "Not only did he lie about William's death, but he won't let her see the books. She has enormous wealth but doesn't know what's happening to it and 'lives like a pauper,' she says. She begs us not to tell anyone else that William is alive. You didn't tell Agnes, did you?"

"No. Do your sons know?"

"I never told them, Thank God. All they know is that they are spies for the King, and everything is secret, even from Michael. Lady Cathryn wants me to beg King Henry for protection from the Crown for her, if we can get out of here."

Nicola gasped. "If we can get out of here? Is it that bad?"

"It could be. As I said, she is afraid of Peter Fitzpole. And his wife, too. Especially now that she knows they were drugging her posset."

Nicola was fearful herself. She had expected to help with a misunderstanding or at worst, to spy for the King and disable cannons rightfully his. She had not expected danger to anyone, least of all to Lady Cathryn. "What did you tell her?" she asked.

Margaret swallowed hard, and pulled the leather satchel in her lap closer to her body. "Only that I was accompanied by two King's men and there were others nearby. And I was sure we would be rescued, because I am one of the Queen's ladies. Nothing about the cannons, or treason. She thinks we—you and I—should leave tomorrow, after Christ's Mass. She will insist we all go to Mass. We will be safe in the church."

"But it is snowing. Can we even get there?"

Lady Margaret glanced out the window at the night sky. Large flakes of slowly falling snow glistened next to the leaded glass, in the light from the fireplace. "Christ's Mercy, I don't know."

"I had better spike the cannons tonight," Nicola said. "If I can. What was in the letters she handed to you?"

A door slammed, and heavy footfalls sounded in the hallway. Two voices spoke, one male, the other that of Alice Fitzpole. "You did what?" the man said loudly. "Shhhh," came the response.

Margaret waved Nicola back into her corner, and composed herself, eyes closed as if she were napping. The argument in the hallway continued, but not loud enough to overhear.

The door then opened and a large man stepped into the room, his back to Nicola. "Lady Margaret. How lovely to see you. I am sorry I was not here to greet you. We only just received your note."

Margaret pretended to awaken. "Messengers are so unreliable these days," she said, after a pause. "I am glad to find Lady Cathryn doing well. Considering her age."

"Dinner will be served as soon as we can find our boys. Wait. I hear them. They're just outside."

A door slammed, and Nicola heard the boys in the hallway, loudly discussing the snow.

Peter Fitzpole opened the door and called to them. "Michael, you are late. You know you are supposed to be inside before dark. Go wipe your feet. Then come here."

They arrived at a run. Geoffrey spotted his mother and skidded to her side. "Mama, it's snowing outside! This is the biggest castle I've ever seen."

"What about Greenwich Palace, where we live?" Margaret responded. Smiling, she brushed the snow from his hair.

"That's not a castle. It doesn't have a moat, or a drawbridge. This one has underground passages and a dungeon. A real dungeon!"

"You saw it?"

"I did! No one was in it."

"We are making snowballs," Reginald announced.

"Oh. Is there enough snow for that?" his mother asked.

"Not yet. We only made little ones."

Michael backed away from his father. "I showed them around," he said. "That was being a good host, wasn't it?"

Nicola could see his father's face in profile. He smiled, but it looked more like a grimace. "You are learning," he said quietly to his son. "Come. It's past time for dinner. Allow me, Lady Margaret."

Margaret took his arm and they left, the boys at a run, completely ignoring Nicola.

Nicola knew they would expect her to head for the kitchen, though she did not know where it was. But she knew she was next to a door to the castle yard. And she needed to spike those cannons, so that she and Margaret and her sons would not end up in that dungeon, or worse. Her heavy cloak, which she had carried all afternoon, had everything she needed. She put it on and left the drawing room. Seeing no one, she walked out into the snowy night.

Snow-covered stairs to castle battlement.
Photographer and location unknown.

CHAPTER 24: SPIKING THE GUNS IN THE STORM

Outside the castle, the same evening

Nicola willed herself not to be distracted by the snow, something she had never seen before. Standing in the castle yard, she saw a torch and firelight in one corner of the castle wall. The narrow stone stairs she and the boys had climbed earlier to view the cannons were built into the opposite wall, far away from the lights. She said a quick prayer of thanks and headed up those stairs.

Snow, she discovered, was slippery. She almost fell but caught herself by throwing her shoulder against the castle wall. "Slow down," she told herself. "There is no rail." Her heart was pounding so violently she was surprised she did not hear it. The castle yard was strangely silent, as if snow muffled noise.

At the top, she sat on the lower end of the first cannon and brushed the snow off the fuse hole. Hands trembling, she reached into her cloak and pulled out the equipment the Head of Ordnance had given to Sir Henry. She had practiced with him on a piece of wood and was glad of it.

"Put the spike in the fuse hole," she told herself. "It will stop halfway down. Feel it in place. Put the wadding on top to muffle the noise, then tap it hard with the hammer. If you cough, the noise will not be heard. Feel it again. If it is flush with the cannon, you are finished. No one will notice the spike."

She prayed it was so. But what if she were caught? Would they put her in that dungeon that Geoffrey described? Would she ever get out again?

On the first cannon, one sharp tap of the hammer and disguising cough was all that she needed. Elated, she jumped up and went to gaze out from the castle wall in case the guard was watching, wishing her heart would stop pounding. No torch approached so she sauntered to the next cannon. That one, too, required one hard tap and one disguising cough. She realized that her years helping to do delicate metalwork in her aunt's armory were helping her destroy the armory's creations. She knew how to wield a hammer, just as a seamstress knows how to pull out a seam she has sewn.

When she reached the third cannon, she began to feel confident. Too soon. The first spike fell through to its interior with a soft clank, so she needed another. And another. How far did these little noises carry in the soundless snowy night? Sir Henry had warned her—the fuse holes were not uniform so some spikes were larger. With a shaking hand she felt for a big one and inserted it. She had to hammer and cough three times to push this spike flush with the cannon. By the time she was satisfied, she saw a lit torch approaching.

Moving quickly to the castle wall she gazed out, one hand on her chest in a vain effort to quiet her wildly beating heart. She could hear breathing and odd crunching sounds approaching from behind her back—the sound of boots trudging through snow, she realized. She hoped it was not the guard who had manhandled her earlier in the day.

Unfortunately, it was. "I have hot wassail ready for us," he said. She turned to see him grinning at her, closer than she would like, displaying his bad teeth again. "Aren't you cold?" he asked.

She backed away from him. "I never saw snow before," she responded, emphasizing her accent. "That is why I am here. Not to drink wassail with you. As I told you before. It is very beautiful, in the moonlight. Big pieces of snow, falling so slowly. Like dancing." As she spoke, she backed steadily toward the stone tower she had climbed to signal the watching soldiers earlier in the day.

"And the field is so white. And see what the moonlight does to it. *Magnifico. Spettacolare.*"

"It is right pretty," he admitted, staring at her wolfishly through lashes and eyebrows dusted with snow. "Like you. Wouldn't you rather see it from the fire, where it is warm?"

Nicola was both frightened and repulsed. Ugly even by day, the snow-speckled guard looked diseased and threatening in the silvery moonlight. "No," she responded. "As I told you before. I do not drink. Too much light there. Best light here. I stay here to watch the beautiful snow."

He continued grinning at her. "I'm afraid you might slip on the stones unless I help you. You might fall."

"I will hold the wall. Light the torch there," she pointed, keeping him at arm's length. "I will bring it to you when I go. You must walk the walls, yes?"

His grin disappeared. "Yes," he admitted. "Best to do my rounds first, eh? Very well. I will light the torch for you. But you wait until I return. Do you understand?"

"I understand," she promised. "I will wait. Now I watch the dance of the falling snow."

Nicola held her breath as he marched past the cannons. Torch held aloft, he did not even look at them. When he reached the opposite corner of the walls she sat down on the fourth cannon, and tapped the final spike into place. Then she grabbed the torch he had lit and rushed up the stairs of the nearby lookout tower—the one closest to the hidden sentinel, who awaited her signal.

Climbing as high as she could, she held the flaming torch where it would light her face, thanked God that she'd finished her task, and prayed the snow would soon hide the evidence of her sabotage. Then she gave herself a moment to enjoy the beauty of moth-sized snowflakes, drifting downwards to join the undulating white fields surrounding the castle, lustrously lit by the waning moon.

Finally, her heartbeat was slowing to normal. But not for long. It was time to climb down quickly. The guard's torch was approaching as he completed his circuit of the walls.

Peasants preparing a pig, by Pieter Brueghel the Elder, after 1616.

CHAPTER 25: TOO MUCH TO DRINK

In the castle kitchens

She was halfway down the stairs to the castle yard when the guard started down after her. "Are you sure you won't have some wassail with me?" he shouted, from behind her back.

She kept moving as quickly as she dared, both to escape him and to give the falling snow time to cover the cannons. "Oh, no. As I said before. I do not drink," she called out.

Leaning into the castle wall, she dug her boots into the deepening snow with each step down, bracing her leg against the wall at each opportunity; praying she would not slip over the precipice on the opposite side.

"Point me toward the kitchens before you go," she added as she heard his panting breath behind her. "I am very hungry."

'I'll take you there myself," he said, as they reached the castle yard. "Here, take my arm."

He expected her to touch his repulsive arm? She bit back a retort and instead thrust her torch towards him, dropping it when he did not grab it. As he bent to pick it up, she scurried to the door she had left only minutes earlier, and burst inside.

He followed her into the hallway. "We really should go 'round the back," he called to her. Looking back, she saw that his toothy grin had become a full scowl.

She remembered the way to Lady Cathryn's sitting room and hurried in that direction, wishing there were servants about. "Too cold out," she called back to him. "I smell the cooking. I think I know the way."

She remembered a flight of stairs ahead and rushed down them, following savory odors and hearing him behind her. At the bottom of the stairs she began to run. Hurtling into the open door of the kitchen, she was grateful to find it full of bustling servants, all of whom stopped to stare.

"Who's this?" a heavyset woman asked the panting guard, when he caught up to her.

He glared at Nicola. "It's the Italian girl," he responded, pausing for breath. "Lady Margaret's maidservant."

"I am very hungry," Nicola said, trying hard not to pant herself. And it was true, because she hadn't eaten since morning. "Did you want food?" she asked the guard, hoping to stall him a little longer, to give the snow more time to hide the spiked cannons. But he was already stomping back towards the stairs.

She seated herself at one end of the long wooden table, and realized she was exhausted and trembling. The room was warm but her hands were still like ice. Someone paused to put food and a spoon in front of her. She warmed her hands on the pewter bowl, then spooned its contents into her mouth without realizing what she was eating.

The tension was edging away, but she still worried that the guard would discover the spiked cannons, even though he'd already passed them without noticing. Surely the stupid man would not even think to look when he passed them again.

As she ate, she watched the cooks and helpers working frantically. A large boar roasted on a spit that ran from its tail to its mouth, turned by a red-faced boy who looked smaller than the boar. Nicola thought about singing the Boar's Head Carol, but she was too tired even to remember the tune. It was an insane thought anyway—her tired mind was playing tricks on her. She needed to stay as inconspicuous as possible.

"I thought she was dead," someone said. "Then she appears and wants a Christmas feast ready by tomorrow."

"You lost your bet, Jacob. She's alive after all. And as impatient as ever."

"Shut up and stir," said the portly woman who was giving everyone directions. "We have time enough to prepare a passable feast. But only if you whoresons keep moving."

"Will the snow stop Christ's Mass?" Nicola asked, wondering what a "whoreson" was.

The heavyset woman stopped long enough to glower at her. "Course not," someone said. "Nothing stops Mass, especially Christ's Mass."

"I know that," Nicola said. "But can we get to the church?"

"We'll get there," someone said. Not everyone was sure, however. Frantic speculation about the weather continued as the staff scurried around, bumping into each other.

Wine, mixed with fruits and spices, was steaming in a cauldron near the roasting boar, and scenting the entire kitchen. Nicola found a cup and helped herself to some of it.

"Who do you think you are? That wine's not for the likes of us," the heavyset cook said.

"Your pardon—I did not know. In Italy wine is for everyone," Nicola responded. "Can someone help me find Lady Margaret? My mistress?"

"Ask a footman. We're busy," someone else snapped. "Get out of the way."

Nicola returned to her seat and sipped more wine, wondering how to find a footman. Fortunately, Agnes arrived and saved her the trouble.

"There you are," Agnes said to her. "Lady Margaret was wondering where you were."

"I went to look at the snow," Nicola said. "Could you take me to her?"

"Just as soon as I check on preparations for tomorrow's feast for Lady Cathryn," Agnes promised.

Eventually, Agnes led Nicola to the top floor of the manor house by the light of a candle, chattering about the feast the whole way. At the door, she pulled a second candle from her pocket and lit it for Nicola. "Her ladyship retired some time ago," she whispered. "See you don't wake her."

Lady Margaret had been given a small bedroom dominated by a curtained four poster bed. Her sons were draped in blankets and curled up on pallets next to the wall, sound asleep. Lady Margaret peered out from beneath the covers, and gestured to Nicola to join her. Exhausted and a little drunk, Nicola blew out her candle, threw off her cloak, kicked off her boots, and climbed into the bed with all her clothes on.

"I was so afraid something had happened," Lady Margaret whispered. "Is all well?"

"I spiked the guns and signaled the soldiers," Nicola whispered back.

Margaret clutched Nicola's arm. "Did anyone see you?"

"That repulsive guard. But he didn't understand what he saw. I think we are safe. How was dinner?"

Nicola could feel Margaret's body shaking beside her and heard muffled noises—evidently her ladyship was stifling sobs. "You have no idea how I worried," Margaret whispered, when she was still again. "I haven't been this frightened since the soldiers took my brother away when I was a little girl. The boys behaved themselves at dinner. Mostly. Nothing of consequence was said. We all go to Mass in the village early tomorrow morning, God willing."

Nicola reached out to pat Margaret's arm, realizing how motherhood and those two sleeping boys must weigh on her. "I am sorry I caused you such worry," she whispered. "There is nothing else we can do now. Let's try to get a good sleep."

Margaret sighed. "I'll try. Happy Christ's Mass, Nicola."

Effigies, John de la Pole (d. 1491) and his wife Elizabeth Plantagenet
St Andrew's Church, Wingfield, Suffolk

CHAPTER 26: A BLOODY CHRISTMAS

Christ's Mass morning
Wingfield, December 25, 1510

The trudge through ankle-deep snow to the Wingfield parish church for Christ's Mass began before dawn. It seemed endless to Nicola. Lady Cathryn, in widow's black, led the de la Pole household in a horsecart, followed on horseback by Peter Fitzpole and his wife in costly, gaudy colors; then by Lady Margaret in more muted attire. Margaret's boys and Michael Fitzpole wove in and out on ponies, occasionally at a gallop, shouting at each other and ignoring their mothers' pleas to mind their manners. The family was surrounded by guards, also on horseback, who ignored the boys' antics.

The servants and retainers, including Nicola, struggled behind them in muddy wet snow, on foot. Nicola was thankful for the shapeless, wool-lined boots that Lena had bought to replace her fashionable thin Italian ones. Her feet were warm and dry, at least at the beginning. She had found a way to jam her dagger into her right boot, in its scabbard. It rubbed her ankle, but at least it fit.

A few of the servants wore colorful shawls or hats for this special holy day, but most did not have any special clothing. Like them, Nicola wore a heavy wool cloak over a shapeless wool sack that covered a linen undergarment, all in shades of brown. However, between breasts and belt, Nicola carried things the other servants didn't: letters and documents handed to her by Lady Margaret that morning for safekeeping. "This is a report for King Henry from me. This a letter to him from Lady Cathryn, requesting his protection. And this an order from Lady Cathryn to her London bankers, for her husband's expenses," she had told Nicola, who helped her dress. "My kirtle suitable for church is too tight to hide them, and I don't dare leave them behind. You may have an easier time getting away from the household than I will, when the service is finished. I pray you guard them well."

All the way to the church, Nicola worried that she would be accosted by the guard from the night before, but he never appeared. As the sun rose, she wondered if he was in the group of horse-mounted guards ahead of her, attending the family. As she saw only their backs, she couldn't tell one from another. She fervently hoped he'd remained behind, guarding the castle.

The parish church at Wingfield looked colorless and uninviting as they approached it. Made of rough-hewn brown stone with a single square tower, it stood silhouetted against a grey morning sky, surrounded by a white, snow-covered graveyard dotted with leafless black trees.

Once inside the church, Nicola's spirits rose. The sanctuary had been lit with candles and decked in pine-scented greenery for Christ's Mass. The saints and prophets looked out at her from luminous stained glass windows, in vibrant colors, lit to the east by the rising sun. Gratefully, she gave herself over to the beauty of the Mass, and prayed for deliverance from danger.

When the service was over, Nicola joined Lady Margaret, who stood gazing at the stone effigies of a knight and his lady, lying side by side atop a tomb in a side chapel. "Here are John de la Pole and his wife Elizabeth," she said. "She was older sister to King Richard III and King Edward IV. John was the last of the de la Pole men to lead a peaceful life. His oldest son died fighting King Henry's father. His middle sons, Edmund and William, are in the Tower. And Richard, the youngest, is in exile, trying to raise an army against King Henry."

Behind them, a man cleared his throat. "You had best stay here," he murmured. "Thank God you spiked those cannons."

Nicola turned to face Sir Edward Beacham, dressed all in black, whom she recognized from the voyage up the Channel. He spoke excellent Latin. "What has happened?" she whispered.

"We're waiting at the bridge to arrest Peter Fitzpole. He and his family are just leaving the church now. There might be trouble with his guards. Best find excuses to keep Lady Cathryn here, and as many of the villagers as you can."

Lady Margaret gasped. Without a word, she hurried to Lady Cathryn, who was sitting in the Bishop's chair in the chancel area next to the altar, chatting with the villagers lined up to greet her. Sir Edward headed for the main door of the church, and Nicola rushed to walk beside him.

"What happened at the castle?" she asked.

"Quiet," he told her, gesturing at the curious parishioners who stared at both of them.

When they were outside, he shut the church doors behind them, inserted his sword between the two handles, and leaned against them. Then he grinned at Nicola. "Last night, after we saw your signal light, we pried open the wooden outer wall in a hidden corner, and moved in a battering ram we'd made from a downed tree in the forest. Soon as everyone left for church this morning, we sent men inside to spike the drawbridge so it couldn't be closed. Fortunately it was still dark—the guards didn't notice. We'd been watching them, and they don't notice much. Bloody damn fools."

He snickered, then looked guiltily at Nicola. "Your pardon, my lady. Most of the guards had gone with the family to Mass. Most of the rest headed off to begin celebrating, soon as the family was gone. The fools left the outer gate wide open, and the outer walls completely unguarded," he said quietly. "And the inner walls, only scarcely guarded. Just as we hoped. Can you believe it?"

Someone inside the church pushed on the doors. One hand on the hilt of his sword, Sir Edward pushed back and braced himself against the door. "Anyway, soon as everybody headed for church was out of sight, our strongest men got the battering ram going on the inner gate, before the worthless guards inside even knew we were there. The rest of us quick marched through the outer gate and up the causeway, dressed in King Henry's colors. The guards pulled the cannons in to load them, but they never pushed them out again. Would have been a bloodbath if you hadn't spiked them." He looked at her. "Thank you. I'll see the King knows what you did for us."

The door shook. "Stay where you are," he roared in English, his voice suddenly terrifying. "The guards panicked, I think," he continued in his earlier, matter-of-fact Latin. "Because there wasn't much of a fight. We were yelling about treason and stolen cannons. The guards threw their swords down, and gave up. The kitchen staff gave us more fight than they did, when our men ate most of their feast." He laughed. "I only got a taste—had to leave with those who will make the arrest. Which is about to happen."

Centered around the loud colors worn by the Fitzpoles, a cluster of horses was disappearing from view at the opposite end of the village. A sudden movement of shadowy shapes from either side of the road triggered shouts, groans and the sound of swords clashing. Horses reared, and the gaudy figures fell, screamed and struggled against others hovering above them. A female voice shrieked repeatedly. Several horsemen rode off, with others in pursuit. Then all was silent.

"That's it, I reckon," Sir Edward remarked, as if little had transpired. "We'll catch the rest."

Nicola's heart was pounding. She had seen the results of violence many times, but never before witnessed it happening. "If the Fitzpoles are still alive, will they be beheaded?" she asked, keeping her voice calm.

"They're alive—that was our orders—and it will be worse for them than that. This is high treason, and they are commoners. Likely he'll be drawn and quartered. Maybe they'll spare his wife that."

"What is 'drawn and quartered'?"

"Guts removed when you're still alive, then body cut into quarters," he said matter-of-factly, his eyes now trained on the road in front of the church, where people were gathering.

Nicola shuddered. Were Italians this cruel? Which was worse: drawing and quartering, or burning someone at the stake? It horrified her even to think about it.

She decided to change the subject. "I think the other stolen cannons must be near by, where they can protect Richard de la Pole's invasion. There are two castles on the coast less than half a day's ride, according to a map I saw at Greenwich Palace. One was called Caister Fort, noted as a Roman ruin. The other, across the mouth of a river from Caister Fort, was Caister Castle. That's a logical place for an invasion force to land, if they were going to use Wingfield Castle as their base."

Sir Edward turned to stare at her. "We're ahead of you on that," he responded. "We've already sent scouts to look at the Roman ruin. Caister Castle belongs to Sir John Paston, deputy to the Lord High Admiral. Who lives in London, I know for a fact. So he probably keeps few servants at his castle. He may know little about what goes on up here."

Noises in the street drew their attention. "Peter Fitzpole has been arrested by His Highness King Henry for *treason*," Sir Edward roared in English at a group of villagers who stood gawking in the roadway. "*Stay away,* unless you want to be arrested, too."

They stared at him, mouths agape, then broke into a cheer. "Merry Christmas," someone shouted. Other villagers took up the cheers. Some began to dance.

"Guess he wasn't much liked around here," Sir Edward murmured in Latin, as if he were discussing some dry aspect of ancient history. "We'll leave immediately to take Fitzpole and his wife to the Tower, and news to the King. The northerly winds that brought this snow mean a fast voyage south. Do you and Lady Margaret want to go with us? You will need to be ready quickly, if you do."

"I'm ready now," Nicola affirmed, relieved that she could leave right away. "Let me ask Lady Margaret. Would you open the door, please?"

Nicola hurried into the church, past puzzled parishioners. Near the altar, Lady Margaret stood with her sons, Lady Cathryn, the priest, and a group of villagers, all of whom gaped at her.

"Wingfield Castle has been taken by King Henry's men, and Peter Fitzpole and his wife arrested for treason," Nicola announced, her voice echoing in the ancient space. "They are being taken to the Tower."

"Treason?" said Lady Cathryn. Eyes wide, she sagged back into the Bishop's chair and put her hand on her heart.

Margaret's son Reginald, who stood next to her, put a comforting hand on her arm. "Those cannons were stolen from King Henry," he explained.

Lady Cathryn turned to stare at Reginald. "What cannons?"

"So all is well?" Lady Margaret asked, her mouth trembling. She stood behind Lady Cathryn, clutching the chair's finials like an escape ladder.

"All is well," Nicola assured her, watching Margaret grimace to stop the tears seeping down her cheeks.

"If all is well, where is Michael?" shouted Reginald's little brother Geoffrey, who was seated the floor in front of Lady Cathryn, glaring at Nicola. "Are they taking *him* to the Tower?"

Lady Cathryn crossed herself, then put her hands on Geoffrey's shoulders. "They won't put a child in the Tower," she assured him.

"Not Michael, anyway," Lady Margaret told her son. She had controlled her emotions, or at least the muscles of her face. She looked and sounded like a calm, well-born lady again.

The church was in an uproar, filled with loud voices reverberating like trumpets in the high-ceilinged space. When the priest stepped down from the chancel to attend his flock, Nicola joined Lady Margaret behind the bishop's chair. Patting the documents hidden in her gown, she whispered, "Sir Edward is leaving immediately to take the Fitzpoles to the Tower and bring news to King Henry. I think I should go with him. I have everything I need on my body. Do you want to go, too?"

Margaret shook her head. "Take my horse," she directed. "I can ride in Lady Cathryn's cart. And please make excuses to Her Highness for me. Tell her I must assist Lady Cathryn for at least a day or two. She will need help to go through her books and manage the soldiers."

Lady Cathryn, now standing, turned to stare at her. "What soldiers?"

"King Henry's soldiers. The ones who stormed your castle, and ate the villagers' feast," Nicola said.

Lady Cathryn looked at Nicola for a long moment, as if noticing her for the first time. Then she grabbed Reginald's arm, her jaw set. "Lady Margaret, I'm *sure* you will explain," she proclaimed, with a regal frown. "I checked the larder and we seem to have ample food. I am happy to lodge good King Henry's men. And give the villagers their feast. We'll manage somehow. We had best be going."

As Nicola turned to leave, Geoffrey grabbed her hand. "Don't let them take Michael," he pleaded.

"I won't," Nicola told him, patting his head. Then she hurried out, hoping she could keep her promise.

Les Grandes Voyages, Theodore de Bry, 1602

CHAPTER 27: THE KING'S SPYMASTER

On board the *Sovereign*, the same day

As she clung to the doorway in a howling wind, Nicola recognized the documents scattered atop a navigator's chart in the captain's cabin, to which she had been summoned. She had delivered all three, seals intact, to Sir Bartholomew before boarding the *Sovereign*. The seals had been broken, though the letters were for the eyes of King Henry and Lady Cathryn's banker only. Everything on the table slid forward and back with the rolling motion of the ship, which was hurtling south at the speed of a cantering horse.

Behind the captain's table sat the man with the pointed black beard who had stood beside King Henry when Nicola reviewed maps at Greenwich Palace. The Queen had called him "the Spymaster," and even she seemed intimidated by him. Behind him, the captain's windows revealed grey-green rolling waves, marked with the frothy white lines of the wake that followed the ship. Having been displaced from his cabin, the captain himself stood on the poop deck above it, the best vantage point for viewing the entire ship and the seas ahead. Nicola could hear him, shouting at a crew member to be heard above the wind.

The Spymaster waved Nicola inside the cabin. "Close the door," he shouted over the noise of the gale thrumming through the rigging and the waves crashing

179

against the hull. "I read Lady Margaret's report and Lady Cathryn's requests," he announced when she stood before him. "Now sit, and give me your version. And speak up so I can hear you—with this much noise, there is no fear of eavesdroppers."

Nicola sat, grateful for a chair fixed to the rolling ship's deck, out of the cold. She spoke up, declaiming everything, from the time Lady Margaret's boys first banged on the gate at Wingfield Castle until she left Lady Margaret and Lady Cathryn at the Wingfield parish church. "I don't think Lady Cathryn had any idea what was happening," she concluded. "She thought her husband was dead."

The Spymaster stroked his beard, his eyes devoid of pity. "So I read in her letter to the King. He was supposed to be dead. It will be interesting to see if he is still alive when we get to London."

Interesting to see if he is still alive? Nicola wanted to ask questions, but didn't dare. "Lady Margaret and her boys were heroic," she continued instead, willing her voice to stay steady and loud. "The King should not doubt their loyalty."

His face was expressionless. "That will be his decision. When we dock, we go directly to the Tower. I may have another task for you there. Depending on whether Lady Cathryn's husband is still alive."

Nicola's heart was pounding. She did not want to work for this man. He had wanted to put little Michael Fitzpole in the Tower, to use against his traitorous parents. "He'd torture an innocent child?" Sir Thomas exclaimed, when Nicola told him. Michael, his eyes red from weeping, had been escorted back to Wingfield Castle. The Spymaster, watching the horses depart, had thrown Nicola a look so icy that she was now afraid to be near the rail when he was on deck.

Nicola wished she had returned to Wingfield Castle with Michael. Better yet, she wished she had never left London. "I am needed by the Queen," she stammered, hoping to avoid whatever task he had in mind for her.

"You'll get back to her soon enough. And the King will have more reason to be grateful to you. You may go. I'll see you in the morning."

That night Nicola huddled in her cloak on a narrow wooden bed suspended from chains that swung with the motion of the ship, in the tiny cabin an officer had vacated for her. The seaweed and sewage stink below decks was the same as the *Romulus,* but the *Sovereign's* noises were different and the cries of English sailors working the sails in the dark unfamiliar. She was beset by nightmares: the sailors' shouts metamorphosed into a shadowy army of men chasing her with cannons, led by the repulsive guard who'd manhandled her at Wingfield Castle, whose teeth dripped blood.

 Soon after dawn, she realized that the ship had docked while she was dozing. In haste, she straightened her clothing, gathered her belongings, and climbed to the deck. The bearded man had already disembarked. He stood on the dock, conferring with Father Wolsey and a cluster of soldiers. Peter Fitzpole and his wife, both gagged, sat on horses with wrists tied to their saddles and feet lashed to their stirrups. As she watched, the bearded man and most of the soldiers rode off with them.

Two seamen then lowered Nicola to the dock in the bosun's chair. There Father Wolsey waited for her, holding a handsome bay horse, saddled for a woman.

"Welcome back," Wolsey said. "You and I have a couple of tasks to perform."

"I am muddy, hungry, exhausted and cold," Nicola said, as he helped her mount. "The last few days have been horrible. Must I?"

"I'm afraid so," he said. "One of the tasks is something only you can do." Before she could ask what it was, he strode to his own horse, and trotted off, gesturing for her to follow. How could she do otherwise? She didn't even know where she was.

Detail from Old London Bridge from the West
Claude de Jongh, dated 1632

CHAPTER 28: SAVED BY THE BANK

Later that day

They crossed London Bridge at midday. It was a bit like the Ponte Vecchio in Florence, Nicola saw, but with taller, more ramshackle buildings in the half-timbered English style, more shoppers, and a drawbridge in the middle. The soldiers escorting them shouted, "Make way for the King's Men," and people did, immediately.

They dismounted in front of the Fugger bank. Father Wolsey handed Nicola the letter that Lady Cathryn had written to her bankers, its wax seal showing no signs that it had been tampered with.

"Lady Cathryn identified you as a possible bearer of this order, for the money her husband needs. They know you," he said. "After you hand it to them, I will do the rest."

"I am dressed like a servant," Nicola said. "Kindly give me your scarf." It was a costly one, of fine blue wool, which she wrapped around her head and shoulders to hide her servant's veil, and at least part of her cheap cloak.

Wolsey rearranged the scarf around her face, then cocked his head and looked her over. "You don't look like a servant. Nor did you before, really. You needn't worry. Your face is a hard one to forget."

Upon entering, she stepped immediately to the counter, to hide her mud-splattered servant's skirt. "You remember Lady Nicola," Father Wolsey said.

The banker behind the counter smiled. "How could I forget her? And how can I serve you?" he said to her.

Nicola gave him her best smile. "I have just returned to London, from seeing Lady Cathryn de la Pole at Wingfield Castle," she said. "She is most upset that her husband is not receiving the money he needs. She asked me to give you this."

He took the document, broke the seal, and read it. Then he looked at Wolsey. "Why are you here?" he asked, with no hint of emotion.

"Lady Cathryn has asked His Highness King Henry for protection from her steward, whom she believes to be taking advantage of her. I can show you her letter, if you like. I am here to help the King determine the facts. I will also deliver funds to Sir William in the Tower, if you will allow."

"I would like to see that letter," the banker said. He smiled at them after he read it. "I recognize her handwriting," he said. "In both letters. This is a great relief. We wondered about the sudden order to stop funds to Sir William. The hand that wrote it differed somewhat from her past orders. Similar, but perhaps not the same. The Tower assured us that William is still alive, so we sent inquiries to Lady Cathryn. We have not heard from her. Yet, there was no word she was dead."

"She is alive and well," Nicola assured him.

"There is more, though," the banker continued. "We received a second order to transfer much of her funds to our bank in Holland. Again, it did not look like her hand. And both of these orders came by messenger, whom we never saw. We tried to contact her. So far, we have been unable to do so. Hence, we have not made the transfer."

"Praise be to God," Wolsey exclaimed. "You may have saved England from invasion. I am confident Lady Cathryn gave no such order."

The color drained from the banker's face. "Invasion? Are you serious?"

"Perfectly serious. May I see the documents?'

"Of course." The banker scurried to bring them. Wolsey pored over them, muttering and pacing the room. When finished, he slammed them down on the counter. "As God is my witness, these are forgeries. And evidence of high treason. May I have them?"

"May I copy them first?"

Wolsey nodded, clutching the gold cross that hung from his neck. "Of course. Copy them carefully. I'll be back personally for the originals tomorrow. Lady Nicola, let us go."

"Did you require funds for Sir William?" the banker asked. "Now that you have clarified the situation, I have a month's worth for you. If you will sign a receipt." Wolsey signed with a flourish and took the bag of coins.

"Do we go to Greenwich Palace?" Nicola asked, as one of their guards helped her mount her horse.

"To the Tower. Then to Richmond Palace. The court is moving there, as we speak."

The Peasant Wedding by Pieter Bruegel the Elder, dated 1567

CHAPTER 29: THE CONSPIRACY BROADENS

The same day, December 26, 1510

Back at Wingfield Castle, Lady Margaret sat watching Lady Cathryn peruse the castle account books, as Sir Edward searched Peter Fitzpole's office for evidence of treason. Fitzpole had chosen an imposing space for his work. Or perhaps he had furnished it at Lady Cathryn's expense. Margaret did not dare ask.

The two ladies sat in leather chairs facing a fire crackling in a hearth embellished with stone carvings of dragons. Opposite the leaded glass windows on Margaret's left hung a large tapestry of a hunting scene. Costly Turkish carpets covered portions of the planked wood floors.

Margaret sat in silence as Lady Cathryn moved her finger across each line of the accounts, occasionally making notes. Sir Edward, similarly quiet, stood riffling through documents piled on a large table near the windows.

In the quiet, Margaret could hear her boys and Michael Fitzpole playing in the remains of the snow in the castle yard, where servants were busy cleaning up after yesterday's feast. It had been as jovial and merry a Christ's Mass day as any Margaret could remember.

Loudly glad to see Peter Fitzpole gone, the villagers and village brewer had pitched in with food and drink from their own larders, while sharing recipes, teasing, and jokes. They had all sung the carols Margaret had rehearsed at Greenwich Palace, and some she had never heard before. The soldiers made up for eating everything in sight when they first conquered the castle by carving and plating the boar for the villagers, when it finally finished roasting. While everyone waited, they paraded its head and sang the Boar's Head Carol.

An impromptu orchestra of handmade instruments and soldiers' trumpets played raucous music, inspiring even more raucous dancing. Margaret had danced with her boys, giddy with relief that God had spared them all from the Fitzpoles' vengeance. Now, she felt exhausted.

A cracking noise called her attention to Sir Edward, who was poking and prying at the floorboards with his sword. "Aha!" he called out, when he found a board that moved easily. Margaret handed Lady Cathryn her cane, and helped her to her feet. They watched as Sir Edward began removing objects from the cache.

Wordlessly, he passed a bag of coins to Margaret, who set them aside for Lady Cathryn. With them was a small bundle of letters, which he read, one by one.

"As I suspected," he said. "Richard de la Pole promised Peter Fitzpole that he would be declared William's legitimate heir, if he assisted Richard with the invasion from Holland."

Lady Cathryn sniffed. "How? William never married that hussy."

"It's easy enough, using a falsified proof of marriage, backdated before he married you. Providing there are no objections."

"Which is why they needed William dead," Lady Cathryn observed, her voice grim. "He would certainly have objected. Particularly since he'd lose any claim to my property as a bigamist. I would have objected just as loudly. I wonder whether Peter would have poisoned me, if I didn't die soon on my own."

"Unknowable," Sir Edward pronounced, still looking at one of the letters. "Do you know who Paul Brown is?"

Margaret felt Lady Cathryn clutch her arm. For an old woman, she had surprisingly strong hands. "How odd you should ask," Her Ladyship responded.

"Yes. He is the steward at Caister Castle, which is close by. Peter Fitzpole was giving him money for 'supplies." She pointed her cane toward the account book she had left on her chair. "It's the only odd expenditure I have noted so far, not counting all the outlays for the foodstuffs he was squirreling away in my larder."

"I suspected something like that," Sir Edward responded. "Our scouts reported back late last night. They spotted what they think are the missing cannons on the walls of the deserted Roman fort that faces Caister Castle. The cannons were facing *away* from Caister Castle, and not visible from it. Instead of cannon balls they seem to be supplied with rock and chains, deadly against soldiers at close range. Which suggests that the cannons were hidden there to protect ships moored in the river between the fort and the castle.

He gazed at the fire, his face troubled. "Before dawn this morning, most of the soldiers here marched off to take the ruined Roman tower. With God's mercy, we'll attack before the traitors there know that Wingfield castle has been taken and garrisoned—that's why we sent men so quickly. The scouts think there is only a small company protecting those cannons."

He began to pace. "But what of Caister Castle? That's where we may need your help. If Peter Fitzpole bribed the steward there, the absent owner—who happens to be deputy to the Lord High Admiral, and living in London—may know nothing about it. The cannons are hidden across the river, so perhaps no one knows but the steward. We could certainly turn the cannons on Caister Castle, order up some iron shot, and blast its walls into rubble. But Vice Admiral Paston would not be pleased. To say the least. We believe he is loyal to Henry, though we cannot be sure."

"How can we assist?" Lady Cathryn asked.

"By getting us in to the castle. If we can get a few men inside, we can probably take the place and arrest the steward without having to go to extremes. I doubt John Paston has more than a token staff there."

Margaret felt herself panicking. Her throat tightened, so she could hardly breathe. He wanted her to do what? "Sir Edward, I am a loyal servant to King

Henry," she said, as politely as she could manage. "But there are limits to what is reasonable. Both Lady Cathryn and I feared for our lives when I first got here. I came with two of the King's soldiers, who disappeared into the bowels of this castle after we arrived. We never saw them again." She felt her voice rising, but she could not help it.

"We were very afraid that we—or my sons—or all of us—would be taken as hostages, or worse. What would you do if that happened now? Destroy John Paston's castle *and* kill a loyal friend and servant of the Queen? And a great Lady who offered gracious hospitality to King Henry's soldiers? And two little *children*?" When she spoke of her sons, she was almost screeching. She swallowed and bowed her head, feeling ashamed of her fears.

Sir Edward stared at her stony-faced, the way her deceased husband did when she became too emotional. "I had not realized that," he said softly. "Your sons will remain here, where they are safe. And I promise you, it will not happen again."

"I, too, am a loyal servant to King Henry," Lady Cathryn said, in a regal tone. "But there are limits on what I can do, too. And the first one is my age. I haven't ridden a horse in ten years. And you expect me to gallop off to Caister Castle? After everything I have already been through? It could be the death of me, Sir Edward. That is a great deal to expect."

Sir Edward paced and stared at the floor, then the window. "There is not a moment to lose," he finally said. "I am going to order your cart, Lady Cathryn. And pillows, and a good driver for you. We'll figure out a plan that will keep you safe while we travel. And keep you safe I will. And the boys, too. I promise." He left the room.

Lady Margaret and Lady Cathryn stared at each other. Wordlessly, Margaret helped the older woman back to the chair next to the fireplace. "My bones will ache like I was set afire, but I don't suppose the cart ride will kill me," Lady Cathryn said, as she sat down, put aside her cane, and stared into the fire.

"Certainly not," Lady Margaret said, in a soothing tone. "We are pawns on a chessboard, and our King needs us. All we can do is think about what best to do next. And pray. At least my sons and Michael will be safe."

Lady Cathryn sighed. "I pray you are right."

An Upper Chamber in the Tower of London
by George Cruikshank (1792 – 1878)

CHAPTER 30: THIRTY SEVEN YEARS IN THE TOWER OF LONDON

At the Tower, the same day

A Tower guard, who recognized Wolsey, ushered him and Nicola into the Tower through the city gate. Wolsey strode toward the Thames, forcing Nicola to trot to keep up with him, limping from the blisters she'd gotten on the long march to Wingfield Church, only the day before.

"What am I to do here?" she asked him. She sounded surly to her own ears, but felt too cold and tired to care.

Wolsey did not seem to mind her tone. "Maybe nothing. I need to inquire about the Fitzpoles and William de la Pole's health. And other matters. If you like, you can wait for me on the battlements overlooking the Thames. There, you can watch the court move to Richmond Palace. Custom requires the Queen to display her pregnant belly to her subjects, before going into confinement. They will dock across from here, and process across London Bridge. Head up that way." He pointed, and left.

Nicola saw that five Biaggi cannons had been installed overlooking the river, on the top of the curtain wall. Their wheeled wooden carriages were new and sturdy. Neat pyramids of stone cannonballs stood next to each. She wondered where they kept the gunpowder.

Below, the boats moving along the Thames included many flying the King's royal standard, all loaded with boxes, barrels, chests and other miscellany. In center stream, a red and gold gilded galley moved in stately fashion, its oarsmen invisible below the ceremonial deck. The King and Queen sat on cushions beneath a tasseled pavilion, surrounded by their guards and members of the court. The Queen wore an ornate headdress and high-waisted kirtle in scarlet and cloth of gold, visibly pregnant even at a distance. King Henry wore a crown, and was similarly resplendent: all in gold it seemed, from where Nicola stood.

Their Highnesses disembarked at London Bridge, and began their procession on foot, surrounded by guards. The Queen walked slowly, her hand on King Henry's arm. Nicola wondered how she felt about displaying her pregnant belly to the multitudes, and how she was feeling generally. The royal couple was invisible once on the bridge, but Nicola could hear the people's cheers.

"Are you ready?" Nicola flinched at the sudden voice at her shoulder. She turned to see Father Wolsey. "Ready for what? I don't know what you require from me," she snapped.

"It's quite simple," he said. He handed her the bag of coins they had received from Lady Katherine's banker. "You are to visit William de la Pole and deliver this money to him. And tell him the truth. More or less. That you saw his wife at Wingfield with Lady Margaret, that his wife is well and sends her greetings. And has ordered the resumption of funds for his comfort. That she apologizes for the mistaken report that he was dead."

"So he is not dead," Nicola said.

"He has been ill, but is recovering."

"What should I say about his bastard son being thrown in the Tower for treason, and the King taking over his home and garrisoning it with soldiers?" Nicola asked.

Wolsey stared into her eyes, with a look that made her shiver. "Nothing whatsoever. Not to him, or anyone else. Except the Queen. You left before all that happened. You know nothing about it. Understood?"

Nicola nodded, suddenly wide awake. "I pretend that I left before Christmas. Why did I leave Lady Margaret behind?"

"Again, truth is best, up to a point. Tell him that she stayed to help Lady Cathryn, because Lady Cathryn seemed sleepy and confused. Also, try to find out why Sir William thinks he was being poisoned. And who he thinks was doing it. You heard this from the soldiers escorting you, not from me."

"Poisoned?" Nicola repeated.

"So he thinks. He has been very ill."

Nicola absorbed this, and nodded again. "You are not here, as far as Sir William is concerned?"

"Correct."

"But you will be listening, won't you? Or someone will, from somewhere."

"Also correct. Remember to speak up."

Nicola let out a long sigh. "Thank you for not making me the bearer of bad news. Instead, I will be doing him a kindness," she said. "He should be relieved that his payments are being resumed. He doesn't need to know what has happened to his bastard son, yet. I will do my best. But what has become of Peter Fitzpole and his wife?"

"Sent to the torturers. We need to know where Lady Cathryn's money was supposed to go in Holland. And who brought those cannons to Wingfield, and where the other four cannons went. And most of all, when Fitzpole expected the soldiers who would have eaten all that food he stored in the Wingfield larders."

Nicola had wondered about all these questions, and suspected the Fitzpoles would be tortured to get the answers. Italian princes and the Church used torture freely for such purposes. From what Sir Thomas had said, England was no different. Still, she was unhappy to find herself responsible—at least partly—for someone being put to torture.

"What about his wife? Are women also tortured in England?" she asked.

"She will watch. Often that loosens tongues. The chief torturer does not like using his skills on women but yes, it happens. Again, you will tell William de Pole nothing of this."

"Certainly not. I have no wish to cause him unnecessary pain."

Wolsey led her down the stone steps and into one of the towers built into the outer wall of the castle complex. "This is known as 'the Bloody Tower,'" he remarked. "Said to be haunted by the ghosts of two young princes housed here long ago, in one of the nicer cells on the upper floors."

As they climbed the interior stairs, screams reverberated against the stone walls around them, emanating from somewhere below. "Accommodations down there are not as friendly," Wolsey noted. Nicola shuddered, wishing her task were complete.

The screams ended in a shriek and stopped, just before they reached the top of the stairs. There, they passed through a heavy wooden doorway, into blessed silence. On the other side was a torchlit hallway, guarded at either end and punctuated by several doorways that had small barred openings. Nicola wondered if torture were going on behind those doors—but no, it was far too quiet. These were prison cells.

Wolsey left her with a yeoman warder, who led her to the far end of the hall, unlocked a heavy wooden door, and thrust his head inside. "Lady visitor," he announced. "Are ye decent? He's asleep I think. Stay here. I'll wake him."

The warder emerged shortly, a reeking chamber pot cradled in one arm. "He's decent. I'll be right here if you need me."

From the doorway, Nicola saw a large whitewashed room, sunny from barred windows on two sides. The space appeared clean, though it smelled of excrement. A fire burned low in the fireplace, and above it, shelves, lined with leather-bound books, ran the length of one wall. Against that wall was a table that held quill, paper and ink.

The linens were clean, but the man in the bed was not. Greasy, disheveled brown hair crowned his gaunt, white face. He stared at Nicola from sunken eyes with circles so dark that she thought, at first, that he had been beaten. Yet somehow she knew that this was once a handsome man.

He attempted a smile that was more of a grimace. "Pardon that I do not rise. I have been sick, near to death. To what do I owe this pleasure?"

She sat in the chair next to his bedside, and tried to hand him the bag of coins. "I come from your cousin, Margaret de la Pole. Whom I just left with your wife, Lady Cathryn, at Wingfield Castle. Your wife is well. She received a mistaken report that you died. But now she has ordered her bank to resume payments for your comfort. These coins are the first payment."

Sir William pushed the coins away. "Give them to the Constable's wife, please. And tell her I thank her again for her kind care. Pray you tell her also, that I will pay her generously to continue feeding me from her family's pot. I was being poisoned—though everyone said I was just complaining that the common food was bad. But when I got sick enough, the Constable's wife fed me gruel with her own hands, and then part of her family meals. And I got better immediately."

Nicola dropped her jaw and put her hands to her cheeks, trying to look shocked. "Someone was poisoning you? But who would poison you, Sir William? And how?" she said loudly.

"My brother Richard, that's who. The 'how' part I can't explain. Someone with access to my food."

"Your brother Richard?" Nicola repeated, in the same loud tone. "But isn't he in the Tower too?"

"It's Edmund who's here in the Tower. Not Richard. Richard's on the other side of the Channel, trying to raise an army for the two of them. Edmund's the oldest and has no reason to poison me, and no way to do it either. He's closely watched."

He shifted in his bed and scratched his head with both hands, as if fleas were biting him. "It's Richard who needs me out of the way, because he's the youngest, see? I'm a threat to him because I inherit before he does, and I don't want anything to do with deposing King Henry."

"Does Edmund ever visit you?"

"In the Tower? We've seen each other from a distance, when we're allowed to walk in the castle yard. But we haven't spoken in years. This prison's a palace compared to most, as long as you have money. But being able to visit my traitorous brother? Too much to expect."

"How long have you been here?"

"Close to ten years."

"Ten years," Nicola repeated. "Why, after ten years, would your brother suddenly decide to kill you?"

"Maybe it's the first time he had access. Someone here is being bribed. I told the Constable, but he doesn't believe me."

Remembering she was supposed to be a servant, Nicola jumped up and put more wood on the fire. "Would you like to write a note for your wife?" she asked.

"Who decided I was dead just because someone told her so? I'll write when I feel less angry. Assuming I survive."

Nicola returned to his side. "I'm sorry you are unwell. You must miss your wife and home."

He stared at the ceiling for a long moment. "Cathryn and I did not always get along," he finally said. "She held the purse strings. I can't honestly say that I miss her. But I miss the hunt. And a good brandy by the fire. And the countryside. And the ladies. But there are consolations here. I can read whatever I want, and play chess. And cards. And swear all I want. Because they trust me, I am permitted to walk the grounds—under guard, of course. I can see London from the walls. I can talk to guards and priests and the Constable and his wife and their lieutenants.

Now that I have funds again I will have servants to clean up after me and fetch what I want. No weapons, of course, but food or liquor. Or women, when I feel up to it." He gave her a sly look. "It's better than certain aspects of running an estate. And infinitely better than the life of a soldier, in a country torn by war."

"Rest well. I'll give the money to the Constable's wife." Nicola curtseyed to him, and tapped the door to be let out, feeling suddenly exhausted. She breathed a sigh of relief when the Warder locked the door behind her.

Wolsey was coming down a steep set of stairs as she emerged at the other end of the hallway. "Well done," he said. "Let's find the Constable's wife and hear what she has to say."

The Constable's wife sat them before her fire, thanked them for the coins, and had plenty to say. "I told my husband something was amiss. Sir William had bloody flux, when no one else was sick. Roger didn't believe me, at first. Now he is worried."

Wolsey nodded. "Edmund de la Pole is fine?"

"Edmund is fine. More prideful and difficult than William, but healthy."

"Can we determine which guards served William his meals?" Nicola asked.

She shook her head. "No. It's whoever is available. That's what's frustrating. It was someone with inconsistent access, or William would have died. Too much poison, you know, leaves a taste. He threw away some of his meals, so the poisoner needed to use less and return frequently. If we had known sooner, we could have done something. But at first, when his money stopped coming, William sounded like a rich man who didn't want to eat common food from the common pot. I've heard that before."

She showed them to her door. "I'll keep feeding him from the family pot. I'm not going to expose him to a poisoner again, on the off chance of learning who was trying to kill him. He's a decent man. The warders all like him."

"He's important to the King, as a buffer against Richard de la Pole," Wolsey said. "By all means, keep him alive."

A View of Richmond Palace fronting the River Thames as built by Henry VII, printed by James Basire, 1765

CHAPTER 31: THE QUEEN'S CONFINEMENT

Richmond Palace, the same day

Wolsey left Nicola at Richmond Palace as the sun was disappearing behind its multitude of domed towers and turrets. The Queen had told her that Henry's father built it to be the most magnificent and luxurious of the royal residences. According to the Queen, it even had a central heating system, something Nicola had never heard of before.

Nicola was immediately taken to the chambers that had been made ready for the Queen's confinement, and escorted to the Queen by Lady Maud Parr. The rooms were as dark and unwelcoming as Her Highness had predicted. The tapestries of flowers and plants were supposed to be soothing, but the light was so low that it was difficult to see them. Nicola peeked into the Queen's bedchamber, which had two beds: one, the usual canopied, curtained four poster with costly feather mattress and linens; the other, a simple table with a thin pallet and sheet, obviously for childbirth. Underneath it, partly hidden from view, was a birthing chair. Two new female servants—expert midwives, according to Lady Maud Parr—stood silent and waiting.

There was only one window in the entire suite of rooms, but it was a comfort: it looked out over a topiary garden, green even in winter, backlit by a pink and orange sunset. The Queen sat in a comfortable chair raised on a dais, her feet propped on a footstool, watching the sky. On either side of the dais were smaller chairs. Nutmeats, dried fruits and pink marzipan candies in the shape of Tudor roses sat on a gold tray next to her.

The Queen beckoned Nicola to take the chair next to the tray. "You are back," she said. "And must be famished. Eat. Where is Lady Margaret?"

Nicola was both hungry and exhausted, but hunger won out. Her mouth watered as she helped herself to several marzipans. "Thank you, your Highness. I have not eaten all day. Lady Margaret begs your forgiveness. She felt she had to stay at least a day or two, to help Lady Cathryn. Who is no longer young, and seems confused by what is happening. Lady Margaret is going to help her look through her steward's ledgers, to sort things out."

The Queen waved Lady Maud away. "Margaret did right," she said, when they were alone. "But I hope she arrives in time for the birth. After five children, she would surely be of great help. Cover my feet with that shawl, please."

Nicola did so, then grabbed another handful of candies and nutmeats. The Queen smiled and motioned for her to sit again. "Now. The King told me the glorious parts," she said. "With his usual enthusiasm. How his soldiers took a formidable castle by surprise, on Christmas Day, with no loss of life on our side. Thanks in part to your cleverness in spiking the cannons, but mostly to their bravery and daring. According to Henry. The brave boys rescued an elderly lady being victimized by her steward and arrested the traitorous steward. Again, with no loss of life. Very romantic. Very chivalrous. And very, very secret, because Henry is hoping to lay a trap for Richard de la Pole. So you must not say a word to anyone."

"The Spymaster already warned me, Your Highness. I will say nothing."

The Queen stared out the window for a moment, looking tired, and older than her years. "Now, you tell me the parts that were not glorious. And anything else I need to know."

Nicola told her how frightened Lady Cathryn was of Sir William's bastard son, whose wife had been forcing sleeping potions on her. And how frightened Lady

Margaret and Nicola became themselves, after Lady Cathryn predicted they might not escape. Then she told of her visits to Lady Cathryn's banker and to Sir William de la Pole in the Tower. "His brothers may be guilty of treason, but I don't think Sir William is," she concluded. "And if he is right, there is a traitor inside the Tower. Who is a poisoner."

"Not a very skilled one," the Queen commented. "But yes. That is very, very troublesome."

She stood suddenly, and bent from side to side, grimacing. "My back is cramping. I am afraid I will die in childbirth. But even more afraid that my back is going to hurt for the rest of my life."

"May I assist you somehow?" Nicola asked, knowing she could not touch the Queen's person unless asked. "Your back will be fine once you give birth. When do you expect the child?"

The Queen sat again. "There is nothing you can do for me. Except listen while I tell some secrets. You must promise not to breathe a word to anyone."

What else could she do? "I promise," Nicola said.

"First of all, I am due any day, because I lied about when my menses stopped. I was pregnant before—gave birth to a stillborn daughter—and the boredom of a full month in confinement nearly killed me. It also sent Henry into the arms of one of my ladies, who is now in a convent. I didn't want to go through that again."

Nicola knew from Margaret about the lady-in-waiting the Queen had sent to a convent. She was Anne Stafford, sister to the Duke of Buckingham and a married woman herself. Anne Stafford's adultery with Henry had doomed her to a solitary life bereft of the luxury she was accustomed to, and hours a day in enforced prayer. Hearing the story the first time, Nicola had felt sorry for Anne. Now her heart went out to the Queen.

"Your Highness, I am so sorry," she said. "How terrible to lose a child late in pregnancy, and your husband to another woman at the same time. But Henry loves you—anyone can see that. Perhaps Anne Stafford was a temptress. Or a tool of her ambitious brother."

Katherine's face twitched into a smile. "You are a good woman—not like some. That is why I trust you." She helped herself to a piece of marzipan. "Thanks to you, the King has his cannons, and a secure castle. If Richard de la Pole had taken it, it would have been disastrous. Wingfield Castle is close to the Channel across from Holland, easily accessed by invading soldiers, and virtually impregnable when properly guarded. Especially if guarded with cannons."

"I am sorry I was not able to find the other four cannons. But Sir Thomas is checking a nearby castle—one we saw on the maps the day you took Lady Margaret and me to look at them. There is a good chance the other cannons will be there."

"Let us hope so. At any rate, you have done what Henry wanted."

"I have found only four of the missing cannons, and none of the murderers," Nicola responded. "That is not what he wanted."

"You did what he needed instead. That is more important."

The Queen leaned back, and closed her eyes. Nicola quietly devoured nuts and marzipan, and waited for the Queen to sleep, hoping she could shed her filthy servant's clothing and sleep herself. But a cacophony of singing, cymbals, horns and shouts grew closer and louder, until it seemed to come from behind their backs.

The Queen stirred, and opened her eyes. "It's Sir Charles Brandon, with Henry and others. I hear Henry's voice. Sir Charles is playing the Lord of Misrule for this year's revels—I talked Henry out of doing it himself. Not seemly, for a King. They probably want you and my other ladies to join them."

"Must I, Your Highness?" Nicola said. "I am tired and filthy and want nothing to do with them."

"I am glad. Because I require you here."

Maud Parr joined them, carrying a candle. "The Lord of Misrule commands Lady Greensleeves to join him and his court in song and dance," she announced.

"Tell His Lordship that I require her here," said the Queen.

"I am exhausted and not properly dressed," Nicola said. "And I do not know how to dance."

Lady Maud stared at her. "You are oddly dressed, but that is perfect. Everyone out there is oddly dressed. All you need is a mask. We can give you one. But you don't know how to dance?"

"I was raised in a convent, where I learned many things," Nicola explained, hearing the fatigue in her own voice. "Latin and a bit of Greek. Nursing. How to read music. But nuns do not dance. So no, I did not learn to dance."

Others among the Queen's ladies had gathered around them. "We will teach you to dance," one of them said.

"I don't want to learn," Nicola responded.

"It might amuse me to have her learn, later. While I wait for this baby to be born," said the Queen. "Right now I am not amused. I require her here."

"May we join the revels?" asked Elizabeth Boleyn.

"No. I require you here, too. Tell them they are disturbing my rest. I require them to leave. And light the other candles. I hate how dark it is in here."

The ladies fluttered away, followed by the midwives, leaving Nicola and the Queen in the dark despite the Queen's orders. Loud voices in the hallway, accompanied by toots from a krummhorn, lapsed into sudden silence. A quieter discussion followed. When all was finally silent, the Queen's ladies returned.

"You were gone a long time," the Queen observed. "And where have you been, Lena? I see you are carrying a mask. Were you with them?"

The ladies looked at each other, and Lena looked down. "I was. I am sorry if I did wrong. But the midwives do not want me here. And I saw something you should know. Charles Brandon is flirting outrageously with Princess Mary. Who is flirting right back."

"Outrageous indeed," the Queen sniffed. "Princess Mary is fourteen years old, and betrothed to Emperor Maximillian's heir. And Charles Brandon is twice her age and married, several times over. She should know better. Light candles, Lena. Please."

"They were all somewhat drunk," Elizabeth Boleyn said, as if this were an adequate excuse. The Queen shot her a poisonous look.

"Are you going to tell the King?" Maud Parr asked, her eyes wide.

"He is there, and has eyes in his head," the Queen responded. "He knows."

Nicola saw that the Queen was angry, and felt her own anger flaring, too. "Sir Charles Brandon tried numerous times to get into my private quarters, on the ship from Rome," she told the ladies. "He even tried the door lock, when I wouldn't let him in. And he kissed me against my will, when he thought no one was looking. He thinks he is very attractive. I don't."

Nicola regretted her words immediately, because the Queen's ladies crowded around her, begging loudly for details. She listened, but spoke little. Sir Charles was a commoner and a rascal, someone said. He had impregnated his first betrothed, then married someone else for money, said another. That wife got the marriage annulled, so he was forced to marry his first betrothed. Who was now pregnant again, so he was prowling. Princess Mary was spoiled. She should know better. But she was very young. And Sir Charles was very charming. If he would only shave his beard, he would be handsome, some thought. Others disagreed.

"Enough," the Queen said, waving a hand. She looked exhausted. Nicola felt guilty for her part in disturbing the Queen's peace of mind.

The clamor quieted, but continued. "Enough," said a louder voice behind them. Every head turned, to look at the two midwives they had all forgotten about.

Both midwives looked angry. "The Queen must have rest and quiet," the taller of them said. "You woke her up, and you are keeping her awake. She is facing an ordeal. The more rest she gets, the easier the birth. Go."

They fled, except for Lena, who had finished lighting candles. "I would like to retire," the Queen told her. "Would you help me up, please?"

Nicola rose to help, but the midwives glared at her. "We will take care of the Queen," the taller one said. "You should not be near her. You are filthy, and smell of horses."

"If you will take care of the Queen, I will take care of Mistress Nicola," Lena said, turning to her. "Would you like a hot bath?"

Tears sprang to Nicola's eyes, to her surprise. "More than anything," she said. "Except perhaps sleep."

Ruins of a Roman *pharos* somewhere in Britain,
photographed in 1869, other details unknown

CHAPTER 32: DRUNKEN TRAITORS

The day after Christ's Mass, 1510

Robin Fox awoke to a splitting headache. A beam of bright sunlight blasting the side of his face had turned the inside of his eyelids a nauseous orange. He was afraid to blink, much less turn his head. His squad had drunk the entire keg of ale sent from Caister Castle for Christ's Mass all at once, carousing far into the night. He had drunk more ale in one night than in his entire previous life.

He groaned and crawled to his feet, clinging to the outer stone wall of the ancient Roman tower. He needed to piss. The others were still passed out on the stone floor around him, spared from the bright sun by the narrow windows, barely wide enough to shoot an arrow through.

The piss buckets were all full or worse, so he emptied one out an arrow slit, not caring that most of it spilled down the wall.

After he used it, he headed for the stairs to take care of the rest of his business and eat some clean snow. His stomach was too sour for anything else. And his mouth tasted like some tiny creature had died in it while he slept, after sucking it dry.

The stone stairs were wide enough only for one man and wound in a tight corkscrew, so defenders could have their swords in their right hands. Looking down made him nauseous and dizzy, so he closed his eyes and made his way by leaning against the outer wall; clinging to the stonework as best he could with his non-sword hand. God only knew where his sword was.

Strong arms and stronger fear grabbed him when he emerged through the door into bright sunlight. "We captured your cannons and killed your sentries," hissed a voice in his ear. "Swear allegiance to King Henry or you'll all be drawn and quartered."

"Don't think you can wait it out," another voice said. "We'll pound that tower to rubble with iron shot before the day is out, if you don't surrender."

"We don't have iron shot," Robin mumbled, wondering if he was dreaming. Or hallucinating.

"But we do," said the voice.

Half-blinded by the bright sun and still woozy, he forced his eyes open. He was surrounded by grinning men wearing jerkins trimmed in green, with a pink rose and crown on the shoulder. Royal livery. Lord have mercy, he thought. We are outnumbered. Surrounded. Doomed. He felt vomit rising to his throat.

"Your pardon," he said, and bent to spew out the contents of his stomach. The men closest to him stepped away, while others mocked him and made rude noises.

Once his stomach was empty, he felt a little better, though fear overwhelmed every other sense. Two of the King's men yanked him to his feet.

"I will swear allegiance to the King," he told them, his voice shaking. "And the others will too. We didn't know we were signing on with traitors. They promised us handsome pay but we never got it. A man must eat."

The man pinning his arms from behind spat, barely missing him. "Go tell the others, then. Tell them how they will die, if they don't pledge loyalty to the King." He shoved Robin toward the tower. "Say that before they surrender, every man is to push his sword and dagger out one of the arrow slits. And come out with hands held high."

Robin nodded, his head throbbing. "Watch out for a rain of swords and daggers."

*****

Later that day, Lady Margaret and Lady Katherine arrived at Caister Castle in Lady Katherine's brightly-painted cart, accompanied by soldiers wearing blue and gold sashes—the de la Pole family colors—over their shoulders. Across a long open field, they faced a tall stone curtain wall similar to the one at Wingfield Castle. Lady Margaret was thankful that this time, she did not face cannons.

"Hurry! Let's get on that drawbridge while it's still down," Lady Cathryn said.

The driver who sat between them whipped the horses into a trot, forcing the soldiers into a jog. They barely fit on the drawbridge, with the cart pulled as far forward as the horses would go. But at least they had made it that far. And it would be nigh impossible for the castle guards to close the drawbridge, with all those people on it.

Lady Margaret watched as Sir Edward dismounted, strode to the heavy gate, and banged on it.

"Open for Lady Cathryn de la Pole and Lady Margaret de la Pole," he roared, in the thunderous voice he had used to intimidate the villagers in Wingfield. "Who come with seasons' greetings and gifts for Sir John Paston,"

A peephole opened in the gate. "Sir John is not here," said a tentative voice.

"Doesn't matter," Sir Edward yelled. "Lady Cathryn has gifts for the steward and staff as well." He gestured toward the wagon, which was piled with provisions. "Sir John will be displeased, if he hears that these two ladies have been treated rudely."

The heavy gates slowly creaked open. Sir Edward grinned at Lady Cathryn as her driver urged the horses forward into the castle yard. To Lady Margaret's relief, soldiers flowed around and behind their cart, staying close, as they had been ordered.

A handsome man in a brown leather jerkin, wool breeches and white stockings came towards them with a smile on his face. "Paul Brown," Lady Cathryn said loudly. "How nice to see you."

"And you, my lady. May I help you down?"

"I am staying right where I am, thank you," she responded.

His smile faded and his jaw dropped. "What is happening?" he asked, looking behind her.

Margaret turned to see two soldiers climbing up to thrust iron bars into the drawbridge chains. Behind them, more men poured across the field surrounding the castle, running for the drawbridge, the fastest carrying the royal red, green and white pennants. "The King, the King," they shouted as they ran.

Margaret's spirits soared as she watched them. No one was falling, and there was no sound of gunfire. Sir Edward's soldiers had formed a phalanx around their wagon, as he'd ordered them to do. She prayed that she and Lady Cathryn were safe.

"I have no idea what is happening, Master Brown," Lady Cathryn snapped, in response to Brown's question. "Sir Edward?"

"Paul Brown, I arrest you for treason, in the name of the King," Sir Edward said. He had dropped his sash bearing the de la Pole colors, to reveal the rose and crown emblazoned on his jerkin, signifying he was one of Henry's chosen men.

"Treason?" Brown's face turned white as he tore past Sir Edward, and tried to mount Lady Cathryn's wagon. Margaret screamed. Lady Cathryn brought her cane down hard on his head. "Traitorous cur," she shouted, as he crumpled and fell.

King Henry's soldiers cheered for her, joined by those spilling across the drawbridge. Some of John Paston's staff cheered as well, Margaret noticed. Soldiers wearing Sir John Paston's colors were pouring down the castle walls, weaponless, with hands raised in surrender. It was over. They were safe. Margaret lowered her head, and gave silent thanks to God.

"I think we are finished here," Lady Cathryn announced. "Now. You," she said, pointing at a grinning female servant who was watching the men pouring through the gate. "Take me to Sir John's bedchamber. Because I very much need to lie down."

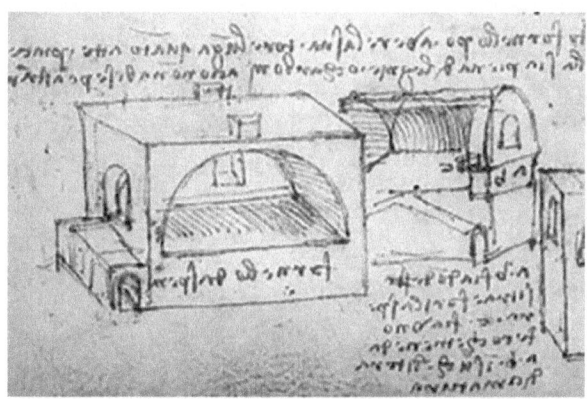

Plans drawn by Leonardo da Vinci for a reverberatory
(smelting) furnace, c. 1488

CHAPTER 33: TESTING CANNONS AND PATIENCE

The next morning

Nicola pulled her blanket over her head, to stop whoever was shaking her shoulder.

"I am sorry, Lady Nicola. The armorers demand you come. They have built the blast furnace, and want to test it. You must wake up. Wake up. Are you listening?"

Nicola sat up, feeling confused. She peered at Lena through tangled hair, still damp from her bath the night before. "Say that again?"

Lena knelt behind her so she could not lie down again, and began combing her hair. "The armorers want to test the blast furnace." She spoke loudly and slowly, as if Nicola were deaf. "They want you to be there. The King will be there. He wants you in your green kirtle and sleeves. Lady Maria and Lady Maud and I will go with you."

Nicola had started to fall back asleep when Lena began brushing her hair. She woke up abruptly when she realized she might have to face the King.

"I am so tired," she said, feeling as if her mouth were not yet working. "I have not slept well in days. How will we get there?"

"There is a wherry waiting for us at the docks."

"Why does the King want me in my green kirtle?"

"I don't know, and I'm not going to ask," Lena said. "But I have it ready for you here. You are in the King's service, and green and white are the colors of his servants. It is right that you should wear it."

"I suppose so," Nicola said. She climbed to her feet, stark naked. "Lord have mercy," said one of the Queen's ladies.

Lena slid one of her *camicias* over her head. "Not this one," Nicola said, feeling more awake. "The best one. The silk, with the shirred embroidery around the neck."

By the time her sleeves were being tied, four ladies were working on her. "Too tight," she said to the one pulling in the laces behind her stomacher. "You are tiny. Show it off," a voice said. "You need a proper headdress," said someone else behind her. "Wait," said another. "The Queen is loaning her the emerald necklace." Both ornaments went on her in succession.

Hands pulled her to a mirror, and she looked at herself. Her eyes were still puffy with sleep and her hair, newly washed, was creeping out around her veil. She pushed it back.

"Leave your hair be. It is perfect," pronounced Elizabeth Boleyn.

"Is this headdress the right color?" Nicola asked. It was heavy and felt odd.

"It is perfect. Black and gold goes with everything. Here, I will fix your hair again."

Someone heavy-handed was banging on the outer door, where Lady Maud, Lady Maria de Salinas and Lena waited.

"Are you almost ready?" Maria demanded.

Nicola squared her shoulders, grabbed her best cloak and a freshly-baked bun from Lena, and headed for the door. The wherry that took them to the Tower moved downstream quickly. They docked and entered the Tower through the waterside gate. By that time, Nicola was fully awake.

*****

Behind their forge, the armorers stood next to the new blast furnace, several wearing heavy leather aprons and gloves. Two others took turns working the bellows. A cannonball mold had been placed near the base of the blast furnace, where the molten metal would emerge.

Nicola walked around the blast furnace, observing. "It looks to be working," she said. "I regret I could not be here to check it while it was being built. What are we waiting for?"

"The plans were clear. We didn't need you here," said John Smith, the Master of Ordnance. "We're waiting for the King." He was flushed and sweating—whether from nervousness or from the heat of the blast furnace, Nicola could not tell.

A young page ran into the building. "He's coming! The King is coming!" he announced. The two men at the bellows bent to their work, fanning the coals until they were white hot. The others took a knee when the King, Sir Charles Brandon, and several other members of the court entered. Nicola and the other ladies curtseyed.

"Lady Greensleeves," the King boomed. He strode over to her. "Are we ready?"

Nicola stepped away from him. "I believe so, Your Highness."

Within moments, the onlookers gasped as liquid metal began flowing from the bottom of the blast furnace, so hot that it glowed orange like the sun. When the first clay-lined crucible was nearly full, an armorer closed the sluice with a long pair of tongs. Two others, wearing heavy leather gloves, lifted the crucible and carefully poured molten metal into the holes at the top of cannonball molds. Two more armorers had lined up behind them, filling another crucible and then more of the molds. They repeated this process until the supply of molten metal ceased. The armorers working the bellows then stood and all of them bowed, their faces pink and sweating.

"That's it?" the King demanded.

"It's working as designed, your Highness. That is what we are testing." Nicola said. "We must let these cannonballs cool completely. Then they have to be rounded—sometimes a bit of metal gets into the joints between the top and bottom of the mold. Then we will test them, by firing them into a hillside. To see how the metal holds up."

"Bring them to Richmond Palace for the test. I will fire the guns myself," King Henry announced. Then he turned to Nicola. "And you *will* sing for the revels, Lady Greensleeves. Beginning tonight, dressed precisely as you are now. Because I require it. But you need not dance."

Nicola curtseyed deeply, to hide her burning cheeks. The other ladies moved closer to her.

"Let me know when it's time to test these cannonballs," the King said to John Smith. He turned to the page. "Are our horses ready?"

Nicola and her attendants watched as the King and Sir Charles galloped towards the other end of the Tower yard. "I must make sure these men know how to round the cannonballs," Nicola told her attendants, motioning them to follow.

The armorers stood near the forge, laughing and bellowing insults at each other, or slurping water from a barrel, using a ladle or their cupped hands. All sound and motion stopped when saw the ladies. They stood and stared, as if the four of them had just descended from Mount Olympus.

"The shot needs to be rounded before it can be used," Nicola said.

"We know that," growled John Smith.

"The technique differs between stone shot and iron shot," Nicola continued. "You should be able to open the top of the mold now. Let us see what we have, and talk about it."

It took only a few minutes for Nicola to assure herself that the armorers knew what was necessary. They seemed hostile at first, making Nicola wonder how many times she must prove herself. The discussion became more respectful when it turned to the differing ways that Italians and Englishmen performed the same task.

"Your ideas are good, but try both ways," she advised. "When I return to Italy, we will do the same. More ideas mean better weapons."

She started to leave, but thought better of it. "I should be present when the King fires these cannonballs. You will inform me, yes?"

John Smith touched his forehead, the English gesture that meant respect. "We will do our best."

Man being tortured on a rack, illustration from *The National and Domestic History of England* (1867) by William Hickman Smith Aubrey.

CHAPTER 34: A RENAISSANCE MEAL

The same afternoon

Lady Maud Parr led Nicola and Maria to the Queen's Presence Room as soon as they returned to Richmond Palace. "Those monks have been waiting for you and Maria for hours," she told them. "You are supposed to sing with them tonight. The Queen sent in other ladies who can sing, and they are working on carols. But it appears they want you."

Nicola could hear the singing as they approached the room. "What did the Queen say we should do?" she asked.

"Sing for the King, because he demands it. She says you must return as soon as the singing is over tonight. Elizabeth Boleyn and I are to dance, but we are to return as soon as the dancing is done. Elizabeth has been invited to play a part in a masque that Henry wrote, where he will be Sir Loyal Heart and Elizabeth will play Lady Virtue. I'm not sure the Queen has given permission for that, though."

Nicola wondered about Elizabeth Boleyn, who was much older than Henry, but still a handsome woman. Henry, who called himself "Sir Loyal Heart," had not been loyal to his lady wife. So perhaps Lady Virtue was not virtuous? From what she had observed of Elizabeth, it seemed possible.

"They are singing one of the carols Brother Michael and I worked out while you were gone," Maria said. "We already sang The Boar's Head Carol, while you were away. So we need to do a new one."

"How did that go? Did the King kill a big boar?

"*Dios Mio*, it was a huge one, with an apple in its mouth. The singing went well, but we missed you."

The bearded monks had evidently missed her, too. Brother Michael stopped the rehearsal as soon as she and Maria walked in the room, exclaiming "Welcome back, Lady Nicola. Come see what Lady Maria and I have done. Ladies, please step aside for them."

Over the course of the next hour, they rehearsed four part harmonies to two carols until they were in tune, and sounded well. When the ladies were invited for supper, the monks left.

The Queen emerged to join them at the dining table, a beautiful one with inlaid mosaics, set up expressly for the ladies' use during the Queen's confinement. After one of her ladies sampled the dishes to ensure they were not poisoned, the meal began with bread and a hearty soup. Next came the meat course. "More boiled beef," the Queen said, grimacing. "I so long for roast pork instead."

"Pork will cause the baby to be humpbacked," one of the midwives cautioned.

The Queen sighed. "So I have been told. Beef will do. But bring me dried fruit, well stewed, to go with it. And some of that ale that doesn't have a strong flavor. Or wine, if it doesn't taste like vinegar."

"Wine is healthy, but the doctors do not recommend fruits or vegetables. Except stewed spinach," the other midwife said.

"My body is telling me what it needs," the Queen snapped. "And it is not stewed spinach and boiled beef." She ate the stewed fruit, but not much of the beef, and called for cheese to be served to her by the window. "Nicola and Maria, you will join me. I am curious to hear how the test of the new blast furnace went this morning."

She dismissed Maria after hearing that the test went well. "Turn your chair so we can be sure no one is listening, and push it close to me," she told Nicola, after Maria was gone.

Nicola did so, wondering why the Queen wanted to talk privately. "Good," the Queen said. "Now bend towards me, because I am about to tell you more secrets."

She helped herself to cheese and a nutmeat, and gestured to Nicola to do the same. "I see Henry every morning in my Privy Chamber, after he sees his doctors and before he attends Mass," she began. "We are disobeying his grandmother, who decreed that a woman's confinement should only be attended by women. But as King, Henry can do as he likes. And he likes seeing me."

Nicola grinned. "I am sure he does. Your strength is an inspiration to me, Your Highness."

The Queen smiled back, and popped another sweetmeat in her mouth. "Henry is also defying his Council, which is very pleased to have me out of the way. They hate Wolsey because he is a commoner, and me because I am a woman. Never mind, that I am of better birth than they, and the daughter of the strongest reigning queen since Cleopatra."

She took a sip of the wine in her cup, and grimaced. "Vinegar," she pronounced. She put her cup down, and, her hand on her belly. "The baby is moving. Can you see him kick?"

Nicola nodded. The Queen's belly was moving visibly. "That's a good sign. Instead of bad wine, I recommend you try a hot *tisane* of mint and chamomile, which will help you to relax. I am happy to prepare for you."

"Sounds delicious. Please do so. But first, here is the news: Henry's torturers were too enthusiastic with Peter Fitzpole. He died on the rack. His wife was there, and confessed to sedating Lady Cathryn. So they beheaded her immediately—which was a kindness, really. Considering the alternatives. Unfortunately they both died without telling us much."

Nicola had expected their deaths, though not so quickly. She was a little surprised the Queen was so nonchalant about them—but then, she was a queen, and the daughter of a queen with a reputation for ferocity against enemies. What must it be like to grow up in such a family? "We learned nothing from them?" she asked, trying to sound equally unmoved.

"Only that Richard de la Pole's invasion would come 'soon.' Whatever 'soon' means. They claimed they did not know the person who delivered the cannons to them, or what happened to the other cannons. Wolsey has already installed a clerk who will become Lady Cathryn's steward. Due to her age—and because she asked—the Crown is taking over management of her estates."

"I am relieved for her, Your Highness. Though now that Peter Fitzpole is dead, she might be able to manage on her own. Lady Margaret will know."

The Queen waved a hand dismissively. "Never mind about her. England is going to be invaded—'soon.' The King is aware. More soldiers are moving to garrison Caister Castle and Wingfield Castle, as secretly as possible. But what is the Queen's next move on this chessboard? I can do nothing myself, obviously." She gave her belly a pat. "But I can send others. Is there anything we can do now, except wait?"

Nicola did not want to be sent anywhere by the Queen—except home. Still, she wanted to help. "I am sure Sir Edward is ransacking Wingfield Castle to look for evidence of the traitors' plans. Perhaps he will find something. Have you heard from him, or from Lady Margaret?"

"Not yet." The Queen helped herself to a piece of cheese.

"We need to hear from them, before we do anything. I'll try to think of a way to be helpful. I wish I didn't have to sing for the court tonight."

"I wish you didn't look quite so beautiful. Henry insisted on the green kirtle, because the Great Hall has been decorated in greenery for the twelve days between Christ's Mass and Epiphany. But I insisted that you and my other ladies return right away. And he agreed. You should not worry about those threats he made. I'm sure he has forgotten them."

Remembering the look in Henry's eyes when he ordered her to sing, Nicola was not at all sure about that herself. "How may I serve you until I must leave to sing?" she asked. "Shall we continue reading Dante?"

"We have reached the Circle of the Violent, have we not? My confessor does not think I should read about violence and Hell right now," the Queen responded. "Everyone is telling me I must stay calm and relaxed to prepare for the birth. But perhaps you could read me some of those English psalms you have been studying to learn the language? Choose one that is comforting."

"I know a number of them by heart. Do you like the one that begins, 'The Lord is my shepherd, I shall not want'?"

Portrait of Mary Tudor and Charles Brandon
Attributed to Jan Gossaert (1478–1532)

CHAPTER 35: A FESTIVAL IS RUINED

That evening

Nicola and the other singers stood outside the Great Hall, waiting for their turn to perform for the court, and watching the dancing. The vast two story space, wainscoted in dark wood and hung with bright new tapestries, was festooned with greenery for the twelve days of celebration that follow Christ's Mass. It smelled of pine and the spiced mulled wine that servants were pouring generously from large pitchers, all around the room.

"Who is the girl dancing with the King?" Nicola asked.

"His sister Mary. They have been dancing together since they were children," Maria explained. "Only months ago, she was still a child. How quickly girls change at that age. Her household is at Eltham Castle, where Henry was raised. But she joins him for the holy days."

"She is certainly a beauty. Flawless skin. And beautiful teeth."

Like her brother, Princess Mary was lithe and graceful. They were best among the dancers, all of whom moved through steps, skips, pirouettes and promenades in unison, their postures erect and proud. All had smiles on their faces, but the ones on the faces of Henry and his sister seemed genuine. They smiled at each other, their affection obvious.

After the dancers finished, the singers filed in and lined up to face the high table where King Henry and Sir Charles Brandon sat, on either side of Princess Mary. Sir Charles wore a paper crown, tilted to one side, and an outlandish motley gown. Nicola remembered that the King had appointed him Lord of Misrule for the twelve days between Christ's Mass and Epiphany. He looked drunk, which seemed fitting. His nose was red and he'd sloshed wine on his chest and the white damask tablecloth.

The Lord of Misrule was like the King of Saturnalia in the Latin poems of Catullus she had found in the convent library, Nicola realized. She wondered if Julius Caesar's soldiers left Saturnalia behind when they abandoned England.

Nicola and the other singers performed "Christ Was Born on Christmas Day" and "Lully Lullay, Thou Little Tiny Child" flawlessly, to polite applause. Then they bowed, and began to file out the door they had entered.

"Lady Greensleeves," Sir Charles Brandon called out. "Sing us a song in Italian. A song about *love*."

Nicola felt her cheeks go scarlet. She was tempted simply to walk out, but Lady Maria stopped her, a pleading look in her eyes. "You must not be rude," she whispered. "Sing something."

Nicola returned to the center of the room, closed her eyes, and breathed deeply. She was angry at Sir Charles for forcing this on her, and appalled by what she had recently learned about his pursuit of young Princess Mary. A familiar melody came to mind, one useful for singing the verses of Dante's *Divine Comedy*, because its rhythms matched the *terza rima* of Dante's poetry. Italian singers made the tune sad or happy or angry by changing a few notes or their inflexion, to match the emotion of Dante's words.

By the time she had prepared herself and chosen a verse, the room was quiet. She faced Sir Charles, but watched the King out of the corner of her eye. She sang:

> Al'inferno ch'a cosi fatto tormento
> enno dannati i peccator carnali,
> Che la ragion sommettono al talent.

She tried to make it sound like a love song, which it really wasn't. She recalled, belatedly, that the King knew a little Italian. Judging from his face, he understood what he was hearing. And was not pleased. Blushing, she curtseyed quickly, and walked rapidly towards the door, as the court politely applauded her.

"Wait," said Sir Charles Brandon. "I command you to return."

She glanced at Lady Maria, who signaled her to go back. She did so, becoming angrier and angrier with every step. She loved sacred singing, but took no joy in being a spectacle or performing for strangers, like a trained monkey. Especially drunk strangers. And she hated being forced to please Charles Brandon, who was despicable. How long was this going to go on?

Sir Charles gulped wine from his cup. "This time, I command you to sing it in English," he said, slurring his words.

Nicola felt herself blushing again. "You will not like it," she warned him.

"As King of Misrule, I am the judge of that. Is it about love?"

"Yes. But..."

"Then sing it in English."

She looked at King Henry, who shrugged. She took a moment to translate the verse in her mind. Then, staring straight at Sir Charles, she sang:

> In hell are tormented
> those damned for their carnal sins,
> who lost their reason to carnal lust.

This time, shocked silence followed her as she curtseyed and left the hall.

When she arrived back at the Queen's rooms, Nicola undressed and huddled under blankets on her pallet. She was simultaneously angry at herself, frightened, and very tired. She was certain the King would take what she did personally. Inevitably it would remind him of the way she had refused his advances. How could she be foolish enough to throw the King's adulterous behavior in his face again? She had been focused on embarrassing Sir Charles, but he was the King's best friend. If anything, that made matters worse. She had ruined the evening of the entire court. Was King Henry petty enough to take revenge on her? Even, possibly, by accusing her of involvement in the murders she was hoping to solve?

Useless questions, she realized. She hadn't had a proper night's rest in days. She was too tired to think straight, so she should stop thinking at all. She closed her eyes and prayed for sleep.

Lena stooped beside her, and picked up her green kirtle. "The Queen wants to see you, Lady Nicola. I will hang this for you."

"I am wearing only my *camicia*," she protested.

"What does it matter? We are all women here. Wrap a blanket around yourself. Here, I will help you." She pulled Nicola to her feet and tucked a blanket around her, clucking like a mother hen. Nicola picked up the emerald necklace the Queen had loaned her, and sought her out.

Her Highness was sitting in her nightdress in near darkness, wrapped in a shawl, in the chair that faced the window. Lady Maria and Lady Elizabeth Boleyn sat on either side of her. Maria's candle and a thin sliver of moon, visible through the window, were the room's only light.

Nicola went down on her knees, facing the Queen, pushing the emerald necklace towards her on the floor. "I am so sorry for what I did, Your Highness. I was angry at Sir Charles for singling me out, and very tired after two nights with almost no sleep," She paused to choke back tears. "Is the King very angry with me?"

"Why would he be?" asked Elizabeth Boleyn.

Nicola looked up at her, stomach churning, wishing she could read Elizbeth's face in the darkness. "What happened, after I left?" she asked.

"Tell her," said the Queen. Her face was also in darkness; her tone inscrutable.

Elizabeth Boleyn wriggled, as if eager to tell her story. "Everyone was quiet, for a moment," she declared. "Then the King laughed, and said, 'She has trumped you,

Charles. The King of Misrule has been overruled.' A very clever remark. So of course, we all laughed with him: Ha. Ha. Ha. Even Sir Charles."

Nicola, still on her knees, began to feel better. "I am glad the King understood that the song was directed at Sir Charles."

"Of course," Elizabeth said. "It's custom to play tricks on the King of Misrule, just as it is custom for him to play tricks. So what you did was in the spirit of things, and clever. Particularly since there are nasty rumors circulating about Charles' behavior these days. It was a little mean, but he deserved it."

She paused for a moment. "After that came the masque, where I played Lady Virtue. The King wrote it and it was all very proper and correct, Your Highness. You would have approved of every word. It ended up feeling like another rebuke of Sir Charles. Who sat there, looking unhappy, and getting drunker. I left immediately after that. Just as you instructed, Highness."

"I don't know if Henry is mad at you, Nicola," the Queen said. "But I am not. Though of course, I was surprised by your behavior. You sang that verse from Dante, where he meets adulterers in the first circle of Hell, correct? It certainly was not what Sir Charles wanted. But it may be what he deserved."

"Her singing was beautiful," said Maria. "I think that is all that most people noticed."

The Queen wrapped her shawl more tightly around her shoulders. "I warned Henry about Charles' behavior towards his sister. He said they had been children together—he couldn't imagine that Charles intended anything but brotherly teasing. But he knows that people are talking. And if Charles is cheating on his pregnant wife—not with Mary of course, but perhaps with some strumpet— Henry knows that too. It does no harm to remind both of them that adultery is a mortal sin."

Knowing the rumors about Elizabeth, who was married, Nicola wished she could see her face. "I did not ruin the evening?" she asked.

Elizabeth chuckled. 'No. You spiced it up. Your songs will be the talk of the court tomorrow. Twelve days of nonstop feasting and drinking gets to be too much, towards the end. I, for one, am getting tired of it. An excuse for vicious gossip is just what everyone needs."

"But King Henry likes everything to be perfect. And I doubt he likes surprises," Nicola said.

"True," said the Queen. She sighed. "He likes to be witty, but generally he plans those remarks. If he's angry, we'll know tomorrow. Try not to worry about it, Nicola. Lady Margaret is back from Wingfield Castle—we'll see her in the morning. Go now—back to your slumbers. You have earned a good rest."

"May I first give you this necklace, Your Highness? Thank you for allowing me to wear it."

The Queen sighed again. Nicola realized how tired she must be herself. "Lena, take the necklace. I'm sure you were lovely in it, Nicola. Now go."

Tudor-era cannoneer swabbing the cannon

CHAPTER 36: GIFTS, AND A TEST

December 31, 1510

Nicola woke to discover that she was the last of the Queen's ladies to arise. "Her Highness left orders you were not to be disturbed," Lena told her. "That you had earned your rest. Come, I will help you dress."

"Can I wear what I like, or has the King ordered my attire again?"

Lena laughed. "No one told me to dress you in a particular way today. I washed your nuns' habits while you were at Wingfield Castle, as you asked. Is that what you would prefer?"

Nicola felt a surge of joy for blessings she'd taken for granted: a good sleep, a clean body, and clean clothing. "Lena, thank you. First for the hot bath when I returned, and now for the clean garments. You are an angel. Yes."

Nicola was tucking her hair beneath her veil when Margaret Pole appeared in the mirror. She turned to hug her. "How long have you been back?"

"Since yesterday afternoon. Wolsey summoned me when I was barely in the door. He wouldn't even let me take my boys back to their tutor. He and that man with the pointy beard—who reminds me of Satan—took my dispatches and questioned me for what seemed like hours. I have not even seen the Queen yet. Is she well?"

Nicola clung to Lady Margaret for a moment, savoring the hug. "He questioned me at length too. The Queen is as well as can be expected, for a woman about to give birth. How are Lady Cathryn and her husband's grandson faring?"

Margaret patted Nicola's back, then pushed away to look at her face. "The same. The Queen wants to see us both. She will want to know everything. I might as well tell the story to both of you at the same time."

The Queen was sitting in her chair facing the room's only window, with her stockinged feet on her footstool. Lady Margaret stood in front of the window to face her, and curtsied deeply. "I hope you will forgive me for taking time to help Lady Cathryn de la Pole," she said. "I left as soon as I felt I could."

"You did right," the Queen said. "Sit. Both of you. And pull those chairs so you can look at me."

Dark circles around her eyes and a stiff frown suggested the Queen was uncomfortable, and had slept poorly again. Her voice showed no sign of it. "You both showed your loyalty by performing a great service to the King," she began. "Who intends to reward you for it tomorrow, on New Years' Day. That is the day we exchange gifts here," she explained, looking at Nicola. "The King spends the entire day on his throne, giving and receiving gifts. He always gets more than he gives." She stopped, and smiled. "In your cases, I am sure Henry will give more than he expects to get."

Nicola was astonished. "I had no idea that the King expected a gift from me," she said. "What should I give him?"

"Nothing," the Queen assured her. "Don't worry about that. I meant only to say, that I expect he will reward you both for your good and dangerous work at Wingfield Castle."

"He knows I have little money," Margaret said. "But I have been embroidering something for him."

"I don't have time to embroider," Nicola said. "And I don't dare give him anything personal—it would suggest—He might think..."

The Queen waved a hand to silence her. "I agree. Don't dare give him anything personal. He does not want your wages back so forget about giving him a gift. Even if he thinks it rude, why not be rude to him? He has not always treated you with courtesy." She grimaced, and adjusted the pillow behind her back. Lady Margaret started forward to help her. The Queen waved her away.

"Now Margaret," she continued, "the midwives tell me that I am near my time. So I am very, very glad you are here to be with me at the birth. Henry's Council is glad to be rid of me—they do not like a woman advising him. And the midwives want me to clear my head of the clutter of court business. Even my confessor says I have taken on too much, for now. So I have tried to distance myself from the worries of the realm. I have spent much of the time since I last saw you in prayer, which has done my soul good."

"How may I assist you, my Queen?" Margaret said.

"By thinking carefully about what happened at Wingfield and Caister Castle since Lady Nicola left, and then telling me only what you think is most important. Only the things I need to hear. Because that is all I want to know, for now."

She stood suddenly. "My back is spasming. Lena, heat a brick for me, please," she called out, eyes still on Margaret. "Understand," she continued quietly, "Nicola has told me what happened while she was there. And early this morning, Henry gave his version of what his Spymaster extracted from you yesterday. He went on about the cleverness of his men, to take Caister Fort and Caister Castle with no loss of life. But he mentioned you being in the lead wagon at Caister Castle, and Lady Cathryn smashing the traitor there with her cane. So in a general way, I know everything. Tell me now, Margaret, what else I need to know. What is most important? What do you know as a woman, that the menfolk have likely ignored?"

Lady Margaret nodded. "You are wise, my Queen. Let me think, and consult with Lady Nicola. She also needs to know what happened after she left, and I need to hear from her. Once we have spoken, I can burden you as little as possible."

"Consult all you like," the Queen said. "First, though, pour me some of that hot *tisane* that Lady Nicola recommends. It comforts me."

"I am glad you enjoy it," Nicola said as she filled the Queen's cup. The midwives had approved the mixture of mint and chamomile that Nicola recommended, and prepared it with well-boiled water, as she also recommended. When the tisane was ready, so was Lena with the hot wrapped brick for the Queen's back.

While the Queen warmed her back and enjoyed her *tisane,* Nicola and Lady Margaret whispered together close by. "Does Lady Katherine know that her steward tried to send much of her fortune to Holland?" Nicola asked.

"What? No!" Lady Margaret said. "We were unable to find any records of transactions with her London bank in the papers at Wingfield Castle. She has sent for an accounting."

"We stopped the transfer, so there is no need to worry her. The thing about Holland is very secret."

"It is all very secret," Lady Margaret said. "That bearded man forbade me from saying anything, except to the Queen. Nor would he tell me his name."

"Even the Queen does not know his name. He frightens me. Did he say anything the Queen might need to know? That King Henry would not have told her?"

"How would we know what King Henry told her? One thing you need to know, though. Those cannons were right where you said they would be, in the Roman ruins near Caister castle. King Henry's soldiers captured them, before we took Caister Castle. So all eight of the missing cannons are now accounted for."

Relief flooded through Nicola. She breathed deeply, and gave silent thanks to God. All the cannons had been found, though the murderers had not. But at least half the mystery was solved.

"I am *so* thankful you told me," Nicola said. "Surely King Henry told her that part. Is there anything else she needs to know?"

Margaret frowned. "I have a long tale to tell, but this may not be the time. I keep thinking about little Michael de la Pole, my boys' playmate. Lady Cathryn dreads having to tell him that his parents were disloyal to her, and to King Henry. And that they are in prison, or even dead. She won't do so until she knows for sure."

"Peter and Alice Fitzpole are already dead," Nicola said, deciding that Margaret looked too exhausted to hear that Peter died while being tortured. "They revealed nothing," she added.

Lady Margaret gasped. "So soon? The bearded man did not mention that. Poor little Michael. But perhaps this is not the time to tell the Queen about his sorrows."

"Best avoided," Nicola agreed. "She is about to give birth. She does not need to hear sad stories of orphaned children. But we could say that Lady Cathryn is doing well, and taking good care of her grandson."

They went back to the Queen, to tell her that Lady Cathryn and her grandson were doing well, and to be sure she knew that the missing cannons had been captured by King Henry's men.

"Henry told me about the cannons, and your parts in locating them, and in capturing Caister Castle. Though of course he gives the entire credit to his men. You must be relieved that your cannon mystery is solved, Nicola."

"But the murders are not," Nicola said. She thought about reminding the Queen that the murderers could well be here, in King Henry's court. Then she thought better of it.

*****

That afternoon, Nicola was summoned to a corner of the Richmond Palace curtain wall that faced an embankment, accompanied this time by Lena and Lady Maud Parr. Two of the Biaggi cannons had been placed on top of the wall, with iron shot neatly piled beside each. John Smith and several of his armorers stood nearby, waiting. They looked her up and down, brows furrowed, apparently startled to see her dressed as a nun.

"I need to look at these cannonballs," Nicola said to John Smith. "You will allow?"

Smith nodded, and gestured toward the nearest pile. Nicola picked up each shot, rolled it in her hands to feel for irregularities that her eyes might miss, then handed it off to one of the armorers. As the neat pyramid of shot she was examining diminished, they built an identical one next to it, at her direction. "Shut your trap," Smith said to the only man who grumbled.

"My arms are getting tired," she finally said. "I see that you have done very well. I will trust that the rest of the cannonballs are as smooth and round as these. Have you put in the gunpowder?"

"We have," said Smith. "You choose the shot."

She picked up another one, looked it over, rolled it in her hands, and kissed it. "This one," she said. The armorers grinned. They loaded the first cannon while she picked up, examined, and kissed another cannonball. The armorers loaded it, still grinning, and put fuses in both cannons. A small fire already burned, well away from the gunpowder, so that the fuses could be lit.

"Now we are ready for the King," Nicola announced.

They waited in silence. The quiet was near absolute, because a defensive space had been cleared around the palace, between its moat and the embankment they would soon pockmark with cannonballs. It was likely built for that very purpose, Nicola realized. The newest cannons could now crumble castle walls like so much bread—but not so earthworks, built beyond the walls, which simply absorbed the shot.

Richmond was a new palace, built by Henry's father, who had surely used the latest building techniques: the dirt dug out for the moat had probably been used to build the embankment. Crows sat in the tree tops visible beyond it, so far away that their occasional caws were muted by distance. Nicola wondered whether the King was hunting, somewhere in those distant woods.

"Are we ready?" boomed his voice, from behind her. Nicola turned to join the other ladies in curtsey, while the armorers took a knee. "We are, Your Highness," said John Smith.

Before they could rise to their feet, Henry had lit a piece of kindling and applied it to the first fuse. He laughed as the embankment exploded, raining mud and rocks in a circle the size of a room. The armorers hastened to pull the carriage back so they could swab out and reload the gun. King Henry fired the second one, with the same results.

"Step well back, your Highness," Nicola warned. "I know nothing about the gunpowder they are using. Sometimes cannons explode."

The King backed up and motioned to the guards and courtiers who had accompanied him to do the same. They took turns aiming and shooting off the cannons, amidst much laughter. Nicola watched anxiously, fearful that the armorers would forget to swab out the cannons, or do it poorly. To her immense relief, the armorers took care to do their jobs properly, and the guns did not explode. The embankment, however, soon looked like an army of giant moles had attacked it.

King Henry grew tired of the sport long before they exhausted the ammunition. He took Nicola aside. "Is this sufficient for the test, Sister Greensleeves?" he asked her.

"Yes, Your Highness," she responded, ignoring the reference to her nun's attire. "Careful, the gun is hot," she warned. Too late. The King already had his burned forefinger in his mouth.

"These cannons have survived an imaginary battle, without exploding," she explained. "They passed the test. We will dig out most of those balls and examine them, to see how they held up."

"You have passed a test, too, Sister Lady Greensleeves," the King remarked. "Has she not, my fine men?" he called to the armorers, who nodded.

"Hard to b'lieve she knows what she's doin'," one of them said. "But she does." John Smith glared at him. Several of the King's courtiers looked shocked, whether because a commoner dared speak to the King or because the man gave credit to a woman, Nicola could not tell.

Henry, though, laughed his high barking laugh. "Of course she knows what she's doing. I wouldn't hire someone who didn't."

He looked at Nicola, who was grinning herself. "Sir Charles will no longer ask you to sing any song he selects," he continued, more quietly. "This he has promised. But I do require you to continue singing carols. And possibly participate in a motet or two, chosen by the monks. You do not object to music chosen by monks, I assume."

Nicola's delight in being recognized for her expertise vanished. She swallowed hard. "Brother Michael and I could choose music for many voices together. Holy music. And practice it, with the others."

"Holy music suitable to the season," the King snapped. "And yes, you should practice it. I'll have him sent to you. But you can't dress like *that*, even though you will be singing with monks. Wear something suitable. With the green sleeves." At that he left, trailing his retainers.

Nicola's sense of dread returned. The King was telling her how to dress again, and demanding she perform for him. He had praised her for being good at her occupation, yet still treated her as if her function was to look beautiful and entertain him. She longed again to go home.

✶✶✶✶✶

Brother Michael appeared at the Queen's rooms later in the afternoon, with a selection of music. He was turned away. Lady Nicola could no longer be spared, he was told. She was needed by the Queen, who had gone into labor.

Woodcut of a woman in a birthing chair, 1554

CHAPTER 37: THE QUEEN GIVES BIRTH

The same day, New Year's Eve 1510

Nicola watched the consternation and panic that seized the Queen's ladies when they learned that Her Highness was in labor. Lady Maud leaped to her feet, upsetting the card table where several were playing. "It is too early," she wailed. "She will lose another baby." Several other ladies who had been watching the game joined in, exclaiming and wringing their hands.

"It is not too early," Lena said. She shouted, "Do you hear me?" when no one paid attention. And shouted again, "It is not too early!" When she saw she had the ladies' attention, she continued more quietly. "I wash the queen's rags, from her monthlies. And I know how to count. So believe me, she is not early." The ladies looked shocked. Lena, who had always been quiet and self-effacing, was breathing hard and glaring at them.

Fearful that the whole group was on the edge of hysteria, Nicola searched her mind for something comforting to say. "The Queen is a small woman with a very large husband," she remarked. "If her belly had gotten much bigger, she would be having great difficulty now."

"Calm yourselves, for her sake," said Margaret Pole, her own voice calmer than anyone around her. "She will feel your fear through these walls. The midwives told her that her time was near. They know best. All is well."

Lady Margaret then took quiet and capable charge of the ladies. Those who were agitated, she simply sent away. She put Elizabeth Boleyn in charge of most of the others, and sent Lady Maria to comfort Henry.

"The King is in the Presence Chamber with his sister Mary and Sir Charles," she told Nicola. "Pacing up and down with Charles, telling him how to handle tonight's revels alone. And changing his mind about it, at every turn they take of the room. Charles is trying to calm him. Princess Mary is huddled in a corner, looking miserable. I trust Lady Maria to be a comfort to both of them."

She took Nicola by both hands, and looked into her eyes. "The Queen wants you in the birthing room. Can you stay calm?"

"I can," Nicola assured her. "I have attended a number of births. And I know the value of calm."

When they entered the Queen's bedroom, she was lying on the narrow birthing bed with a midwife at either side, working to soothe her. Queen Katherine was more stoic than any mother in labor Nicola had seen. She took direction quietly, and scarcely made a sound when the pains took her.

She and Lady Margaret moved to the side of the room. "The midwives seem very capable," Nicola remarked.

"The best money can buy," Lady Margaret agreed.

"The blue cloth Her Highness holds against her belly—what is that?"

"A holy relic from Westminster Abbey. It's a cincture—the Virgin Mary herself wore it, or so it is said. It is supposed to protect from the pains of childbirth."

"I hope it gives Her Highness comfort." Nicola had ceased believing in the authenticity of any of the hundreds of supposed relics in Rome when the nuns showed her the pig bones they believed to be those of Saint Sisto, for whom the convent was named. She never had the heart to tell them about their unintended fraud. Relics brought churches and convents income and comfort to many, whether they were real or not.

"Margaret!" the Queen called out, her voice raw with pain.

Margaret hurried to her side, gesturing to Nicola to follow. "How can we help you, my Queen?"

The Queen was panting. "Pray the rosary with me. And tell me all will be well."

"It's a normal birth," one of the midwives said. "All will be well."

"Indeed it will," Lady Margaret promised.

They prayed the rosary, over and over. When that became difficult for the Queen, Nicola held her hand and recited comforting psalms, in Latin and then in English.

When her pains came close together, the midwives shooed them aside. With practiced hands, they moved the Queen to the birthing stool, which they called "the groaning chair." One supported her shoulders, while the other knelt, cheek on the floor, watching for the baby's head.

"It's coming. It's coming, my Queen. Keep pushing, keep pushing. I see the head. I see the head!" shouted the kneeling midwife. "Help us put her back on the table."

With the midwives supervising, Nicola and Margaret helped lift the Queen back onto the birthing bed. Lady Margaret then ushered several of Katherine's ladies into the birthing room to act as witnesses, and sat them in a corner where they could see the baby emerge from the birth canal. Nicola wondered what Margaret had said to keep them calm and quiet.

Prince Henry was born at half past one in the morning on New Year's Day, 1511. He cried lustily when the midwife slapped his bottom. "It's a big, healthy boy," she told the Queen, who burst into tears. "Tell Henry," she sobbed.

"In good time," said the midwife. "The afterbirth is coming. He can wait."

There was something about the baby's cry that did not seem right to Nicola, but she said nothing. The boy was bigger than any newborn she had seen. Surely that was a good sign. The Queen's color was good and her lips wore a slight smile. She was resting. She deserved it.

After the chord was cut Lady Margaret took the baby to wash him, while Nicola stood at bedside, waiting with the midwives for the placenta. She saw the pile of herbs they had set aside to staunch excessive bleeding, if it occurred. "Thanks be to God," the head midwife breathed, when the placenta emerged normally. She put it immediately into the fireplace, where it sizzled and stank.

"Look you well," the midwife shouted to Nicola and the others in the room. "No one will ever accuse me of witchcraft. When the afterbirth is completely burned we will throw all these ashes in the Thames, in front of witnesses. You are invited to witness."

Lady Margaret returned holding Prince Henry, swaddled in white linen embroidered with "HRH" in gold thread. The royal prince had a halo of reddish hair.

"Who would like to help me tell the King?" she said. All the Queen's ladies, including Nicola, followed Lady Margaret into the room where the King and his sister waited, slumped in their chairs and looking miserable. "You have a healthy son," Margaret announced.

The King jumped to his feet. "A son!" he shouted, his face exultant. Then he looked at Nicola in horror. "Is the Queen dead?" he cried.

She looked down at the blood-smeared apron she was wearing, regretting that in the tumult of the birth she had forgotten to take it off. "The Queen is alive and in good health," she announced loudly. "There is always a little blood. It was a normal birth. All is well."

Henry put his hands on his knees and wept, loudly and without restraint. Henry's sister patted his back softy, as if she might hurt him. "I must see her," he sobbed.

"Wouldn't you rather see your son first?" Lady Margaret suggested, her voice gentle.

He stood, swallowed his tears, and walked up to the baby. "He is very small," he observed. "And red."

Lady Margaret smiled at him. "He is actually large. Red is normal. Though red hair is unusual."

"Not in my family. Nor Katherine's. She is descended from a daughter of John of Gaunt, you know." He touched the baby with his forefinger, then withdrew his hand, as if burned. "When can I see her?" he asked.

"Whenever you like," Lady Margaret said. "She is waiting for you." He rushed into the birthing room. Margaret quietly shut the door after him.

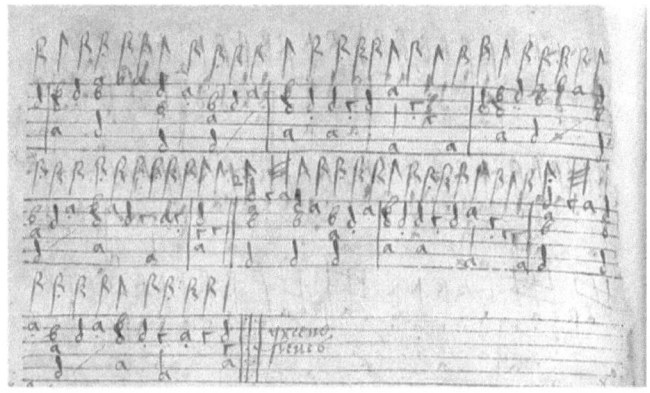

One of the ealiest known sources for the tune *Greene Sleues*, in lute tablature, from *MS. 408/2*, an anonymous amateur anthology dated c. 1592–1603.

CHAPTER 38: GIFTS AND A MUSICAL THREAT

New Year's Day 1511

Nicola and Lady Margaret de la Pole waited in a long line of well-wishers that stretched from the doorway of the King's Presence Room. Neither had wished to leave the Queen and her newborn son, but they had been given no choice. The King was giving and receiving gifts. Attendance was mandatory.

The line, overwhelmingly of sumptuously-dressed men giving gifts of coin, moved slowly. "This is going to take a long time," Margaret remarked. "Last year—his first on the throne—King Henry was gracious, but little was said. Now just listen to him, shouting for joy that he has a newborn son. Everyone in the line needs to express their joy, too. Not only for him, but for the kingdom. We may be here for hours."

When they finally reached the front of the line, Lady Margaret presented her embroidered waistband to the King, then curtseyed. Nicola handed him a small Venetian silk bag with a few shiny Italian coins, then curtseyed herself. The King smiled on them both. "You have done us good service, both of you," he said. "Katherine told me last night that you were of particular help to her during her labor. These gifts were prepared before then. I will not forget what you have done since."

Henry rose from his throne, and handed leather packets to both of them. As they curtseyed again, he took Nicola's hand, guided her to her feet, and kissed her fingers. She saw his desire when he looked into her eyes, and felt her fears returning. The King was still determined to have his way her, no matter how she felt. Or what his adulterous betrayal did to his wife, who had just risked her life to bear his child. Nicola hated him so much she wanted to spit at him. But she was too afraid even to protest, because he had threatened to accuse her of murder. That threat still hung like the sword of Damocles over her head.

With as much dignity as she could muster, Nicola fled. Lady Margaret followed her.

"Nicola, let's sit on this bench," she called out, when they were close to the Queen's suite. "I, for one, need to get off my feet." Nicola sat, her heart still pounding and her stomach queasy.

Margaret did not appear to notice her discomfort. "Come, let's look at our gifts," she said. Margaret squeezed hers, and frowned. "No coins. I am disappointed. He knows I have little property, and little money." She read the document she pulled from the sealed packet, and began to cry.

"What is it? What has he done to you?" Nicola asked, hating the King for being cruel to her friend again. He had accused Margaret of being a "Judas" before they went to Wingfield, for no good reason—but she had proved her loyalty there, risking both her life and the lives of her boys. How dare he lead her to expect a generous gift, then play a nasty prank on her? The man was a monster.

Tears streamed down Margaret's face. "He has made me Duchess of Salisbury, in my own right," she responded, her voice choked. "And restored the lands seized from my brother when he was executed. And I am to be one of Prince Henry's attendants. Which will come with a stipend." She began to weep in earnest.

Nicola hated the King so much at that moment that she had trouble believing he had been kind and generous. Was it even possible? "You are crying because you are happy?" she asked.

Margaret laughed through her tears. "After my husband died I wasn't sure how I would feed my children," she sobbed, mopping her eyes with an embroidered handkerchief. "'Happy' doesn't begin to describe it."

Nicola patted her shoulder, relieved she had mistaken happy tears for sad ones. Lady Margaret had the future before her that she deserved. Doubtless the Queen had much to do with this.

Margaret swallowed her sobs, dabbled her eyes, and looked at Nicola. "Come now Nicola. It is your turn. What did he give you?"

Nicola shuffled through the sheets in her leather packet. One was a bill of exchange, payable to her on her bank in Rome. "A generous gift of money," she said, shocked by the amount. "Very generous. And a song. Evidently King Henry has written me a song."

She folded and pushed the bill of exchange into her bodice. Then she looked at King Henry's composition. Its lyrics brought back all her fears.

"Margaret, he is still pursuing me," she said, feeling suddenly queasy again. "I need to escape. I need to go home."

Margaret dried her tears, and looked at the music Nicola was holding. "I saw how he kissed your hand. And this is a love song. No denying it," Margaret said. "Can you sing it?"

Nicola sang, very softly:

> Alas my love you do me wrong
> To cast me off discourteously;
> And I have loved you oh so long
> Delighting in your company.

Greensleeves was my delight,
Greensleeves my heart of gold
Greensleeves was my heart of joy
And who but my lady Greensleeves.

"What a lovely melody," Lady Margaret said, continuing to dabble the tears oozing from her eyes. "You should be flattered."

"I'm sure he intended flattery," Nicola responded. "But I feel tired and frightened instead. I want to go home."

Margaret sniffled, and blew her nose. "What more do you have to do here, to fulfill your obligations?"

"For the armorers: only one thing. For the King: find the murderers."

Margaret wiped her eyes again. "I'm sure you can do the first. Are you any closer to the second?"

"I don't know, Margaret. Something keeps rattling around in my brain. I saw something that I'm not remembering, that would solve the mystery. Or heard something, perhaps. Or both. But I haven't put it together yet."

"I pray you do soon. Because Henry is very determined when he wants something. And it's obvious that he wants you. Once the Queen is churched, she may recapture his attention. The King is pushing for it as soon as possible. But it will be several weeks, at least."

"Churched?"

Margaret smiled. "It's a church ceremony that welcomes a new mother back to the world after her confinement. And to the arms of her husband. The delay is for the sake of the baby."

Nicola thought about it. "More likely for the recovery of the mother. The Queen will be beautiful again, with her breasts big from milk. Henry will either lust after her, or...just lust. For several weeks? *Madre di Dio.*"

A sudden thought struck her. "Margaret, since you are now part of the baby's household, you must help keep the new prince safe. If my instincts are right, baby Prince Henry is in great danger. Possibly from someone in this castle, whose identity no one suspects."

Lady Margaret stared at her. "He will have nothing but breast milk for a long while, Nicola. I think he will be safe."

"From poisoners, yes. But from assassins? Think about it. You did not see the severed heads of the murdered men like I did. Whoever did that could cut a baby in half before you knew what was happening. So you must be very, very careful. No one should be let near that baby except the people who absolutely must be there. Trust no one, until we find the killers."

"Surely no one would do that to a baby," Margaret protested, her eyes round.

"What about those dead little princes you told me about?" Nicola responded. "Someone did it to them."

W. Neade, *The Double-Armed Man*, (pike and bow) 1623

Chapter 39: What the Fireworks Revealed

That evening

That evening, the first of the new year, England rejoiced at the birth of a son to their new King and Queen. Church bells rang and bonfires burned all over London. Free wine, a gift from the King, flowed from barrels opened around the city so his subjects could toast the health of the new prince.

There were fireworks, too. A yeoman warder, armed with a longbow, stood at his post on the walls of the Tower of London, watching and listening to the distant explosions. The Tower guards were on high alert, for reasons the warder did not understand, so he was careful to do his duty as well. The moonless, cloudy night made it difficult to see into the Tower Yard. Still, he thought he detected movement in one corner, where no movement should be. As he peered in that direction, a flash of light from the fireworks lit the area for an instant, and erased his doubts. Armed men were trying to open the door of the stone building that housed the cannons and small arms that had recently been put there.

He had his orders, and knew his duty. After waving a torch to signal the other guards, he used it to light and shoot a fire arrow at the men attempting the break-in. A cry told him he had hit one of them. Other torches waved and a bell began clanging continuously. He sent two more fire arrows to the same spot.

When fireworks lit the yard again, four more fire arrows flew there from other points on the wall. Weeds next to the building burst into flames that showed two men sprawled on the ground. Other men scattered and ran into the shadows, pursued by guards converging from their barracks. Swords clashed; men screamed.

Another yeoman warder standing on the curtain wall overlooking the Thames heard the melee and turned his back to it, to do his duty. When fireworks lit the river, he thought he saw something. When fireworks flashed again, he was certain he did. The light glinted off the helmets of armed men, crouching in the bottom of a large wherry that was fast approaching the dock.

He had his orders, and was ready to stop the wherry from reaching the Tower. The new cannons had been loaded with fresh powder that morning, and he had checked the aim himself when he went on duty. He waved a torch to signal for help. Another fireworks flash showed him it was time. As others joined him, he trotted the length of the wall, lighting one cannon fuse after another.

A fireworks flash showed them the large boat near the dock just before the guns exploded, and the screams began. Screams continued until the next flash, when they saw a few men clinging to floating wreckage, hopelessly weighed down by their armor. The next flash showed nothing: bits of debris swept downstream, and disappeared. The Thames had swallowed everything.

The yeoman warders stared at each other, too shocked to speak. Their boring routine had erupted into something monstrous that disappeared just as abruptly, like a sea monster in old sailors' tales. Had they not all seen the wherry seconds earlier, they would have sworn that nothing had happened.

Nearby, William de la Pole lay in his bed, listening to the shouts from the yard and then the cannons, and wondering what was happening. He jumped to his feet when he heard someone fumbling at his door lock. At first he thought it was a yeoman warder, trying to let him out because of a fire. But warders would have known what key to use.

"Who's there?" he shouted.

"We're going to get you out of here, William," said an unfamiliar voice on the other side.

"Help! Murder! Treason! Treason! Treason!" William screamed, convinced that whoever had tried to poison him had come to finish the job. He flung and propped his bedstead against the door, and kept shouting until he heard men pounding up the steps near his cell, and swords clanging in the hallway. The familiar shouts, screams and grunts of men killing and dying in battle that had haunted his dreams for years were now a living nightmare, playing out within feet of his head. Heart pounding, he sat on the floor with his back against his bedstead, prepared to resist if anyone tried to open his door.

"They're all dead," someone yelled, over groans, whimpers and then cheers in the background. "So's Ben," someone yelled back. "George and Bill are hurt. Bill's hurt bad."

 Whoever had won, it was over. William listened as the surviving men called out to each other for help with the wounded. Were they King's men? He could not tell. What would his brother Richard do to him for alerting the guards, if the rebels had managed to take the Tower? Death, surely—but would he escape torture? He crossed himself, and tried to pray.

When all was silent, a familiar voice said, "Is all well with you, William?" And he began to cry.

****

The people of London assumed that the cannons of the Tower were shot off that night in celebration of the birth of Prince Henry. By morning, there was no sign—at least from the outside—that anything unusual had happened

The barrel of a bronze saker cannon inscribed with a Tudor rose and a monogram of King Henry VIII.

CHAPTER 40: THE SECRET OF CASE HARDENING

January 2, 1501

Nicola smelled a whiff of gunpowder when she and Lena arrived by wherry the following morning, but thought nothing of it. She sent the wherry to deliver a note to Captain Napolitano of the *Romulus*, which was docked across the river from the Tower. She and Lena then entered the river gate, and headed to the armory.

Today, several armorers were working on chain mail. Nicola picked up the corner of a mail shirt to see how heavy it was. "Ours are lighter than this, but yours are probably stronger. What happened last night?" she asked John Smith as she piled the mail shirt back on the table. "I see there was a grass fire next to the storage building where all the cannons are housed. Is all well?"

"Just a little fire," he assured her. "All is well."

"But the door had been shot full of arrows—I saw the holes. Are you sure?"

He looked at her, his face a mask. "We aren't supposed to talk about it. Come see what we have done."

Several of the armorers stood grinning around a large, gleaming bronze cannon, emblazoned with the Tudor rose. They had obviously cast it with metal from the blast furnace, in one of the molds Nicola had brought from Italy. "Excellent work," she said, after she inspected it. "Did you use the Biaggi formula for bronze, or your own?"

"Our own," Smith said.

"I thought so, from the color. You can test to see which works best for you. Where are the cannonballs the King fired from the walls of Richmond Palace, and how did they do?"

"They're over there. They held up well."

Nicola examined them. "Excellent. Your iron is of good quality. That means I have only one last thing to teach you, before I return to my homeland. Are you ready?" She spread a piece of paper out on the table that held the drawings of King Henry's new ships.

"What is it?" Smith asked.

It's a description in English of how to make good, reliable cannons from cast iron—with small amounts of other metals, listed there," she pointed. "Much cheaper than bronze. The important thing is how you finish them. When they are cool enough to handle with heavy gloves, you wrap each one tightly in one of those cow skins we sent—put some pieces of skin inside the cannon, too—then pack them tightly in one of the wooden crates we sent, or ones like it. And seal the case, and leave it in the hot sun or near the heat of the forge for at least a week. When you open the case, there is a smell you will learn to recognize. Somehow, this hardens the cast iron. You can use the cow skins a couple of times before replacing them. We call the technique "case hardening." It is very important that iron guns be case-hardened. That includes the arquebuses."

"We have never had much luck with pure iron guns," Smith said.

"I cannot promise you that you will have better luck in the future. Depends on your metals, and maybe even on whether English cow skins are different from Italian cow skins. I have heard rumors that other armories are working with other materials from cows—hooves, or bones. But these are rumors—no one wants to give away their secrets. I can promise you that we have had good luck, using this technique. And our cannons are the best. You will need to experiment, then test, test, test."

"Of course,' Smith said. He smiled at her, which he had never done before. He was missing several teeth. "We have cow skins a-plenty. This will save the King a fortune, if we can do it right."

"One more thing," Nicola said. "On this piece of paper is a copy of a mutual promise we made in our contract with King Henry." She doubted he could read, but at least he would have a copy. "It says essentially, that you will inform us of advances made with this technique, and we, the Biaggi arms firm, will inform you of the same. Father Wolsey can show you the original, if you like."

Smith held the piece of paper by one corner, staring at it as if it were alive, and about to bite. "We never did that before. But if that's what it says, you will hear from us."

"The same," Nicola responded. "Now I must say 'Addiò.' Farewell in English, I think."

"You going home to Italy?" one of the armorers asked.

She nodded. "Soon, I hope. I may be back, but I cannot be sure. I am trusting you will tell Reverend Father Wolsey that I showed you how to cast and case harden iron guns, and gave you these writings. Show them to him, please. Addiò."

As she and Lena walked away, she heard "Go with God" and "God go with you" and "Fare you well" and "Good bye" from the men. She turned and waved, then headed for the river.

*****

At the docks, they were joined by the King's Spymaster, who shared their wherry back to Richmond Palace. "What happened here last night?" Nicola asked him.

"Why do you think something happened?" he snapped.

"Because there was a fire next to the building where all the guns are stored, and arrow holes in the door. I asked the armorers, but they wouldn't tell me anything."

"As they were ordered." He stared at the riverbank for a moment. "This is not a place to share secrets," he said, glancing at the oarsmen, and Lena. "I'll tell you when we get ashore."

Nicola sent Lena ahead when they reached Richmond Palace. As she and the King's Spymaster walked toward the entrance, he said, "You are not to repeat this to anyone, understand? Edmund de la Pole tried to escape last night. He had help, and they tried to steal some of the Biaggi weapons. The attempt failed. He is being questioned now."

"What about William de la Pole?" she asked.

"He helped sound the alarm. He should be fine. Edmund likely will not be. Five good men died in the attempt, including the Keeper of the Keys. There were eleven traitors inside. They are all dead."

Nicole looked around, to ensure no one was listening. "I assume this relates to Richard de la Pole's planned invasion?" she murmured.

"Assume whatever you like. You heard nothing from me. We did not have this conversation and you know nothing that happened last night at the Tower. As far as you are concerned, it was an ordinary night. Understood?"

"Understood." Lady Margaret had called this man "Satan." It fit, Nicola thought. She wished she were already on the ship to Italy.

When she arrived back at the Queen's rooms, several ladies-in-waiting with flushed faces were sitting at the dining table, with a flask of wine.

"How fares the Queen?" she asked them. "And where is the baby?"

"She is resting. So is he. So are we. Have a cup of wine," said Maud Parr, with a crooked smile.

"The prince is in his household. He is to have his own chaplain and groomsmen—probably close to a hundred attendants," said Maria.

"A wet nurse and plenty of guards are all he needs for now," Nicola responded.

"Yes. He has a wet nurse. And a chief nurse. And Margaret Pole. She is helping set things up," said Elizabeth Boleyn. "Henry is full of plans for him. He is also planning a huge jousting tournament for next month, to celebrate Prince Henry's birth. I am to play a queen called "Noble Renown." I am sure there will be a part for you, Lady Nicola. Though I don't know what it is yet."

"Who is running the kingdom while Henry makes these plans?" Nicola asked.

"Probably no one," said Lady Maud. The ladies laughed.

"The Council. Or so they think," said another lady, giggling.

"Probably Wolsey," said Elizabeth Boleyn. "He does anyway. When the Queen lets him." They all laughed even louder.

Nicola regretted her question, and wanted no part in this conversation. She wondered if the new prince had enough guards. "I'm going to find Lady Margaret and see the new nursery," she said.

She caught up with three of the bearded monks on the way there. One held a lute and another a tambourine that jingled as he walked, in step with the others. "We are going to sing for the new prince," Brother Michael said. "The lullaby carol we sang for the court. Would you like to join us?"

"I don't think Prince Henry is being shown in the public yet," Nicola warned, feeling uneasy. A host of people, from courtiers to cooks, was converging on the baby prince's nursery. She sensed danger, but perhaps she was being irrational.

When they reached the new nursery wing, a crowd had already gathered in the hallway. Lady Margaret stood in the doorway, flanked by Yeomen of the Guard, with Prince Henry sleeping in her arms. The crowd struggled to catch sight of him, exclaiming about his red hair in whispers, so as not to wake him.

Nicola spotted Lambert Simnel in the crowd ahead of her. She could not see whether he was wearing a knife at his belt. She also saw the Duke of Buckingham in profile, magnificently dressed and followed by two of his knights. He held what was apparently a gift for the baby. On his right hip hung a large jeweled sword.

Something was tugging at her mind. Something she had missed. Something that had to do with the murders. What was it? And why was she feeling so nervous?

Her mind found the answer when the crowd forced her and the monks to a stop. She knew what she had seen without noticing earlier, and why she was feeling fearful for the young prince. And she knew who the murderers were. The more she thought about it, the more obvious it seemed.

Heart pounding, she sidled around the monks and towards the doorway, jostling several servants. She still could not see if Lambert Simnel wore a knife, but it did not matter now. "Take the baby inside and close the door," she hissed at Lady Margaret when she reached her. Margaret looked puzzled, so she spoke more urgently: "Take the baby inside and close the door."

Prince Henry solved their problem by starting to cry. Lady Margaret murmured apologies to the crowd, backed into the doorway, and kicked the door closed behind her. Nicola placed her body in front of the door handle.

By the time the hallway was empty, Nicola had calmed herself. She asked one of the guards, "Where is your captain? And where is the King?"

He stared at her. "I think the King is playing tennis. I can take you to Sir Henry."

"You stay right here and guard this baby," she scolded him. "He is in *danger*. Just tell me where Sir Henry is."

Court Paume (older version of modern-day tennis)
player, 1580. Artist unknown.

CHAPTER 41: AN ANCIENT THREAT

An hour later

"If I am wrong, we simply apologize," Nicola said. "It will all blow over in a day or two. But if I am right, the entire royal family is in grave danger."

She sat in the wainscoted meeting room where she had earlier examined maps, this time with Reverend Father Wolsey, the King's Spymaster, Sir Henry Marney, and one of Marney's subordinates, an enormous man with hair the color of straw, dressed in green and white livery embroidered with the Tudor rose.

"I see no harm," Wolsey said. "But I would prefer to consult King Henry first, as a courtesy. If this danger exists, it has existed since the time of Henry's father. It can continue to exist for a few more hours. I'll find him and brief him—I think he's playing tennis with Sir Charles Brandon. We have other matters to discuss."

When he left, Sir Henry turned to Nicola. "I had a man try the door, and it's locked," he said. "Do you think you can get them to open it? We could break it down, of course, but that seems..."

"Excessive and bound to call attention," the Spymaster pronounced. "If nothing is wrong, we want to know with as little fuss as possible."

265

"I think I can get you in the door," Nicola said. "I have something that will help. I'll go get it."

When she returned, a rolled document in her hand, the King sat at the table with the others. He wore a white linen shirt and knee-length pants with a plain codpiece and stockings, evidently his costume for tennis. His face was flushed, and the room smelled of his sweat.

Henry frowned when he saw Nicola, who was dressed as a nun. "So you think you have found our murderers, Sister Lady Greensleeves?" he called to her. "I am skeptical."

"You have reason to be, Your Highness," she responded, with a curtsey. "But there is no harm in looking for the evidence."

"They could have killed us long ago, if you're right," he said. "Both the Queen and me. Why do you suppose they haven't done it yet?"

"Because they don't want to die themselves. Particularly not in the horrible ways your nation deals with traitors. I think they are waiting for a signal of some sort, from Richard de la Pole or someone who supports him. A signal that they will be safe, or at least have a chance of it. They may have expected it to come this week."

"You know what happened at the Tower yesterday, then."

"I do, because I was there. I saw where the arrows hit and the grass burned. But they may not know what happened yet. They may be assuming the attack at the Tower was successful, and that orders to kill you will come at any moment."

King Henry looked at his Spymaster. "Could it be so?"

The Spymaster's face showed no emotion. "It could. It may not be likely, but it could."

Henry stood and looked at the Captain of the Yeoman Guard. "Well, then, take care of it. Do it now. It is only risky for you if she is right. If she is wrong, it will at least be amusing. Try to take them alive. If they are guilty, I want them to suffer."

"I beg your Highness to stay where it is safe," he responded.

"I am going to see the Queen and my son before supper," the King barked. "With the usual guards. I should be safe there."

Leg-hook technique from a fencing manual
by Paulus Hector Mair (1540-1550)

CHAPTER 42: MUSIC, MAYHEM, AND KEYS TO THE MYSTERY

The same day

Nicola and at least a dozen Yeomen of the Guard made their way silently across the palace in small groups, using circuitous routes. When the guards were assembled and deathly quiet, Nicola knocked on the door.

"Who is it?" said a voice within.

"It's Lady Nicola," she said. "I have something that the King has written, that he wanted me to share with you."

When the door opened only slightly, Nicola put her foot inside it and pushed as far forward as she could, holding out the music King Henry had written for her New Year's present. Frowning, Brother Michael took it to examine, which allowed her to push her way in further. Behind him she caught a glimpse of a wall lined with wooden chests. Several puzzled monks stared at her, from a table where they were playing cards.

Then someone yanked her from the doorway and a group of guards piled inside the music room, one after another, swords drawn, shouting "Surrender or Die" or "Traitors Die" or just shouting. Nicola watched as guards stationed themselves in front of each chest, and behind each seated monk.

"What is the meaning of this?" thundered Brother Michael. "You may not open those chests. They are none of your business—" Someone large punched him hard in the jaw. He crumpled and fell.

Sir Henry Marney rifled through a chest, then turned to his men, eyes wide. "A trove of weapons," he announced. "Arrest them."

Guards immediately sat on the monks' chests. One laughed as he swung his sword back and forth, keeping the monks at bay. "Never fought while sittin' on me arse before," he shouted. "I *like* it. I'll slit your belly, ye whoreson traitor!"

Nicola stood frozen, watching with her heart pounding. She hadn't entirely believed her own theory until the weapons proved it true. Now she could hardly believe how hard the monks were fighting. Were they really monks?

"Get out of the way, woman!" a guard shouted at Nicola, shoving her aside as he rushed into the music room, where men were bellowing and screaming. A monk tumbled into the chapel. Two guards followed and wrestled him to the ground. More guards rushed from the chapel into the music room melee.

Someone tapped Nicola on the shoulder. "Come," said the Spymaster, ushering her away from the door. Nicola heard shouting, then sounds of a struggle, then weapons clanging, then cries of pain. Another monk rushed out of the music room, a sword in hand. He looked at them, then was knocked down from behind.

Nicola and the Spymaster glanced at each other, and wordlessly fled to the hallway outside the chapel. He closed the door and put his back to it.

Nicola's heart was pounding, but the Spymaster showed no emotion. "It appears they found your evidence," he commented, as though they were discussing the weather. "I hope it doesn't get too bloody in there. The King will not be pleased if they ruin his beautiful chapel."

"Surely it will be over soon," Nicola said, hoping it was so. Sir Henry had done well to have his soldiers guard those chests. Yet one of the monks had gotten hold of a sword. That did not bode well.

"You have not completely explained how you deduced this," the Spymaster said. "I should have seen it. That is my job, and I failed. Tell me now. The whole story. How did I miss it?"

"It was the sound of chain mail that gave them away,' Nicola said. "I know that sound, because our armories make chain mail. I heard it at the Tower armory this morning, then again when I lined up behind the monks to see the baby prince. They always carried tambourines, to disguise the noise, but I heard it when everyone was shifting around to see the baby. Understand, they didn't always wear chain shirts. But I believe they did when they thought they might need them. I have no doubt they were wearing swords, too, under those big monks' robes. It was all invisible, but it made them a little bulkier."

The Spymaster waved away two scullery maids who had stopped in the hallway to stare at the chapel door. They curtseyed and bustled down the hall. The shouting within continued intermittently, but sounded less frantic.

"I don't hear weapons anymore," Nicola said.

"Nor I," the Spymaster responded. "It will soon be over. Continue."

"The monks had always struck me as a little odd," she said. "In Dover, they knew exactly when to blow their horns to time them with the firing of the cannons. I didn't think about it then, but I did today. How would monks know that? And those beards. I have never seen monks with beards. I'd decided it was an English affectation. Now I think it was a disguise. They are all big men, who carry themselves like soldiers. I saw them walking in step, a couple of times, including this morning. I don't think they were even aware of it. Do monks march? Nuns don't. They walk slowly, contemplatively, with small steps. And of course, the tambourines. Monks with tambourines? They had lutes and horns, too. Monks and nuns sing. Mostly ancient chants, but also the beautiful and holy new music, written for many voices. But monks don't dance, and their songs do not require instruments. I assumed they had adapted to their roles as court musicians."

"They adapted so beautifully that they became invisible," the spymaster responded. "Henry's father came upon them somewhere—no one remembers where, or exactly when. They have been waiting to strike for a long time."

"I remembered one more thing that had nagged at the back of my mind. When we first arrived at Greenwich Palace, I saw the monks at the end of the line of courtiers, when I was going to the docks. They were marching along, jingling that tambourine. But three of them were missing. Which is the number of assassins whose footprints I saw the next day, when we examined the second set of bodies. I'm pretty sure that Brother Michael—the biggest among those big men—was one of those missing when we arrived at Greenwich. He and two more must have been the assassins. After they delivered the cannons to the French ship, they must have ridden the missing horses to Greenwich, abandoned them somewhere, then slipped quietly into the Palace. No one would have missed three musician monks, for a few days. And, they could have arranged the rendezvous point with the French ship while the court stayed at Canterbury. Likely they were housed with other monks—Canterbury is full of monasteries. The monks there would have known the Archbishop's woods. And it would never have occurred to them to be suspicious when Brother Michael questioned them about it."

The spymaster put his ear to the door. "Things are quieter. That's a good sign," he commented. "When King Henry and I discussed the murders with the Queen, she claimed that the beheaded men knew their killers because they hadn't defended themselves. And their faces, frozen at death, showed they had been surprised. I was skeptical—I am always skeptical—but it fits."

"Who would suspect that a musical monk was about to kill you?" Nicola agreed. "Or that monks singing lullabies could possibly want to assassinate a baby prince? That was the first thing that bothered me this morning. They wanted to sing "Lully Lulay Thou Little Tiny Child" to baby Prince Henry. That's a Christmas carol that we sang to the court last night. But it is actually a song about King Herod, who ordered the deaths of all the Jewish babies in Israel—he feared the prophesy that one of them would become king. It was a very inappropriate song for a baby prince."

"But perfect for the occasion of his assassination," the spymaster observed, in an appallingly ordinary voice. "It's quiet in there now. Let us see what has happened."

The chapel stank of blood and sweat. Piled next to the altar were suits of chain mail, and next to that broadswords and battle axes. A guardsman was bandaging soldiers who stood in line, quietly joking with one another. Nicola thought about offering to help him, but he seemed capable. No one was bleeding heavily.

One of the monks lay on the floor, obviously dead. The rest were roped together, hands tied behind their backs. Many of their faces bore cuts and bruises, and one a bite mark.

The Spymaster walked up to Brother Michael and said, "Who are you?"

"I am Brother Michael," he spat. "A monk. That is all I am going to say."

"We will take them to the Tower," said the Captain of the Guard. "The torturers will get their names, soon enough."

"Before you do that, have the Royal Barber shave them," said the Spymaster. "And have the oldest members of your company look them over. Someone might know them."

"Ask Lambert Simnel, too," Nicola said. "And anyone else around that was involved in those long-ago struggles for the English throne."

"What about the dead one?" the Captain asked.

"For now, put him and those weapons in the music room, and lock the door. Clean up in here immediately. I'll get Wolsey in to resanctify the place so it can be used. I'd like to keep this quiet, if possible. If you hurry you can get the traitors through the halls while the court is at supper."

Nicola crept into the music room, which was in shambles, while guardsmen dumped weapons and a monk's body onto its floor. Music lay scattered everywhere, some of it written on ancient vellum; all of it costly and irreplaceable. She picked it all up, and made as neat a pile as she could. After placing King Henry's "Greensleeves" carefully between sheets of holy chants and motets, she put the pile of music in one of the chests, where she hoped it would be safe.

Katherine of Aragon as the Madonna,
by Michael Sittow (c. 1469 –1525)

CHAPTER 43: A FAREWELL

The following afternoon

Nicola was summoned to the Queen's bedchamber the following afternoon. Katherine lay in her royal bed, dressed in a white linen nightgown trimmed with lace, gazing raptly at the redheaded baby nursing at her breast.

Nicola had never seen her so happy. "Your Highness, you are glowing. And so beautiful. If my Raphael were here, he would paint you as the Virgin Mary, to capture that look on your face. And he would put you on the walls of the papal palace, so that others could see you forever."

The Queen glanced up at Nicola, and smiled. "I wanted, just once, to nurse my own child. Leave us, Lena. Lady Margaret, you stay."

Her eyes went back to her baby. "Margaret told me about the song that Henry wrote for you, and what you said when you saw it," she continued. "I agree with you. You need to go home. For everyone's sake, including you and your betrothed. But not without hearing the end of the story. And not without saying goodbye."

Tears sprang to Nicola's eyes. "I spent the morning writing a letter to you, Your Highness. I would not leave without saying goodbye. But I am afraid that the King will not let me go."

"I'll get you to your ship. You still have your servant's costume, don't you?"

"I do. And I will leave my chests of Italian finery behind, for your ladies. I am sorry we never finished Dante's *Inferno*. But you can read it yourself now, and beautifully."

"Your finery will delight my ladies," Queen Katherine said, while continuing to gaze at her son. "And I will read how Dante punishes the violent with Henry. It may teach him something. When will the Italian ship be here?"

Nicola wiped the tears oozing down her cheeks with the back of her hand. "Late today or early tomorrow, at the very latest. How did you know?"

"Lena watches what you do. She saw you send the note to the ship, and explain 'case-hardening' to our armorers. It was not difficult to deduce your intentions."

She shifted Prince Henry to her other breast, then kissed his head. "Do you want to hear the end of the story of your cannons?"

"Of course. Do they know who Brother Michael is?"

"Lambert Simnel recognized him and several of the others, once they were shaved and had their hair cut. Brother Michael is really Viscount Francis Lovell, who fought several times for Richard III against Henry's father, and later for one of the pretenders to his throne. He disappeared at the Battle of Stoke, when Henry 's father finally defeated the last of the pretenders. And took refuge in a monastery, apparently, with some of his followers."

"I remember Lady Margaret mentioning him, when she explained the War of the Roses. How did they get from a monastery to the court of Henry VII?" Nicola asked.

"That remains a mystery."

"I assume they will be executed? Will they escape being drawn and quartered, because they are nobles?"

"Henry hasn't decided how they will die. But it will be done quietly. It's best the people do not know how close they came to losing their royal family." The Queen again kissed her baby's head. "He is asleep. Will you take him, Margaret?"

Nicola had never seen Lady Margaret looking so happy, either. She picked up the baby prince, gazed into his eyes and smiled at him before putting him on her shoulder.

The Queen buttoned her nightgown. "The other good news, Nicola, is that Henry's spies in Holland sent word that Richard de la Pole's army has deserted him. They were all mercenaries. It seems he was unable to pay them, so they refused to take ship to England."

"All is well, then." Nicola said, wishing that tears were not coursing down her cheeks. "How are you feeling, Your Highness?"

"My back feels much better, as you predicted. Now it's my breasts that hurt. I have a gift for you, Nicola. To thank you for all you have done for me. I embroidered it myself. Margaret, can you hand it to her? Open it, Nicola."

Nicola began to sob in earnest when she saw the word "amica"—Latin and Italian for "friend"—embroidered on the drawstring black *brocado* bag that Margaret handed to her. The Queen's emerald necklace was tucked inside with a document: the final payment for Nicola's services to England's armories, including the amount that had been withheld for the missing cannons.

"I will take the payment," Nicola said. "But the King has already been generous to me. Please keep the necklace. Think of me when you wear it."

"I will think of you, whether I wear it or not," Queen Katherine said. "I will miss you, Nicola. Very much. I am very glad our paths crossed. Not only because of your help, but also because of your friendship. Take the necklace, please. Think of me when *you* wear it, and write to let me know you are safe. Any of our emissaries in Rome will carry the message for you."

Nicola swallowed hard, to keep from sobbing. "I have not had a friend my own age since the convent," she said, her voice choked. "I will miss you, too. And yes, I will write to you." Tears streamed down her cheeks as she put the necklace on, and tucked it under her nun's costume.

Prince Henry burped. "A royal belch," Lady Margaret announced, smiling. She glanced at the Queen. "Please don't be alarmed, Highness. This is normal. It is why I was patting his back."

The Queen's look of horror relaxed. She giggled, and held her arms out for her baby. "It's amazing that something so tiny can make so much noise," she said.

"The King is here," announced someone behind them.

The Queen looked at Nicola. "Go with God," she said. "Go now."

"Addiò," Nicola responded. "I am gone."

AFTERWORD

Chapter 1 Considerable circumstantial evidence suggests that Henry VIII contracted syphilis, then rampant, as a very young man. This includes his wives' numerous miscarriages, stillbirths, and gynecological problems (both Katherine and her daughter Mary had false pregnancies, possibly indicative of swelling and infection); his own late life symptoms (paranoia; an open wound that would not heal); Katherine's mysterious early death at age 50 and his own at 55; and the early deaths of all of his children except Elizabeth, some or all with symptoms of congenital (inherited) syphilis. Elizabeth I was conceived immediately after Henry's marriage to Anne Boleyn, likely before he infected her. (Syphilis spreads best through an open wound. It was custom then to refrain from sex during pregnancy.) After Anne's next three pregnancies ended in miscarriages, she was abruptly beheaded.

Academics who reject this circumstantial evidence point out that Henry's medical records do not show that he was treated for syphilis or otherwise received mercury, the treatment of choice for syphilis for another 500 years. (His doctors did create "the King's Grace's Ointment" for "his inflamed member.") Also, Queen Katherine never once blamed Henry for her numerous miscarriages and stillbirths during their bitter divorce.

I have chosen to show Henry as syphilitic because the circumstantial evidence is strong[10]. He may have suffered the visible "pox"–if at all—as an adolescent, when he mysteriously disappeared from public view after his older brother's death, several years before he married Katherine. He would have been treated secretly to preserve his chances to win a European princess bride. His doctors may even have pronounced him cured when the visible signs of the disease disappeared. In that era, revealing this secret would have been considered treason—little wonder his doctors wrote nothing down. With care and luck he could have hidden the visible "pox" from Katherine, as it occurs, if at all, in the early stages of the

---

[10]https://journals.lww.com/greenjournal/Citation/1953/05000/DIAGNOSIS_IN_RETROSPECT__Mary_Tudor.13.aspx

disease, and is often hidden in women. Syphilis hides during later stages, which can last for decades. Death, which was inevitable during Henry's time, occurs much later, at the final, "tertiary" stage.

Chapter 2 Henry VIII invented and preferred the honorific title "Your Majesty," but later in his reign. Hence this book refers to Their Majesties as "Highnesses." Conversely, this book avoids proper terminology, particularly involving clothing, that might be confusing to modern readers. Nicola's knife is always a "dagger" rather than a "stiletto," and her nun's clothing is rarely referred to as a "habit." The English ladies' "gabled hoods" are referred to as "headdresses" because "gabled hood" sounds like a stove part and does not remotely resemble a modern "hood."

Chapter 3 The evolution of cannons and small arms roughly parallels the evolution of computers in the twentieth century. Essentially, both became smaller, more versatile and more powerful over time. The earliest European cannons, which date to the thirteenth century, were little more than firecrackers, good for little but scaring the horses. The first truly lethal cannon was an enormous tube, build in place because it was far too large to move, used by Sultan Mehmed II to destroy the walls of Constantinople and eject the remains of the Christian Byzantine Empire in 1453.

By Nicola's time, smaller, lighter, and far more powerful muzzle-loaders had evolved, wheeled for use on the battlefield and on ships. The arquebus, first precursor to the modern day rifle, was essentially a downsized cannon, a bit like a modern mortar. Because the flintlock had not yet been invented, its users actually carried coiled fuses over their shoulders, unless they had a "wheelock," which ignited the gunpowder with sparks emitted by a wound spring, coated with iron pyrite. (Leonardo da Vinci is credited with inventing the wheelock, pictured in his drawings.) The arquebus later evolved into the musket, then the rifle.

It is also true that early in his reign, Henry imported cannons and other inventions from European artisans, including Italians, and sought to have them teach their more advanced techniques to their English counterparts.

Chapter 4 Though this court journey is fictional, Henry and other monarchs in that era spent much of their time traveling from royal castle to royal castle, to survey the realm and mete out justice. The castles described in this chapter still exist between Dover and London. Though Rochester Castle is largely a ruin, Dover Castle is intact and was used by Britain for close to a thousand years, until after World War II. It is well worth a visit.

Chapter 8 Whether Queen Katherine was actually a virgin when she wed Henry, as she always insisted, has been debated endlessly by scholars. Obviously, there is no way to know the answer. This narrative chooses Katherine's story as the most probable, because she was a deeply religious woman who would have quailed at lying under oath. Instead, her testimony that she remained a virgin until she married Henry was consistent, emphatic and impassioned over the course of several years. If her first husband, Henry's older brother, died of tuberculosis as some scholars insist, his illness was already severe at the time of his marriage, and undoubtedly hidden from Katherine's parents during the marriage negotiations. Was Henry VII, father of both her husbands, "Machiavellian" enough to do this? Emphatically, yes.

The beheadings of Henry VII's unpopular counselors occurred in August 1510, three months before this book begins. As Nicola predicts here, both King Henry and Queen Katherine died young for well-born, well-nourished individuals: Katherine at 50, Henry at 55. Katherine's death was rather mysterious, and has been attributed, very tentatively, to cancer. As described at greater length in the notes to Chapter 1, Henry's symptoms were consistent with a death by syphilis, as are the early deaths of all his children, legitimate and otherwise, with the exception of Elizabeth, who may have been conceived before her mother was infected.

Chapter 9 The royal residences mentioned in this book all existed, but most have long since been demolished. Originally a 15th century manor house, Greenwich Palace was enlarged by various monarchs including Henry VIII himself. The description of the exterior is consistent with early drawings. The interior, other than the tiltyard, is entirely imagined. There is more evidence for the appearance of Richmond Palace, which was also demolished in the 17ᵗʰ century. The description of the rooms set aside for Katherine's confinement (including its solitary window) is taken from "The Private Lives of the Tudors," written by historian Tracy Borman. The royal residence in the Tower of London, built in the early Middle Ages, had deteriorated by Henry VIII's time and was thereafter used most often for royal prisoners, most notably Elizabeth I, before she was queen. It, too, was demolished in the 17ᵗʰ century. Brideswell Palace, which also existed in central London, was the residence of Father (later Cardinal) Wolsey at this time, as historic fact. It later became a notorious prison and mental hospital. Eltham Palace still exists as a privately-owned manor house.

Chapter 14 Renaissance Italy gave birth to many financial innovations, such as double-entry bookkeeping and regional, then international banking. "Personal banking" necessarily had a much more literal meaning back then. Banking families and their customers knew each other well, and operated to a large extent on trust. The Medici, the Italian bankers who led Europe in these innovations early in the era, made mistakes and were no longer ascendant by this time. The Fuggers of Germany were instead the primary bankers of the early 1500s. They did have London offices, but perhaps not in Fleet Street.

A pound was an enormous amount of money at the beginning of the 16ᵗʰ century—more than 450 of today's pounds, according to online sources. A "testoon" was Henry VII's label for what came to be called a shilling.

Chapter 16 In 1674, the bones of two children were found buried under a set of stairs in the Tower of London, and later re-buried in Westminster Abbey. Though they have not been re-examined or tested, it is assumed they were the bones of the two princes who disappeared into the Tower of London in 1483, at ages 9 and 12. Their uncle Richard, then Lord Protector, put the princes in the Tower, allegedly to prepare Edward V for his coronation. He then seized the throne himself and had the princes declared illegitimate. They were never publicly seen again. Historians have debated who was responsible for their murders, ever since.

Chapter 15 Henry VIII is known as the father of the British Navy, and the stories relating to ships in this book are true. The number of guns carried by the Mary Rose when she launched is apparently unclear, but Geoffrey Morehouse, author of *Great Harry's Navy,* reports that she had 91 cannons when she sank thirty-five years later, plus smaller ordinance on the stern (rear) decks. The Mary Rose was towed up the Thames to London for fitting out when completed in the summer of 1511, a few months after this book ends.

While the Biaggi armory is fictional, the problems Nicola spots with the Mary Rose are not. It sank rapidly in 1545 during a battle because water entered its lowest gunports. This resulted in the death of all aboard—somewhere between 400 and 700 men.

The enormous hull of the Mary Rose and various artifacts were located and raised in the last century. The remains of the Mary Rose can now be viewed in a purpose-built museum in Portsmouth, which is well worth the visit.

Blast furnaces and case-hardening were both developed during this time. Leonardo da Vinci sketched out his ideas for the smelting of bronze in the early 1480s. At the time this tale occurs, da Vinci was actually working on anatomy with a doctor in Pavia.

Chapter 17 The Christmas carols sung in this book are ancient ones, first written down and published decades after this story. Henry reportedly wrote one himself. Many familiar carols that sound ancient may not be. "Deck the Halls," for example, was first published in 1794. *Solfeggio* was invented in twelfth century Italy, and had many local variants over time. For simplicity I have used the version popularized by Julie Andrews in The Sound of Music. Henry VIII definitely sang (tenor, reportedly), read and wrote music, including polyphonic music. Nothing I have seen indicates whether he knew *solfeggio,* however.

Chapter 22 The ruins of Wingfield Castle and its well-preserved and lovely parish church, St. Andrews, can still be seen in Wingfield, Suffolk. The tombs of John and Elizabeth de la Pole, as well as others in that august family, are still intact. The description of Wingfield Castle in this book is based on an archeological reconstruction of the castle as it existed circa 1500, found here: https://www.youtube.com/watch?v=M9cjlkYT_As . It passed from the de la Poles when Henry VIII gave it to his sister Mary and Sir Charles Brandon as a wedding present. (They married hastily after the death of her first husband, King Louis XII, much to Henry's consternation.) Lady Cathryn lived into her eighties, elsewhere. (I changed her real name, "Katherine," to "Cathryn" to avoid confusion. Unfortunately I chose "Caterina" for the name of Nicola's mother when I wrote the first of the Nicola mysteries, not realizing I would end up with three Catherines in one book.)

Chapter 30 Sir William de la Pole spent 37 years in the Tower of London, until he died there. It was the longest imprisonment in the Tower of London in history. Since he was never beheaded, it is likely he was guilty only of having a better claim to the throne than the Tudors, and therefore treated tolerantly.

Chapter 31 The Tudors were very fastidious about the cleanliness of their castles and clothing, if not their persons, according to Tracy Borman's *Private Lives of the Tudors*. The linen undergarments worn under costly raiment were frequently laundered, which helped keep body odor down. Though baths were frowned on generally as unhealthy, both Henry and his daughter Elizabeth had elaborate baths installed in their palaces, and no tolerance for smelly courtiers. Being from the Mediterranean, Lena and Nicola might have felt less aversion to bathing.

Chapter 32 Caister Roman fort, once on the coast near Great Yarmouth, is less than 1000 feet from Caister Castle and now half a mile or so from the English Channel, as the crow flies. You can visit both ruins, though little is left of the Roman one. At the time of this tale, Caister Castle was indeed owned by John Paston, who was a deputy to the Lord High Admiral. However, the coast had moved and the stream between the old Roman fort and the castle (apparently a tributary of the Bure River) may or may not have existed by 1500. Great Yarmouth—once an island—has now almost entirely covered the large estuary that was once at the mouth of the Burre, Yare, and several other rivers.

Chapter 34 There seems little doubt that Henry—who often chose "Loyal Heart" as his sobriquet—had an affair with Mary Boleyn, Ann Boleyn's older sister, after this book occurs. There were also rumors of an earlier affair with Elizabeth, mother of both Boleyn girls and reportedly a very attractive woman. Quite a family.

Chapter 37 The descriptions of the Queen's confinement, dietary restrictions and birthing regimen come from "The Private Lives of the Tudors" by historian Tracy Borman. The "tisanes" prepared by Nicola are my invention.

Chapter 38 Legend has it that Henry VIII wrote "Greensleeves" himself, for some mysterious lady. The lyrics to "What Child Is This," the Christmas carol set to its tune, were not written until the nineteenth century.

Henry VIII made Lady Margaret Pole the Duchess of Salisbury and gave her brother's lands back to her in 1513, two years after this book ends. Edmund de la Pole was executed that same year, when his brother Richard declared himself king and attempted an invasion from France. These events likely had a connection but my research has not revealed what it was. The attempted Holland invasion I have described is fictitious, but consistent with the de la Poles' behavior. Richard de la Pole was planning yet another invasion when he died in Italy in 1525.

Chapter 42 Italy's famous bearded monks, the Capuchins, had not yet split from the Franciscans when this story occurs. (The white "beard" on a cappuccino coffee is named for them.) It was considered quite scandalous when the pope at this time, Julius II, grew a beard. As the portraits of Henry and Charles Brandon show, beards were becoming fashionable among the laity in the early 16th century.

Rumors that Edward Stafford, Third Duke of Buckingham, felt his claim to the throne superior to that of the Tudors surfaced early in Henry VIII's reign. (He was the oldest male descendant of John of Gaunt's youngest son.) However, Buckingham was not executed for treason—reportedly, on slender evidence—until 1521.

PARTIAL BIBLIOGRAPHY

Borman, Tracy. *The Private Lives of the Tudors: Uncovering the Secrets of Britian's Greatest Dynasty*. Grove Press 2016

Christopher, John. *The Mary Rose Story*. The History Press 2012

Moorehouse, Geoffrey. *Great Harry's Navy*. The Orion Publishing Group Ltd. 2005

Hutchinson, Robert. *Young Henry: The Rise of Henry VIII*. St. Martin's Press 2012

Gilbert, Felix. *The Pope, His Banker, and Venice*. Harvard University Press, 1980

Kelly, Jack. *Gunpowder: The History of the Explosive that Changed the World*. Basic Books 2004

Aligheri, Dante: *The Divine Comedy: Hell*. Sayers, Dorothy L. *Trans*. Penguin Press 17th Ed. 1971

The author in Renaissance garb at Stanford

ABOUT THE AUTHOR

Maryann Philip (a nom de plume) is the author of four Nicola Machiavelli "real history mysteries" spanning the Italian Renaissance that consistently average more than 4 out of 5 stars after over 225 reviews on Amazon. The mysteries are the candy coating to the real history at the core of each one. The series begins with the Borgia family history in *A Borgia Daughter Dies*, followed by the history of persecution of alleged homosexuals including Leonardo da Vinci by the horrifying Florentine Night Office in *Da Vinci Detects*, then the story of young Martin Luther, horrified by the corruption of the papacy and Rome in *Martin Luther and Murder*, and finally, the story of the early English Renaissance under the youthful Henry VIII, the father of the British Navy in this book.

Maryann graduated from Stanford University with honors in "Renaissance Studies" (a self-created major) having spent part of her junior year in Florence, researching her honors thesis using original Italian texts. She then attended law school (University of Chicago) and spent several decades doing civil litigation, with occasional time out to sing music, especially Renaissance music. Now retired, she devotes her time to her family, travel, pro bono legal work, and writing about the Renaissance.

www.ingramcontent.com/pod-product-compliance
Lightning Source LLC
Chambersburg PA
CBHW030034180626
46810CB00001B/361